THE FREEZE

For Matthew,
   Hope you enjoy
   the trip!

     Robin.

"Emotionally resonant and briskly paced, this apocalyptic vision of a world plagued by disease, conspiracy, and silenced voices will hook you early and keep you guessing until the very end. With his sophomore novel, Stevens has accomplished something truly impressive: written a book unlike anything I've ever read."
Benjamin Roesch, author of *Blowin' My Mind Like a Summer Breeze*

"An adrenalin fuelled adventure in a fresh-feeling, near-future world, with a tormented protagonist who's swept along by events, desperate to make amends for what he's done."
LA Weatherly, author of the best-selling *Angel* series

"Full to the brim with concepts, cinematic locations, heartfelt characters raging against a broken world, and tons of emotive action and adventure... something truly original in the dystopian genre."

★★★★★
Readers' Favorite

THE FREEZE

R. D. STEVENS

Welcome to Thaw!
Enjoy your
first trip....

V

PRESS

Published by Vulpine Press in the United Kingdom in 2023

ISBN: 978-1-83919-493-1

Cover by Rowan Thomas
Seal image © by Rowan Thomas

www.vulpine-press.com

For anyone who's ever lost a piece of themselves and struggled to get it back

"If the 'now' were not different, but one and the same, there would not have been time."

- Aristotle

E.P.R.L. Government Advisory Notice: Living safely with the Temporal Anomaly (the 'freeze') Guidance and Support - Overview

First Published 2042
Version 18 (Updated 2064)
Zone 4 Edition
From: EPRL Security Agency and Freeze Police Department

Contents

- Background
- What is the Temporal Anomaly (the 'freeze')?
- Overview of Current Zonal Restrictions
- Anomaly Safe Behaviour - a reminder

Background

Since the devastating escalation of the pandemic in 2025, the threat of the virus and its continual evolution of new, more lethal strains has been ever growing. Given the significant rapid population decrease, the start of war in Eastern Europe, the growing threat of contagion and the necessary de-globalisation of our world, the European People's Republic of London was created by referendum in 2035. The people of London spoke and our government listened. At a time of extreme crisis, we separated from the rest of the UK and established a new city state that continues to grow and thrive year on year. To protect the 70% of London's surviving population from the virus, the walls went up around the EPRL in 2038. This proud feat of civil engineering was a collaborative effort, a triumph of the human spirit, and did much to protect us all against the transmission of the virus, but there is still more work ahead.

In 2042, with the global pandemic continuing to escalate and war now ravaging Eastern Europe, the Temporal Anomaly (commonly now known as the 'freeze') first occurred and changed the face of human existence forever. In response to this unprecedented event, and the threat of rising crime, in order to protect us all the government constructed the inner walls in 2043 so that the four newly established zones remain independent and protected during 'freeze' state. The four zones that we now all inhabit were legally established and local government structure adjusted accordingly. Now each zone is semi-autonomous with the government overseeing the whole of the EPRL from the Houses of Parliament in Zone 1.

- Find out more about our great nation's history at www.gov.eprl/nationalfoundations

What is the Temporal Anomaly (the 'freeze')?

The Temporal Anomaly is the single most impactful event in human history to occur on a quantum level. Whilst government scientists had speculated about its possibility in recent years prior to 2042, having observed it in other parts of the galaxy through the advancement of deep space technology, no one expected it to happen right here in the EPRL. Here are the key facts to remember:

- The Temporal Anomaly 'locks' in place all sub-atomic particles in the area that it affects for thirty days. This is an entirely natural process, which is the result of sub-atomic random behaviour, the laws of quantum mechanics and the changing existence of 'quantum super-states'. This 'locking' of all particles in an area is commonly known as a 'freeze'.
- The quantum irregularity began unexpectedly in 2042 and resulted in four Zones across London – divided by when and where the anomaly was occurring. Luckily, the current anomaly follows a pattern, with a high degree of probability that this will continue. This means that each of the EPRL's four zones all 'freeze' individually for 30 days in turn. So whilst Zone 4 is frozen, Zones 3, 2 and 1 are not. And after 30 days, when the 'freeze' rotates to Zone 3, it is then the case that Zones 2, 1 and 4 are not, and so on.
- To be 'frozen' as a human, as is the case with everything else, is perfectly safe.

You will not realise that it has happened, there are no known side-effects, and for you it will be as if no time has passed at all.

- You do not change at all or age whilst you are 'frozen' and there is no way to not be 'frozen' when in the relevant zone.

- There are further, more detailed scientific papers regarding the nature, causes and effects of the temporal anomaly to be found on our website at www.gov.eprl/tem-panomaly/research

Overview of current Zonal Restrictions

This is a brief overview of some of the key restrictions to remember to follow, for your own protection and the safety of our great nation:

- You must never attempt to travel into (or 'trip' into, as it is commonly called) a zone whilst it is 'frozen'. This is a serious criminal offence and breaches a number of Zone restrictions, as well as infringing upon the Freeze Rights of those 'locked' in the zone at the time. The maximum penalty for being caught 'tripping' into a 'frozen' zone is life in prison.
- Travel between zones that are not in 'freeze' state requires booking in advance and all the necessary permits and documentation completed correctly. It is not possible to travel through a 'frozen'

zone to get to a zone that is not affected. Contact your local authority for more information on travel restrictions and necessary virus prevention conditions.

- Nothing should be touched, altered, changed or stolen whilst it is affected by the temporal anomaly. The maximum penalty for being caught doing any of the above in a 'frozen' zone, is capital punishment.
- Zonal laws exist for all our protection against crime and the spreading of the virus, and should be respected at all times.

➤ This is detailed further in our Zonal Restrictions and Law page which can be found here www.gov.eprl/zonelaws_restrictions

Anomaly Safe Behaviour - a reminder

Here are some helpful 'dos' for your guidance:

DO

→ Follow zonal laws and restrictions at all times

→ Support your local community by reporting anything illegal or any suspicious behaviour (please refer to the section 'When to consider reporting someone to the FPD')

→ Use your government issue 'freeze countdown clock' so that you know exactly when the anomaly will affect you next and check your interzoner for regular freeze crime updates.

→ Prepare your property accordingly before the anomaly begins in your zone - ensure all relevant security measures are taken.

→ Check your property carefully once you have been affected by the anomaly and report any changes/anything unusual/people you may find.

→ Remember to obey all government curfews and current restrictions.

→ Stay alert and vigilant for any person being a member of, possessing material for, or openly discussing 'Thaw' or any other terrorist organisation. It is vitally important that we all look out for each other in this regard.

➢ For more advice on what to do if you are suspicious of freeze crime, please visit www.gov.eprl/freezecrime/reporting

The EPRL government thanks you for reading this advisory notice and reminds you to remain pandemic and anomaly safe at all times. Thank you.

*This is all bullsh*t! Don't believe their lies!!! Don't look for thaw and we can fight this corrupt government together! #unfreezethetruth*

PART 1: BEFORE

1|

There is a fog of noise that sits thick in the dark, heavy air. Speakers are filling the room with a weird remix of a song that I half recognise, and everyone is talking loudly but I can barely hear them. I've never been to a party before – not a real one – and now that I'm in, and the door has closed behind me, I've got no idea what I'm supposed to do next. My stomach is all scrunched up and I wish my brother were here. He's really good at this awkward intro stuff, he just talks and talks, and I can ease my way in on the back of his wave. People fall in love with him straight away because you never know what he's going to do next. There's something magic about the way he speaks. But his magic goes both ways, and they don't see the other side when it all bottoms out.

'Hey, who are you?' says a boy about my age, stepping right in front of me and throwing me off balance. He's got tousled blond hair and a baggy, faded psychedelic print t-shirt. His bloodshot eyes search me up and down. His breath stinks.

'Sasha invited me,' I reply with the first thing that pops into my head. 'Is she here?'

'Yeah, she's here,' he responds before looking down at my hands. 'Oh, sweet, you brought a drink. I'll take it over for you, no worries.'

He reaches out and grabs it before I can say anything else.

'You didn't bring any devices, did you?' he asks, raising his eyes to mine.

'No, no…Sasha said not to,' I reply, shaking my head.

'Good, good, they can trace that shit you know? Locate you then listen in on anything, whatever they want.' I'm pretty sure that's not true, but I want to get away and find Sasha, so I don't bother replying. As I try to walk past, he puts his hand flat on my chest and blocks my way. 'Don't do anything stupid,' he says, looking me straight in the eyes. 'They find out this is happening and we are all screwed, you get me?'

I nod and he moves his hand out the way. 'I think Sasha's somewhere in the back room,' he says, pushing past me, unscrewing the bottle and taking a swig.

My eyes scan for anything that looks like a back room. I'm in someone's council flat and the whole space has been opened up into one big area. I spot what looks like another smaller one just glowing through at the back. There are lights hanging off the ceiling and massive speakers standing in the corner. No wonder he's worried; if this is his flat then this place breaks a ton of rules even without the party. I don't think I've ever been in a room with this many people.

Stepping forward, I try to act like I fit in.

2|

The smell of sweat and vape sticks to my nostrils as I squeeze my way over to the drinks table. I need something before I can get the courage to talk to Sasha. The table's covered with empty cans and half-drunk cups but the bottle I brought isn't there. Of course it isn't. After a quick glance, I realise the guy who took it has disappeared, so I decide to grab a used cup and down what's left before reaching for another. That bottle I snuck out of my foster carers' cupboard had to be worth a couple of weeks' credit at least. I don't know this new pair very well yet, but I know they'll murder me if they find out.

The liquid in the cup is warm and tastes disgustingly like cheap chemical booze that someone probably made in their bath. It makes me wince and just as I begin to wonder whether I should really be here, I turn to see her standing next to me.

'You came!' she says, smiling before leaning in next to my ear. 'I didn't think you would.'

'Why not?' I reply too quietly.

'Huh?' she asks.

'Why not?' I repeat louder this time, taking another huge gulp of the bath booze.

'I dunno. There's something…different about you.' She leans back, wobbling slightly before immediately pushing herself in again. 'Don't get me wrong,' she continues, 'different is good. Different is *interesting*. Kill me if I'm the same as madame average everyone, right?' She looks down at the floor. 'Look, I just saw you and wanted to get to know you a bit, that's all. That's why I invited you, it's not that deep. Maybe it's because I'm a bit faded that I'm saying this, but…I know I've got something a bit…different in me, and maybe it's a bit dark sometimes,' she says, a smile appearing then disappearing too quickly, 'but when I saw you out on the corner the other day, I thought maybe you did too.'

Her eyes meet mine with something that feels like vulnerability; there's a tiny shift in her body language, some small change that pierces through all that confidence she showed when she first came up to me, all smiles and bravado on the estate. We both stare and I'm sure she can see that I sense it: that tiny whisper of who she really is. Something must give me away too because she breaks the connection, smiling in the knowledge that she guessed correct. Right now, I swear we are the only two people in the room.

'How can you tell?' I ask. I've never thought of it as darkness before; I don't know what to call it. But there's always been something there that isn't what it should be. My social workers call it abandonment issues and trauma, my foster carers call it insecure attachment related aggression. My brother calls it being a dick. Whatever it is, I try to keep it buried because it always causes trouble when it comes out.

'It's on your face. Broken pieces stick together but the cracks still show. I'm good at spotting it, I guess; like finds like. I always get the broken ones. Come on,' she says, taking my hand, 'let's dance. No offence, but I didn't come here just to talk. Life's short enough, right?'

As she leads me through the crowd, we flow like water between islands until she stops. What does she mean, she always gets the broken ones? It doesn't matter – she just held my hand and I'm on a dance-floor at a real party with a girl so cool I'm feeling totally intimidated – it's not the time to get lost in my head right now. I down the other cup and let it fall to the floor as the music gets louder and all the hairs on the back of my neck stand on end. She moves and I move and I'm in the moment as the music lives in both of us.

3|

We are squashed in tight with people dancing, pushed up against us on every side. There is this sense of alliance between us all, some invisible binding bringing us together and tying us up into a whole. I can feel it in the air like electricity and I want to let go of everything else and hold onto it. If only I could capture it and take it with me out there where nothing fits together as it should. I look up at the lights and lift my hands, stretching my fingers into silhouettes and tracing patterns in the air before closing my eyes. My body is right here in this room but my mind is somewhere new, somewhere the darkness Sasha mentioned can't reach. Somewhere that feels good. When I open them again, she is looking at me and smiling. She puts her hands on my chest and leans into my ear.

'Why haven't I seen you at any of these parties before?' she asks, her body pressed against mine. She tucks her dreads out of the way and I tilt my head down to her ear so that she can hear my reply. My nose and lips brush her neck as I'm about to speak and it sparks the electricity in the air.

'I only moved to the estate a few weeks ago. I've never been to anything like this before, though. This is so cool! How often do these things happen?'

'It depends – usually at least once every couple of months, but they always have to be kept really quiet. The details are only let out a couple of days before so that the government can't come in and shut it down. A guy from around the corner got arrested a few weeks ago for trying to organise something like this and no one's seen him since. These new laws they've got, the police can just do whatever they like.' She adjusts the strap on her top. 'It's so unfair. There's no restrictions in place at all in Zone 1; they get to do whatever the hell they want.'

'I can't even imagine what that would be like.' The whole of Zone 1 feels like a foreign country to me. I don't think I've ever been able to do whatever the hell I want. 'Have you ever been in?' I ask.

She looks at me and laughs. 'Are you kidding? Who do you know who's managed to get into Zone 1?'

'No one, I guess.' She's right but it makes me feel small to say so.

'Exactly. No one gets into Zone 1 anymore. I don't know anyone who has even left Zone 4, do you?'

'No,' I reply. I think maybe my old foster parents might have done years ago in the thirties before the inner walls went up, but I don't say this.

'Of course you don't, because the government has got us all cooped up in this pigsty, doing any shitty jobs that come up if we can get them, living on universal welfare and not getting any of the latest vaccines. When was the last time they did a vaccination drive around here? I know we are inside the walls, but outbreaks still happen. There was one only a few months ago from another new strain. I know plenty of people approaching forty who are as good as dead. It's not right.'

She pulls away from me and dances again as a new song starts, but I can tell she's got more to say. She has so much passion and intensity, it's flowing out of her in waves and I'm not sure she can contain them. They feel wild and dangerous, and I wonder if any of her broken people have ever been caught in the riptide. After a minute or so she leans back in.

'They took my mum, you know,' she says, downing another glass, her body still moving to the music. I tip my cup too and then let it fall to the floor again. I've had a few glasses of the bath booze now and everything is starting to shuffle a bit sideways, but Sasha is out drink-ing me two to one and seems to be fine. I'm not sure if I heard her right.

'What?' I ask.

'They *took* my mum.'

'Who did?' I shout into her ear to be heard over the music as it gets louder. A crunching, pulsing bassline kicks in that climbs up my legs and through my ribcage and into my heart.

'The government, obviously, who else?' Pulling back, she looks at me with a glare that makes me feel like I'm stupid.

'Shit,' is the best reply I can offer; she's right, I am stupid. I have to forget the music and try to rescue this; she's really talking to me, actually communicating. I don't remember the last person to do that apart from my brother. 'What happened?'

'One night she was there, then the next day she was gone.'

'They just came in and took her?'

'Yeah. You know they do that now don't you? Steal people from Zone 4 because who gives a shit about them, right? They don't care about us. We are a dead weight to them, just a problem to remove. A stain on the beautiful republic. They're cleaning us out, you know. They can't keep us all on welfare and there aren't enough jobs. And they won't vaccinate us all because they can't keep up, which means we can't leave. It's eugenics is what it is and they're using the freeze to do it.'

She's getting angry now and I can feel that too. I don't understand how with her darkness her emotions can be so powerfully out there in the world. Out there, emotions become something bigger and cause real problems, rather than just the ones in our heads. I have to keep all mine inside, otherwise I'm afraid of what they might become.

'Were you there? Did you see it happen?' I ask. I've heard of this kind of claim before. Each school I got bumped into, there always turned out to be someone there talking about this conspiracy stuff. I mean, people do go missing sometimes, that's true, but that could be for any number of reasons. I never really believed any of the lines about it being the government, but the way she is telling it feels different.

'No, she was there before I went to bed and then just gone when I woke up.'

'So how do you know it was them?' I shouldn't have asked this; her body language changes the second I do and it's as though our connection is lost and she is a million miles away. Stupid question, you idiot.

'Would *your* mum just up and leave in the middle of the night? Would *your* mum just disappear without saying goodbye? Would she leave and never come back? Tell me – would she?' she asks, fire in her face and her hands fanning the flames into me.

I hate it when people ask these kinds of questions. I usually lie or just talk about something else, but there's something about her, something real about this connection, something more that I need to get back, which means that before I've even thought about it, I tell the truth.

'I never knew my mum.'

Her body stops moving, the fire goes out and her hands fall. She wrinkles her nose.

'Shit,' is all she can say this time and it makes me feel a tiny bit less like an idiot. 'I'm sorry,' she continues. 'Christ. I really fucked that up, didn't I? I'm not usually such a bitch, I promise.'

She touches me on the arm and I don't care about anything else anymore.

'No wonder we're both messed up, right?' she says, placing her hands on my cheeks and looking into my eyes. It's too much this time and I have to look away before she carries on talking. 'What happened to your mum?'

'I don't know. I was removed from my parents before I was two.'

11

'So you don't remember them at all?'

'No. Sometimes I have this feeling as if I do. Like something's there but I can't tell what it is. I really thought I did for a while when I was little, but I think I just made it all up.'

I was certain of that memory for years. Her taking me to the park and pushing me on the swings. It was so specific, I thought it had to be true. I was wearing this old, fraying white knitted sweater and she was in pink. She was smoking as she took turns pushing me and my brother. She was talking on her interzoner at the same time and facing away from me as I called out to her to look. I was making the swing move on my own and kept calling but she ignored me. I started to cry and she turned to me and said something, but I can't remember what it was. Whatever it was, she made me feel scared because her face was all fierce frowns and furrows. It wasn't much of a memory, but it was something.

A couple of years ago my brother showed me a photo of our mum which turned up in some file with our latest foster carers. Whoever that woman in my memory is, it turns out it wasn't my mum. I hated my brother for showing me that. He knew what it would do to me but did it anyway. It meant I really had nothing of her which made my darkness, or whatever you want to call it, grow. I don't normally talk about this kind of thing, or even think about it to be honest; it's weird I'm doing it now. It's only my brother and I who share it.

'Why did they remove you?' she continues.

'I don't know, no one ever told me.'

She pauses and looks at the floor before raising her head once more. Our eyes reconnect and her face is now bold, but brittle. Another of her waves crashes over me and this time I want it to pull me under.

'Well, screw them!' she says. 'You don't need to be dealing with any of that anyway, right? Come on, let's get another drink.'

She takes my hand once more and pulls me out of the crowd and the invisible binds of the dancefloor are broken. We are something new now, something all of our own.

4|

I don't know what time it is. Blue and red and yellow halos surround our heads in the dark. The music has dwindled to the quiet mantra of a chillout beat – something way old school from the twenty tens or twenties – and Sasha is lying next to me on the futon, my arm around her shoulders. We spoke and danced for so long but now are simply being quiet together, and it's magical. I wonder if two people's darkness can cancel each other out and become light?

She pushes herself up and says that she needs to go to the bathroom. I lean back onto the cushions and stare at the ceiling, with the music filling my ears and mind. I've always loved how music can make you feel anything at all if you just let it. Music's always been my way out, my place to escape to when there's nowhere else to go. I close my eyes and the feelings come and I can't help it. I barely know her, but I want Sasha to be in this moment with me, and then I want the moment to never end. She's right; life's short enough.

The song finishes and she's still not back, so I sit up and take a look around. A couple of small groups of people sit dotted around the room, most lying down asleep or passed out. I scan the dark to try and pick out her face, but I can't see her. As I'm about to lie down again, a glass smashes and I tilt my head towards the drinks table. Sasha is pressed up against it with the guy in the baggy t-shirt from earlier leaning over her. Sitting up, my head is a bit misty but, squinting, I make no mistake in seeing him grab her and push her up against the wall. She tries to slap him but it makes no difference, he raises a finger and waves it in her face. He then goes to move his hand down and that is all it takes.

Before I'm even sure what I'm going to do, I launch myself at him and we both fall to the floor, cups of warm drinks falling on top of us, and I just keep hitting and hitting. He is throwing punches back but I can't feel anything other than anger, it's everywhere. The darkness is howling out of me; it wants to destroy his face. It wants to tear away everything that exists through him. It wants to rip a hole in the world through his bone and tissue and skin, and I'm not sure how to stop it.

I'm on top of him now, wrestling his hands out of the way and trying to land more punches anyway I can, when suddenly something steals in softly to interrupt. I feel a gentle touch on my shoulder and the electricity from earlier shoots through my body and the howling stops. Turning, I look up to see Sasha's face and everything else – the sweat, the heavy breathing, the strain of my clenched fists, the taste of blood on my tongue – disappears. How she did that, I don't know. Her eyes are lined with steel and something else that I can't pick out.

'Leave him,' she says calmly. 'Come on, let's just go – he's not worth it.'

I drop my fists and pain surges through my knuckles and up my arms as I climb to my feet. He squirms to the wall, feeling his face and touching the blood that is crawling out of his nose.

'You can have her, freak,' he yells, his voice breaking. 'She's that type; I know her. She wanted it, I know she did. She was asking for it.'

I move to throw one more punch, but Sasha holds me back before leaning over and staring him straight in the eyes.

'Little, small man,' she says with ice in every word, 'no one is asking for it unless they actually *ask* for it.'

She spits in his face and then says nothing as she turns to me and we leave. I press the button, the door opens and Sasha breaks into a run, pulling me with her. Racing down the corridor of the block until we hit the stairs, we run and run down flights and flights and flights. As we reach the bottom, she suddenly stops and turns to face me. Her big brown eyes are wide and wild and lost and alive and she moves in close to my lips and stays there. The condensation of her breath passes onto me, and our fast, warm exhales fall into the same rhythm. She waits, breathing hard and looking at me as if she dares me to do it. I want to, but after what just happened, I don't know if I should. I wait, feeling the pain in my knuckles, and then she moves forward and decides for me. We kiss against the cold of a concrete staircase on a grey morning with the sun about to rise, and the world is beautiful.

5|

'So have you ever done it?' she asks in the afternoon sun.

'Done what?' I reply, not sure where this is going. Even though we kissed yesterday, I'm still totally in awe of her and well aware that I've probably not done most of the things she has.

'You know…tripped?'

Sliding her back down the concrete wall, she adjusts to find a comfy position on the floor. Placing one arm behind her head, she twists to face me. I look around hastily to check that no one heard. I'm still hanging from the bath booze from last night so I try not to move too quickly because there's a good chance I might throw up.

'Tripped?' I say in a hushed voice. 'No, never. You haven't, have you?'

'Twice,' she replies, as if it's no big deal.

'What?! You're a tripper?' I exclaim.

'Keep your voice down!' she hisses. 'You never know who could hear.'

My mind is racing through questions and garbles out the first ones it catches. 'When? How?'

'Both in the last month. It was so awesome, you wouldn't believe.'

I am now sitting bolt upright. I knew she would have done things I hadn't, but I wasn't expecting this. 'But how? You did it on your own?'

Sasha casts her eyes around again before leaning closer towards me. 'Thaw. Someone from Thaw found me and got me involved.'

'Thaw? Shit, Sasha!'

'Yeah, I know!'

'If anyone finds out, you're going to be…you know.'

'I don't care anymore,' she announces. 'Don't you want to get answers? Aren't you sick of this life?' Her hands wave at the rusty kids' playground that is falling down around us: the broken seesaw and the bent bars of a busted roundabout. 'Don't you want *more*?'

'I guess so. You didn't tell me any of this last night,' I say, feeling hurt. 'You said you'd never left Zone 4.'

'Come on, we had just met. I didn't know if I could trust you yet. Look, I'm telling you now, aren't I?' She leans over and gives me a kiss on the cheek. 'You don't believe their bullshit about this, right? This amount of order can't come about by some freak of nature. That's so *reductionist*. It *must* be designed.' More waves begin to crash out of her. 'And why did it start? Twenty years ago the freeze just *happened* to begin? In the middle of the worst pandemic in history? The city gets divided into four zones that freeze for exactly thirty days each time on rotation by *chance*? Come on. Things like this don't start on their own, they are caused. *Everything* has a cause. It's basic physics. You can't buy into the government crap about unexplained spatio-temporal phenomena, can you? Naturally occurring time lapses, sub-atomic random behaviour and quantum mechanics and all that shit? Surely?'

I try not to think about it if I can, but I don't say this. The government scientists have explained everything with charts and diagrams and formulae; it's in all the textbooks and lessons at school. The European People's Republic of London divided into four zones, freezing in time in turn as a result of some quantum anomaly. It's always been perfectly possible, they say, and occurs in other parts of the galaxy, it just hadn't happened here until now. It's not so much about time either, apparently, but about the nature and position of sub-atomic states locking and unlocking. I don't really understand any of it and have got no idea if it's made up, but the way Sasha talks makes it feel as though she could be right about everything in the whole universe.

'No, they're just making it all up,' I reply. 'But what can we really do? If it's true then we're stuck here and they're controlling everything from Zone 1.'

Sasha sits up and I instantly regret my words. 'What can we do?' she asks, her voice raising. 'What can we *do*? We can fight back! If they won't give us the answers, then we have to take them. We have to help people stand up against this corrupt government. And that starts by tripping. We trip to show that they don't control us. To break into different zones and buildings and reveal their secrets. To take back some of what they *owe* us. To try and get hold of the vaccines and stop them letting us die.' She pauses and takes a breath as the waves subside. 'Besides, you know what the best bit is – it's *hella* fun! I heard stories of all kinds of crazy shit you can get up to! You could trip too, you know. We need new trippers. Don't you want to see what it's like? Don't you want to get out of here?'

She only waits a second before continuing. Her hand moves on to my leg. 'You should see a zone in freeze state – it's incredible.'

'It must be. What's it like?'

'It's so hard to describe,' she rubs her nose. 'There's a…a feel to it that I can't really explain. The air is static and everywhere. I mean, I know it's always everywhere, but you notice it when it's frozen. It's like moving through a frame of a movie, or entering into a page of a book. And you become the character, but not just the character, you're the author and you write your own tiny piece. God knows how they do it, but I wish I could freeze the world whenever I wanted to. Imagine what you could do…'

She looks up at the sky and rubs her nose again before playing with the ring on her necklace.

19

'You can mess with whatever you like, you know? Take whatever you want. I've got some souvenir tech stuff from when I went. I can't ever use it, obviously, because the minute it's turned on they'll know where it is, but it's cool to look at.'

'What are frozen people like?' I wonder out loud. 'Have you seen anyone?' I hate the idea of someone looking at me when I'm frozen, it creeps me out.

'Never seen one yet,' she says, 'but I'd love to though. Wouldn't you? Saw a frozen dog once, it was mid-wee with this little fixed stream under its cocked leg. Hilarious!' She laughs and I do too. 'I want to catch a Zone 1 prick in freeze state and pull his pants down and put him in the middle of the road for when he wakes up! Now that would be amazing!'

She snorts and throws her head back as she laughs. The way her cheeks rise as she smiles: I can't describe how it makes me feel. Her eyes catch mine again and their chestnut brown shine sees right inside me, lighting up some place I didn't even know was there.

'We should go tripping,' she says, grabbing both my hands. 'Come on, it'd be great. I can introduce you to some guys from Thaw and they'll set us up with something. They'll give us some kind of job to do on the trip, but that never takes very long and the rest of the time we can do what we want.' She smiles. 'I've got some great ideas! Come on, what do you say? You in?'

The shadow of another grey cloud passes over us. I look up at the grey sky, interrupted by grey buildings made of grey concrete and full of grey people. It feels as though everything in my life is some shade of that colour. Except her. Right now, I'd do anything with her if she asked me to. Now I realise that it feels a bit scary, but it's so exciting I don't care. I've spent my whole life moving from placement to placement, school to school, street to street. But they've always been the same; I've never really been anywhere new. And I'm terrified my whole life will end up like this – a life full of nothing but filling time.

'I'm in,' I say, and she does a little squeal before leaning over to give me a kiss.

'We can go see someone,' she says, grabbing my hand. 'I'll set us up a meet. You're going to love it, I just know!'

6|

It's after breakfast and I'm waiting just long enough that I can head out without anyone thinking I've got somewhere in particular to be. They'll switch on the TV and the VR console soon, and then they won't give a shit where I am. It's only been three weeks since my brother and I got placed with this couple and I've already basically got them figured out. Thank God this will be our last placement. We have dreamed of turning eighteen and getting our own housing since we were little. We used to spend nights talking about everything we were going to do once we were on our own. There's just under a year left and the funny thing is even though these carers are as bad as the rest, I don't want to move yet: things here have just started to get interesting.

Foster dad he calls himself; why do they always pretend to be the same thing? He is probably about forty and lucky to be alive considering he's now number one high risk group – overweight, old and sedentary – but he doesn't seem to care about that. His pudgy, rolling barrel belly is sitting twisted away from the kitchen table. He is scrolling through his interzoner with that expression that means he's about to complain.

'They've bloody changed the zonal provision laws again,' he mutters to no one in particular, flicking his thumb up and down. 'How is anyone supposed to run a business if they keep changing the rules about what can be taken across zone lines?'

He complains about this stuff as if he has a job and is not just living off our foster allowance.

'Of course, they allow what's left of the factory jobs to continue here. Low skill, low pay – let's keep those in Zone 4 until they're all gradually replaced by 3-D printers and fricking robots. You can produce as many cheap manufactured goods in 4 as big business allows.' *Big business runs everything* – he repeats this line basically every day. It's so dull to listen to him.

'You know they're even talking about letting big business open up supply lines through frozen zones?!' he continues. 'Order something before the freeze and it's there in literally no time at all! Private delivery in frozen zones! As if that isn't an invasion of basic freeze rights! Fricking Amazon runs the world!'

He moans about this kind of thing every day. I'm not saying he doesn't have a point, but what really annoys me is that he just sits on his arse and complains all the time. He never *does* anything about it. It's like he's comfortable in his complaints – they define him – and he enjoys them. If I could take away all the things he had to moan about there'd be no point to him even existing and he'd slip into pointless obscurity like some kind of redundant robot.

Foster mum clears the plates away. 'They can steer clear of my house, thank you very much,' she spits in that scratchy screech of a voice. 'I'm not having some corporate delivery monkey or half-baked drone with a camera dumping a parcel on my front doorstep whilst I'm frozen upstairs. Think of the things they could get up to!'

I used to get nightmares about people doing things to me when I was frozen. I would wake up in the night grinding my teeth or clawing my pillow. Being honest, sometimes I still do. The scariest thing is that anything could have happened and there's no way you would know. You come back after every freeze wondering if someone did something to you whilst you were out. You wake up like it's been eight hours, but somewhere in the middle of those, you stopped and thirty days passed everywhere else.

I deal with it in my own way. My solution is to set up the room in exactly the same way each time, millimetre by millimetre, so that you know where everything is when you're about to freeze. That way you can tell if anything's moved. Sometimes there are reports of this kind of thing happening. I guess it happens more in Zone 4 – that's what the only good social worker said once, sitting us both down at a new placement years ago with a face of concern – but the only ones that make the news are in Zones 1 and 2. Stories of sexual assault and physical abuse of frozen people. They blame it on degraded, morally bankrupt trippers. But who knows who does it really?

The freeze rights got introduced early on supposedly to protect against this kind of thing, but unless you can stop trippers, you can't stop it. And they haven't managed to work out a way to do that yet. Or they just don't care enough. They say they do, but they don't. Politicians lie – it's what they're best at.

No one cares about me. No one except my brother. And most of the time he doesn't give a shit. It's not his fault, I guess. They're trying him on new medication again, and he's gone weird like usual. He hates it; I don't think it'll stick. He's doing his thing where he pretends to take it then hides it somewhere. He's sliding back to the everything or nothing that he is without them. He has days when his manic, nonstop, uncontrollable talking and ideas and energy are all-consuming and all-at-once, and others when he simply can't get out of bed and hates everyone and everything, including me. I don't know which is worse; I just want him to be like he used to be when we were little. As long as he can keep it together 'til we're eighteen, I don't care this time.

But maybe someone else does care about me now, at least I really hope she does.

Foster dad groans his way to his feet and begins his shuffle towards the sofa. Five more minutes then he'll be dead to this world and killing some random zombie or alien in another. He spends so much time in that world, I wonder if that's his reality. When he's locked in, he senses nothing of this dump. Then I can get out of here. My brother is zoned out half asleep somewhere coming off these latest meds so he doesn't know what I'm up to and I don't want him too. This is my thing. My adventure. My relationship. I can be my own man too. I don't need him this time and I won't let him take it away.

7|

Holding onto the crumbling concrete wall, I take one last look at the grey clouds as they move through the sky. A strong gust of wind tugs at my shirt and rattles the pile of rusty road signs beside me.

I'm terrified.

We only got to meet two people from Thaw – Sara and Drake – for about five minutes before they asked us to go on this trip. They told us which slipway to use and what our objective was, and that was about it. Sasha walked me through the basics of tripping on the way over here, but now the reality of it is in front of me, I'm feeling massively underprepared. She told me not to worry so much about it, we just go to our designated slipway – which is basically a hole in the wall or ground that some trippers have gradually dug out over time – at the designated moment so as to avoid the border patrols, check no one is watching, and pull back the covering. It was strangely easy to do this and now that I'm about to begin my first mission for Thaw, a recognised terrorist organisation that is systematically targeted and hunted down by the Freeze Police Department, the reality of it is hitting me.

I duck down and peer through the hole in the wall to see Sasha standing in Zone 3 on the other side. She's literally in Zone 3 right now whilst it's in freeze state and I'm looking straight at her from Zone 4. If I could travel back in time and tell myself one week ago that I'd be standing here now, there's no way I would believe it. Smiling, she holds out her hand and beckons me towards her.

We shouldn't be doing this.

If we get caught, it's prison at the least. This has all happened so fast; I'm not sure if I'm ready. I only met Sasha two days ago and now I'm about to become a tripper. The one thing society tells me I shouldn't be. One step on the other side of that wall, and there's no going back to ordinary life. If Sasha's right, people disappear for this.

She smiles at me again, so I take in a deep breath, crouch down, squeeze through the gap and enter my first trip.

Who wants to be ordinary anyway?

8|

I straighten up on the other side and Sasha grins widely at me, taking my hand. We start to run and are soon sprinting, adrenaline racing through our bodies; my arms and legs pumping the pent-up excitement out of me as I think of nothing else but her. I feel free. I feel electric.

I feel alive.

Then the silence hits me – the sound of absolutely nothing happening is incredible. It feels like being in one of those sensory deprivation rooms they used to put me in to try and help me stay calm when I was little, as if someone has put mufflers over my ears and all I can hear are my own thoughts. I slow down and try to not freak out.

Seeing my expressions, Sasha stops and pushes me up against a wall. We kiss and it becomes everything we are.

'You'll get used to it,' she says, and it sounds as if I'm listening to an ASMR track and her voice is the only sound in the universe. 'Come on!' she pulls me forwards. 'There are so many places I want to go!'

With her grabbing a hold of my arm, we are off running again, taking deep breaths of the static, windless air around us. The deserted streets flash past; nothing moving, nothing changing. Everyone will be safely frozen inside their timeless homes right now, locked up tight to protect themselves from people like us. Every atom of their body unchanging for thirty days. I look up as we run and the sky is perfectly poised, like a painting. I've heard the stories, but never knew it would be quite like this.

We run past a pigeon, wings open in mid-flight yet suspended in the air. They never show you this kind of stuff on TV; it's always shots of sleeping people or captured trippers. We go through an open square to then take a sharp turn before reaching a sign that says *Montpelier Row*.

'James, the map was right!' she squeals, turning to smile at me as we run. 'It's not far now – come on, I want to show you something first.'

I slow to a walk, trying to catch my breath and figure out what it is that she wants to show me, but she tugs on my arm. 'Hey! Come on! We've only got a few hours, remember?!'

We move off the road and onto beautiful, lush green grass. Its blades initially feel stiff but soften as they brush against my shins. I stop for a moment to run my fingers through it. There is a permanent smell in the air of something sweet. I get my first glimpse of the park's flowers, frozen like perfect fakes in their beds.

We don't have parks in Zone 4. Everything is concrete and cold. The open spaces were initially tarmacked over to put people off social gatherings when the new strain, the big one, came in. That was back when people could still get together whenever they felt like it, when you could still have parties and gatherings and barbecues and night-clubs. Once everything else kicked off they just never bothered to put the grass back.

Sasha pulls me onto a path as manicured flower beds and bushes begin to line our way up the hill. This is only a Zone 3 park; imagine what those places are like in Zone 1.

We keep moving and the lactic acid builds in my legs but I don't care. I'm something more than my body right now; my heart is some-where up ahead carving a path for me to the summit. After half an hour or so, Sasha lets go of my hand and scrambles a last section of grassy bank before turning to face me at the top.

She's resting her hands on her knees and panting but her face is transfixed.

'Look. At. That,' she gulps.

I crawl the last yard and collapse. Taking deep breaths and propping myself up, I raise my eyes to a view over The City.

Sasha sits down and puts her arm around me. Her head leans into my shoulder.

The city stretches out as far as I can see.

'There it is,' she says. 'London. The City. It feels like the whole world when you see it from here. Amazing, right?'

It's bigger than I dreamed possible.

I think it is the most beautiful thing I have ever seen.

9|

As we look across the London skyline, she plucks a butterfly out of the air and examines it. Its static wings are like paper; so delicate and soft. She places it on the palm of her hand then blows and we watch as the butterfly glides slowly down. We're not supposed to change anything in freeze state; there's laws against it. I guess it doesn't really matter now though.

In front of me, rows and rows of houses stretch out for miles. The skyscrapers in the City tower above everything. I've only seen them on screens and didn't realise just how big they are. Their lights don't flash here; the light particles stopped on their way through like everything else.

'It's like the whole of London is frozen,' I say.

'Yeah, it's so weird, right? Knowing that they're still moving but we can't see. That's where we'd be right now,' she says pointing to a grey patch of cuboid buildings. Box after box crammed together with narrow corridors between them. They look small from here; so insignificant.

It's easy to see the wall. Not just the one that separates the zones, but even the one that borders London. It's so big, apparently you can see it from space. Why the hell anyone would want to, I don't know.

She looks down at her watch. 'We've probably got just under a couple of hours 'til the sweeps get to this area. Sara says when they tripped here, they watched the police routes and they patrol closer into the centre first. What do you want to do next?'

She checks the gun tucked into the back of her jeans.

'I honestly don't care, as long as it's with you,' I say.

She pushes me and I topple over onto the grass. 'Oh, shut up!' she says, smiling. Clambering on top of me and, with one hand either side of my head, she places a kiss on my lips. 'Well, look,' she continues, 'we've got a bit of time before we need to add to the map. How about a little shopping?!'

Putting the rucksack on, she rises and puts one foot on my chest.

'Last one to the bottom is a loser!' she shouts, before releasing and sprinting off down the hill.

10|

After running back through the park, Sasha pulled me into a narrow side street with shiny, polished glass fronted shops spanning either side. She has stopped on a bend in the road and is now searching for something to throw. The guys from Thaw said we should get our assignment done and get out, but Sasha doesn't seem to care. We were asked to scout for information on a designated section of the Zone 3 map and then come straight back. Zone 3 is the easiest to trip into so that's why they sent us there for my first trip. Our interzoners only give us access to satellite maps for Zone 4 – it's meant to be for added security against freeze crime – and people at Thaw have been sent some screenshots of maps for other zones by supporters, but they don't include all the specifics of what's on what street and where. Thaw figured that if they were going to make the most of the trips they made, they should record what's on what street, and how often patrols go past and along which routes etc. It's actually pretty smart, but also very time consuming and not much fun – the kind of job they give to inexperienced trippers like us.

I watch Sasha move around excitedly, her dreads sliding over her shoulders as she twists and turns. It makes me smile to picture my foster carers' reactions if they saw me now.

'I don't have anything against people...like her,' foster father said in hushed tones, pulling me to one side after Sasha had come over – I told her not to but she insisted – to pick me up, 'it's just that she's not from *here*, is she?'

When I told him that she was from Croydon he rolled his eyes and said 'that's not what I mean, I mean where's she from *originally*? Look, I don't want you to get mixed up with any gang stuff. You know that these BAME types, or whatever we're supposed to call them, are statistically more likely to get picked up by the police: that's not for no reason.'

When I told Sasha this on our way out, she laughed. 'So because I'm black I must be in a gang?! Does he not think there might be reasons why the police pick up white people less? Has he never heard of racial profiling and police bias? Jesus, what century is he living in?'

She'd soon stopped laughing and the waves began crashing again as she continued. 'What a prick. Can you please tell him to not call me a *BAME type* either, like that defines who I am? I hate it when people call me BAME as if that somehow represents one type of person. Is everyone black, Asian and minority ethnic supposed to be the same? Are even everyone within one of those criteria the same? I define who I am; a label like that tells you nothing of who I can be. So he can piss off with his BAME bullshit.'

I was in awe of her as she continued. Nothing can contain Sasha; she is limitless.

She's found something. She turns her head back towards me and says, 'Watch this!' before launching a rock at the window. It shatters as if in slow motion and Sasha's cheeks fill with glee. 'First time!' she yells.

Of all the stores in these rows upon rows of immaculate terraced buildings, of course she picked a sweet shop.

'Oh my god! You've got to get in here!', she says, clambering over the broken glass. 'This place is insane!'

I pick my way through the shards and step into the window display, holding a pose for a moment as if I were a mannequin.

'Hey, Sasha, look!' I hold the position until she turns around. 'It's a new work of art – urchin breaks into a sweetshop – a post-modernist take on capitalism in the modern world!'

She laughs. 'Stop being weird, James! Come on, have you seen these sweets? I can't decide what to try first.'

I step down onto the shop floor and cast my eyes around. Rows upon rows of glass jars filled with brightly coloured sweets of all shapes and sizes. The shelves stretch from floor to ceiling with each jar polished and perfect. I don't even know what half of them are. Any sweets on sale in Zone 4 are all sugar taxed to death, so they either taste of chemicals or they're so expensive I can never afford them.

There are so many choices, I can't move. It's too much. I don't know where to go, but I'm happy just staring at the displays. Caramels, chocolates, boiled sweets, gummies, lollipops, liquorice, gobstoppers. I pour over them and as I finally make a decision of what to try first, I feel a hand on my wrist and turn to see Sasha chewing on a mouthful.

'You okay?' I ask.

The fun has gone from her face and my eyes dart around to check the freeze police haven't arrived. There's no one else here, but in the corner of the room, by where she was standing, there is a large cardboard cut-out of a grinning girl sucking on a lolly and being held by her mum. It is torn into two pieces on the floor. My eyes move back up to meet Sasha's and she is staring at me with dark intent. I know that look.

'Let's destroy the whole place,' she says.

11|

Launching one last swing, I crash through a final shelf and see the perfect cylinders shatter, each one's contents spilling out and tumbling down like miniature landslides. The floor is a beautiful mess of bright colours and plastic wraps and jagged pieces of glass that glint as they catch the light. My arms feel tired and I drop the broom.

I watch as Sasha attacks a gumball machine, hitting it again and again, each time the cracks in its casing growing and growing until it suddenly bursts and the balls empty out, bouncing in all directions across the floor. She throws the mop handle away and walks towards me, every step crunching loudly on the detritus we have created. Standing breathless, Sasha rests her hands on her hips as we survey the scene.

'I wonder who owns this store,' I say, thinking out loud.

'Screw them,' she says. 'I don't care. They deserve it.'

The total silence of a frozen zone reappears and I remember why we came.

'What about the map?' I ask. 'We need to get that done.'

Sasha checks the timer on her wrist. 'We don't have time,' she replies. 'We'd better go. The FPD will get here soon.'

'Sara won't be happy; they'll have to wait a whole cycle now to get those streets.'

'It's fine,' she snaps. 'God, you really can find a way to ruin a good moment, can't you? Don't worry so much. I'll sort it with her when we get back. Come on, we need to get out of here.'

She clambers past me and out of the shop window. I pick my way through the mess and exit to see her running down the road.

'Hey, wait for me!' I yell.

12|

Sasha doesn't speak to me as we slow to an out-of-breath, fast-paced walk back to the slipway. I keep scanning the road for any FPD agents but there is nothing, and a sense of relief starts to wash over me as the wall comes back into view. She squeezes back through first and then I follow suit. With Sasha replacing the road signs carefully over the hole, I act as look out behind a banged out old car wreck. We are back in Zone 4, with all the noise and bustle of an unfrozen zone, and it feels bizarre. The clouds are moving again and the sound of everyday life is back. It sounds like traffic and footsteps and building works and sirens. But we aren't safe yet – the FPD regularly patrol this side of the wall. No one is allowed within a few metres of it, and if we get seen we'll get an immediate citation.

When time first changed, nobody knew how to react. There's this famous footage of people losing it all over the city. Fights and riots and shouting. London ablaze with fire and anger. The very possibility of it didn't fit into anyone's worldview. The virus had already changed the face of the world – thirty per cent of the world's population gone in a matter of years – add in Eastern Europe descending into war and the ensuing collapse of global trade after that, as well as the separation of London as a state to try and protect those within it; it was too much.

I've tried to understand it the same as everyone else, but it makes no sense. There's two types of people in Zone 4: those who can accept it and those who can't. They say it's happening elsewhere too, but there's no way of knowing if that's true. My interzoner only tells me what it's told to.

Sasha returns the last of the signs and then spins to face me on her haunches.

'See anything?' she asks, glancing around.

The early morning sun bounces off the stained glass of the old clock tower ahead. My eyes squint in the glare making it harder to see. I watch as a flight of pigeons darts off the tower and veers left then right, black dots zigzagging against the blue sky, before settling in the skeleton of a dead tree. The hands on the old face have long since broken, but the tower still stands dominant over the rooftops. A marvel of twentieth century design, now retired like the rest of them.

No one cared about clocks until they stopped.

'Nothing at the moment,' I reply. 'I think we should be safe to…wait, look!'

I point to a spot about two hundred metres down the street where a pair of Freeze Police Department agents appear around the corner.

'Quick, get back!' she growls, yanking my shirt.

'What do we do now?' I ask, panicking.

'Sit there,' she orders, pulling out her interzoner, 'we need a distraction.'

13|

'I'll call Sara, see if she can get down here.'

'Can't we just run?' I ask. 'We could probably make it from here.'

'They'll see us and call for backup,' she replies. 'We won't get away. Besides, if they spot us near here, they're bound to check the wall and then the slipway will be blown after just a couple of uses.'

Sasha pulls the pack off her back and reaches inside for the inter-zoner. It's one of the Thaw tampered ones. She fumbles it open and types in the complicated set of steps to remove government access to her call. If she gets caught with that phone then there will be prison time. Placing it to her ear, I can hear the quiet sound of ringing.

'Come on, come on,' she says desperately.

There's no answer.

'Try again,' I say.

'I am, I am,' she replies, re-entering all the codes and dialling again. 'This is the emergency number on a secure line, it's the only one I can call – they're supposed to pick up.'

The police are further down the street now as the quiet ringing sound continues.

'They're not answering! What are we going to do?'

We both shuffle back further behind the car. There's only one person I could call, but I really don't want to.

'I could call my brother,' I say. 'I have my dumb phone with me – they won't be able to trace that to me – and he has one too.' We found them in the loft amongst a whole heap of junk at a previous foster carers a couple of years back. We hid the relics in our room, along with their charger, and couldn't believe it when we turned them on later that night and they actually worked. They are ancient 'pay as you go' phones and still have a tiny bit of credit on them. We made a pact to always carry them on us just in case, never really knowing what we might use them for. Turns out it was a good decision.

'You have a brother?' she says. 'Why didn't you tell me?'

'It just didn't come up,' I lie.

'Does he know that you're tripping?'

'No.'

'But you can trust him, right?'

I pause for a moment. The birds fly off the dead tree and swoop through the air once more, all together as if they are one.

'James? You can trust him?' she asks again with more urgency.

'Yes,' I say.

'Then get him down here, now! We need someone to create a diversion so we can get out of here.'

14|

'Hey, look! He's here!'

Peering through a gap in one of the car's broken windows, I can see my brother pull up on his bike just down the road. He loves that thing; he found it dumped somewhere one day and brought it home. Pedals, gears and a chain – that's what he enjoyed so much. He spent hours watching old clips on how to fix it up. Ever since he finished, he has taken it everywhere. He never wanted an ebike, not that we can afford one anyway.

Looking over his shoulder, he pulls out his brick phone discreetly and dials, hiding it inside his hood.

The two FPD agents are still talking to each other about fifty metres up the road. It must be ten or fifteen minutes that they have been there now.

My brick vibrates and Sasha looks at me. I push the button to answer.

'I'm here,' he says. 'Where are you?'

'Can you see the beat-up old Tesla parked just over the street?'

He looks up towards us. 'Yes,' he replies.

'We are behind that.'

With her eyes. Sasha pleads with me to hurry up.

'If you look a little further up the road, you should be able to see two FPD agents.'

He turns his head slowly. 'Yep, I can see them,' he says quietly, before taking a sterner tone. 'What have you done?'

'I'll tell you later. Look, can you distract them long enough for us to get away without being seen?'

'Us? Who are you with?'

I hesitate, flicking my eyes sideways. 'I'm with Sasha.'

'Sasha? Well! So I'll finally get to meet this mystery girl.'

'Can we do this later?' I snap. 'Just help us get out of here.'

'Alright, alright. I'll figure something out.'

He ends the call and buries the phone back into his hoodie. Staring at the floor, he rubs his nose before wheeling the bike to face the direction of the police. He jumps on and pulls a pedal round with his foot until it reaches a position to push off.

'What's he going to do?' asks Sasha.

'I'm not sure,' I reply. Most of the time I have a good sense of what he'll do; growing up together for seventeen years will do that. But every so often he completely surprises me. And right now, I've got no idea what hell he'll raise.

He pushes off and begins to pedal as fast as he can. Within seconds I know exactly what he's going to do, and so does Sasha.

'He's going to ride straight into them!' she gasps.

We both watch as the distance closes rapidly and one of the agents yells seconds before the bike ploughs into him. My brother flies over the handlebars and an agent crumples onto the floor, howling out in pain. If my brother doesn't play this right, he'll be down the station, for sure.

'What the hell are you doing?' shouts the other agent. 'On your knees, hands behind your head, now!'

'I'm sorry officer, I lost control of the bike,' bleats my brother. False contrition is a speciality of his. 'I'm so sorry,' he repeats, raising to his knees, with the briefest of glances over in our direction, 'I didn't see you there.'

'Go, go!' urges Sasha under her breath, yanking my shirt as she moves off in a half crawl. We move around the side of the car and she checks once more before tugging me across the road. As we scurry to safety, I can hear my brother's voice.

'Hey, look at this! Look what you did to my bike!' he yells. 'You've ruined it! It's an antique this: you'll have to pay!'

'Stay on your knees!' yells an authoritative voice as we now finish crossing the road and rise to run down a side street. 'You rode into us; I should have this bike impounded!'

'I rode into you? Are you serious?! You came out of nowhere! You should watch where you're going. I thought you were supposed to keep us *safe*, not endanger passing children. I'm a minor you know…'

We move out of earshot with my brother still going. As much as I hate to say it: he's very good. We both know it. And now Sasha does too.

'Oh my god!' says Sasha, still running. 'That was amazing! Your brother is so wild! I can't believe he just did that! I have to meet him once we're out of this. Seriously! I can't believe you never told me about him!'

We keep running and I lean out to try and hold her hand, but it is just out of my reach.

15|

Sara is drumming her fingers on the table. Her, Sasha and I are sitting here sweating in stale air, waiting for Drake to arrive. I don't know if Drake is his first name or his surname, or even his actual name at all, but after one meeting I do know that he is definitely a pretentious prick. After the last trip ended so badly, Drake told Sasha and I in patronising tones that we needed to come in 'for a talk'. I get that he might be annoyed that we didn't come back with the map, but if he's cross with us because we nearly got caught, then, as far as I'm concerned, that's his and Sara's fault for not picking up the interzoner.

The whole Thaw set up confuses me. They've been around now for about five years, apparently, and have built up this reputation as an organised terrorist network. They are constantly vilified by the media and presented as an *existential threat to our way of life*; you hear more about them than the virus. As far as I can work out though based on my limited interactions with them, they are just a bunch of inefficient, self-aggrandizing teenagers who are pretty poor at organising anything. I mean, Sara apparently didn't answer the phone when we called because she was taking a nap. It's almost disappointing to see how far from the truth the portrayal of Thaw really is.

We are sitting in a basement flat on the estate and there are sheets hung over all the windows. Sasha and I are waiting on a beat-up old sofa and Sara is perched on a chair next to two tables which have been pushed together. The air smells musty and unclean, and in the corner of the room the bin is overflowing with junk food wrappers. Dust particles dance in the slivers of light that peek through the sheets. The table is covered with sections of maps, scrunched up pieces of paper, a range of different edition interzoners and a couple of stickered laptops. If this is the hub of an organised criminal enterprise, then the government has nothing to worry about whatsoever.

A rhythmic knock sounds at the door and the guy with a serious face sitting beside it reaches up with his pop gun in hand to press the lock release. A shaft of daylight penetrates the room as Drake's heavy frame appears, before he quickly slams the door shut behind him. He walks over to the table and places his gun down with a clink before pulling out a chair.

'Sorry I'm late,' he says, sweeping the long blond hair out of his eyes. 'I was held up in a meeting at Centre 2.'

Sasha nods as if she already knows about Centre 2 when I'm pretty sure she doesn't. I'm feeling pissed off about this whole thing, so I'm not about to just accept anything the *great* Drake says. 'Where's Centre 2?' I ask.

'Well, I'm afraid I can't share that information with you, James,' Drake replies, as of course he would. 'Let's just say that there are a number of centres right now in different locations and we are working towards relocating everyone to a central hub in the very near future.'

He looks over at Sara and rolls his eyes. Sara glances at something on the table and Drake nods his head. She's got a buzz cut recently and got rid of the high top she had in our first meeting, which means that she keeps drawing her hand over the back of her head. She does it again as she turns to speak to us.

'Look,' she says, 'we are disappointed by the way you handled the trip. You only had one objective and you didn't accomplish it. And then, to top it off, you almost got caught and blew a new slipway on the way out.' She looks over at Drake. 'To be honest, we aren't sure if you are the right people for what we are trying to accomplish here.'

'I'm sorry,' Sasha jumps in. 'I mean, we're sorry. It was a mistake and it won't happen again. I lost track of time and...well, I promise I'll make it up to you on the next one. I'll go again and get double.'

Drake casts his eyes from Sasha to me and then back to Sasha again. 'You've performed better on other trips, Sasha. It's not you we are so worried about. James,' he says, turning to look at me with a face like a foster carer, 'we're concerned you're perhaps not...cut out for this.'

I take in a slow, deep breath. People talking to me like this pulls that darkness out of me, but I have to keep my cool for Sasha.

'Look,' I reply, shuffling my position on the old sofa, 'we didn't do the map, fair enough. I accept that, but I'm pretty sure there will be other chances to do that. But it's not fair to blame us for nearly getting caught. It wasn't our fault that we almost got spotted at the slipway. We came out within the timeframe we were supposed to. We called the right number. We improvised and we *didn't* get caught. That wasn't our fault, and the fact that your new slipway wasn't busted was thanks to us and our quick thinking. And *to be honest*,' I add with extra emphasis, 'if the whole trip had been organised better, then we wouldn't have faced that risk anyway.'

Drake turns towards me in his chair and leans his elbows on his knees. 'Careful, new boy. Don't start having a go when you've only been part of this revolution for five minutes. It has taken a lot of work to get this far, and we've lost a lot of good people, so don't start getting so high and mighty when you're still in the baby pool.'

'Well,' I reply cuttingly, because he's belittling me even more, 'you're going to lose more people if you don't start being more organised. Why don't you have lookouts by the exits of every slipway? Why did you give us a rough window to trip in when it should be down to the minute? If Sara was taking a nap, who even knew we were on the trip? Was there only one person available here? Did anyone else in all of your centres know where we were?'

Sasha turns to me and her face suggests she doesn't know whether to be worried or impressed. Drake picks up a piece of map from the table and starts to turn it over in his hands.

'It's unfortunate that Sara was asleep, I agree,' he says as Sara looks at the floor, 'but it's not as easy as you might think to set this stuff up...'

'Well, it should be,' I interject. I've had enough of this guy and if I'm going to keep tripping with Sasha then things need to change. 'You just need someone to spend the time organising these things in a joined-up way. I know you've got lots of people, so you should use them wisely.'

Drake visibly bristles at this comment. He kisses his teeth and looks me straight in the eye. 'You think you could do better?' he asks.

I turn to Sasha who is totally transfixed by this exchange. There's a look on her face which suggests she might even be impressed by this latest version of me she is seeing. The one who gets pissed off by ineptitude. Who doesn't sit down and just take it. It spurs me on. 'Yes, I do. Give me a trip or day that's coming up. I'll organise it and show you how it should be done.'

Drake turns to Sara and raises his eyebrows. 'What do you think, shall we give the kid a try?' he says, as if he isn't only a couple of years older than me.

Sara rubs the back of her head again and says, 'Well I guess it can't hurt. We've got a busy day tomorrow and I'll be running operations from here. I could do with some help, to be honest. I think we have four trips planned, but I don't know all the details yet.'

Drake chews his bottom lip and turns back to face me. 'Okay,' he says in a deep voice. 'You get back here tomorrow morning and we'll see if you're just big talk or if you can actually help out with any of this.'

'Fine,' I say feeling powerful and proud and rebellious. 'I don't think it's a good idea to keep using the same meeting locations, but we can talk about that later. What time?'

'Nine thirty,' replies Sara. 'We've got an early start.'

'But you listen, and you listen to me good,' says Drake flexing his biceps as he folds his arms. 'If you screw this up, you're out. Understand?'

16|

I double check my watch and it is definitely nine thirty. I'm here and no one is answering the door. It's another cold, grey day and the clouds in the sky are smothering everything. I didn't sleep much last night. When Sasha kissed me goodbye after the meeting yesterday, there was a feeling as if it could be the last time. As if she believed in me only just enough to give me a shot, but not enough to think I could pull it off. I'll prove it to her. I'll prove it to all of them.

I knock again, harder, in the rhythmic pattern they gave me, and finally someone opens the door. Sara peers round, squinting her big brown eyes in the light. She yawns and has definitely only just woken up.

'Oh, you're here,' she says with little to no emotion. 'Come in, I'm just making a coffee.'

I walk in and the door closes behind me.

The guy with the serious face from yesterday is asleep on the sofa. He is curled up in the foetal position with a patchwork blanket over him and looks like a giant baby. Sara points to a chair and tells me to sit. 'I'll be back in just a minute,' she says. 'You want coffee?'

'Sure,' I reply, looking down at the table. The different pieces of map are connected at various points, but interspersed with scrappy pieces of paper featuring names and dates of what look like proposed trips.

Sara reappears with two mugs and, handing me one, starts to filter through the different scraps on the table. 'Okay,' she says half to me, half to herself. 'Today, we have this one...this one,' she hands me pieces of paper each time, 'this one...and this one. Four, like I said.'

She takes a gulp of the coffee before straightening up the four scraps of paper. 'This is what's happening today. I've got the phone should anything go wrong.'

'What do we need to do then?' I ask.

'You tell me, genius,' she replies. 'I thought you were the one with all the bright ideas?' She looks at me with disdain before sinking into a chair and cradling her coffee.

I take a slug – it tastes disgusting – and begin reading the notes. Each note contains the names of the people going on the trip, the rough time they said they would do it, and what the objective is. That's it.

'Is this all you have?' I ask. 'For the whole day?'

She sniffs. 'Yep. It's all been agreed with the majors – Drake included.'

I look at the timings. The first trip isn't due to go out until ten. 'But these aren't the only people working with Thaw, right?'

'Of course not,' she snorts. 'We've got tons of contacts. We don't have everyone going out on trips every day.'

'Right, so we could get in touch with some of them and set them up as lookouts, right?'

'I guess so. We can see if anyone's available.'

'And it's not too late to contact today's trippers?'

'No. Why?'

'We need to get them more specifics. We need to call each of them up and establish exactly what time they are going to be at the wall, when they will be through the other side and what time they will be back out. Do they have staggered entry and exit times?'

'No, we just went with what times they were available.'

'Okay, that needs to change too. You don't want to potentially be dealing with multiple exit problems at the same time when you could just be dealing with one.'

Sara looks at me with tired eyes. 'This is going to take ages,' she sighs.

17|

'Okay,' I say, leaning back in my chair. 'The fourth group should be out in two minutes. I'm going to check with the lookout that they are in position and everything is clear.'

The other three trips have all happened without a hitch. I contacted all of them and set up the details so that we could manage them consecutively one by one. One of the lookouts caught a FPD patrol coming up to the slipway just in time which averted a disaster. We are now on the last one of the day and Drake has joined us in the dimly lit flat. He has apparently been very busy all day, but I've got no idea what he's been doing.

'They're not answering,' I say, having not received any confirmation from the lookout. 'What is he up to? They should be out any moment now. Why isn't he answering?'

Sara, Drake and I sit there in a strange moment of silence. Drake is examining his fingernails, picking dirt from under them, and Sara is scrolling through her interzoner. I almost forget about the fact that we are now all criminals and would go to prison for the rest of our lives just for sitting here, and think of how us three are probably all as messed up as each other. How maybe we are all a bit broken, and we've all got some darkness, and we're all trying to deal with it in our own way.

'Come in, Centre 1! Come in, Centre 1! We've been spotted! We are on the run!' a panicked voice bursts through the speaker.

I grab the tampered interzoner and reply. 'Where are you?'

'Running down Mulberry Avenue! Two FPD agents are after us – we need some help!'

I look down at the map in front of me and trace my fingers from the slipway to Mulberry Avenue. They haven't got far. Drake grabs the interzoner from me.

'Do you have your guns?' he asks.

'Yes,' pants the voice back.

'Then you will need to use them,' Drake barks, panic in his voice too.

'No!' I shout. 'Not yet!' Drake looks at me startled as if he can't work out what just happened. 'If they get caught in a firefight, they're not going to make it,' I say, covering the microphone on the interzoner. 'Come on, you know that. I can get them out of this, just give me a chance,' I say with my eyes fixed on his. He nods and I pick up my interzoner and start searching.

Furiously scanning the map whilst searching for bus routes and times on my device, I get into this state of heightened awareness. It usually happens when I get stressed out or nervous. My social workers used to call it 'hyper-vigilance' back when I was little and said it was a result of my early life trauma and neglect, but I don't know if that's right. Social workers are full of it sometimes. Apparently, I'm so scared of uncertainty and change that in moments of stress my senses work overtime to account for this. Whatever it is, it means when I get flustered, I work double time on what's in front of me.

'Take the next right down Ponting rd.,' I say, tracing lines across the map. 'You there?'

Heavy breathing. 'Yep, there now,' they reply.

'Okay, keep going. How far are they behind you?'

'About a hundred metres, I think,' they pant.

'Take the next left. You're aiming for the bus stop on Church St, okay?'

'Yes, okay.'

My fingers are frantically scrolling down live departure updates. 'There's a bus due in…one minute. Number 37. If they are a hundred metres behind you, you should have time to turn the corner and get on it before they see you do so. Let's just hope the bus is on time.'

'There's the bus! It's coming!' The frantic sound of footsteps speeds up as they start sprinting.

Drake stares at the floor and it feels like everyone is holding their breath. My foot is tapping the way Jake's does when he's hyper.

The next sound we hear is that of a bus door opening and closing with the familiar hiss, shhh and clunk. My foot stops.

'Are you on?' I ask. 'Are you on?'

'We're on,' comes the reply. 'I don't think they've seen us. I can't see anyone following.'

There is a loud exhale of air over the interzoner.

'Thanks,' he says. 'I don't know who this is, but you seriously saved our bacon. Phew!'

Drake, Sara and I all simultaneously slide back in our seats. The tension in the air drops away and I can feel myself smiling. I did it. Drake draws his toes across the floor to bring his feet under the seat. 'Well,' he says quietly. 'I guess we could use you after all, James.'

I smile and Sara gives me a little nod of recognition. 'You're pretty good at this, you know?' she says. 'You want to do it for us again?'

18|

My brother perches himself on the edge of the roof, his legs dangling down. It's been over a week since he saved my skin at the border wall and he hasn't let me forget it. He lost his bike because of it, and got processed at the police station, so I guess I understand. But he's not taking his meds which means he's been pissed at me pretty much the whole time since. I love my brother, I kind of have to, but he can be a real dick sometimes. And I don't know what he's going to try to do to this thing I have with Sasha. He's in one of his moods where I can't predict his actions and, honestly, I'd rather he wasn't around.

When he suggested meeting up with her, I tried to put him off, but in the end he said I owe him so I didn't really have much choice. I've managed to avoid the two of them meeting until now, keeping busy with more and more trip planning at Thaw, but Sasha has been asking after him all week, so I guess it had to happen at some point.

There's nowhere easy to meet when you're mixing households, they make sure of that. We are only ever supposed to meet one on one and, lately, the police have been getting stricter and stricter on people who do, so when my brother suggested meeting Sasha at our spot, it seemed like the best option.

It feels weird bringing her here. This is our thing, mine and his. We found this when we went exploring after first arriving at the estate. It only took a couple of hours to spy the old emergency stairwell at the back of this disused tower block and, after a few attempts, we managed to prise it open, discovering that it led to the roof. It's a flat open expanse above the streets: a surface of scratchy shingle that's covered in moss and puddles and bird shit. But it's private. And it's quiet. And the view over the estate is as good as you'll get. It's the place we go to breathe and escape for a while when the foster home is too much.

We don't talk about how much we need somewhere like this, but we've always made it our mission to find our own spot. It's a kind of ritual we have whenever we move. In every placement we've had, we've hunted down a safe space and claimed it as our own. You get pretty good at finding them after a while. Somewhere private and only ever for us. That's why I was surprised when he suggested bringing Sasha here; we've never had anyone else in our secret spaces before.

'Hey,' comes Sasha's voice from the direction of the stairwell. I turn around to see her leaning on the doorframe, one hand in her hair. 'Well this place is a bit of a shit hole, isn't it?!'

She walks over to where I am standing and peers over the edge. 'Not a bad view, though. We could use somewhere like this to keep an eye on what the pigs are up to.'

My brother spins around, lifts his legs back over the ledge and looks up at Sasha. 'Well you sure know how to have a good time,' he says, rubbing the back of his neck and looking straight at her in that way he does. 'Let's all just sit here and watch for police, shall we? Sounds like a riot! And maybe while we're at it, we can all complain about how terrible our lives are.'

He grins and Sasha smiles back, scratching her shoulder with one hand and giving him the finger with the other. She peers forward, flicking her gaze from each of us in turn.

'I'm Jake, that's James,' he says. 'Got it?!'

'Christ,' she says, 'I knew you were twins but I didn't realise you'd be so, well…identical. You're like weird, twisted copies of each other.' She tilts her head to one side. 'God, it's so freaky! I can't handle it!'

He stands up and puts his arm around me, pushing our heads together. 'Yep,' he says, 'he's a weird copy of me alright. Except I got all the brains and the self-control, and all he got was some twisted-up impulse to be individual and free and unique. Poor guy. It really is a problem. He just will persist in not *fitting in*.'

He always does this: switches us around to play with people's perceptions. He sets me up as the boring one every time. I look at the floor and kick some of the shingle.

'Well, gee,' says Sasha, 'who'd want to be free and unique? That sounds like torture! Aren't we all just supposed to be good little boys and girls whose sole purpose is to contribute to the republic? One more member of the herd, that's me!'

My brother steps forward and paints his arms across the skyline. 'What could be better than being a member of the herd here? Our lovely liberal utopia; the squeaky clean, fake-news free, milk turned sour that is…' He places his hands in the air to make an invisible frame. '*The European People's Republic of London* – such a delightful place! Open to…no one, unless you already live here or are filthy rich.'

I can see Sasha's eyes lighting up as she continues the conversation. 'Life is idyllic in this new Eden! Pandemic safe – cough, cough – with blemish free skin and shiny white teeth! All the latest delicacies of modern cuisine, sponsored trips to the beach through the quarantine channels and tantalising cocktails in your favourite bars! All available to you right here, unless, of course, you live in Zone 4 and then you're fucked!'

They both burst out into laughter and my brother's hand goes to her shoulder as he creases over. As the laughter fades, she looks at him and it reminds me of that night at the party.

'So, anyway,' I say. 'Now you two have met, Sasha and I have got work to do. Another trip to plan, right Sash?'

'Hold on a minute,' he says, turning to me. 'Why can't I come along? As far as I'm concerned, the only reason you're not in juvie right now is because of me.' He stands bolt upright and salutes me. 'I want to join the revolution, sir. I am ready and willing to fight; new recruit at your service!'

'I dunno…' I say, but Sasha interjects.

'Of course you can come along! The more the merrier. We need more soldiers! Come on, they're going to love you down at Thaw. And the two of you together, we could cause some real mischief, I'm sure!'

'Okay, but we can't all go together,' I say, hurriedly looking for excuses. 'We'll get picked up.'

'It's okay,' replies Sasha. 'I can show your bro the way and you can just meet us there in ten. Okay?'

She is already turning to walk off before I reply. He picks up his jacket off the floor and knuckles me on the head. 'See you in ten, big man!' And with that he is off.

I shuffle over to the ledge and sit down, picking up a handful of the crumbling shingle and dropping it off.

That was exactly what I didn't want to happen.

19|

The good thing about a zone being frozen for thirty days is that there are plenty of chances to trip into it. The hard part is trying to make sure that everyone's trips are coordinated so that no one uses the same slipways on the same dates, as well as ensuring that the paths are used on rotation to avoid detection. I've learned a lot about all this since my first trip with Sasha a couple of months ago. I thought tripping was just going to be about having fun, but it's way more serious than that. These people really believe that they are going to change the world. Every so often, I catch myself believing that too.

As long as I get to keep tripping with Sasha, I'm okay with whatever else we have to do.

We are tripping into Zone 2 today. When all this started, I was worried that my foster carers might catch on at some point and ask me about where I keep going, but they don't care. My brother joined a while ago too, and we've both been out of the house a lot since then, but they aren't interested in what we're up to. As long as they keep getting paid their foster allowance, they don't give a shit. The only thing they keep telling me is that I should get a job, like they can talk.

I don't know anyone my age who has a job; Zone 4 isn't exactly full of opportunity. I live on the same universal credit as everyone else. It's hardly anything at my age, but at least I'm not stuck packing boxes in some delivery centre all day. I guess I could try for something better, but what's the point? I only finished school last year and my GCSEs weren't bad, but they aren't about to set the world alight. I'll probably be out of here soon and have to move again anyway, and I've got plenty keeping me busy with all the jobs Thaw sends me on. Sometimes I get to keep some of the money I find on the trips, if I see any. One day I'll get a job, but not yet.

'You ready?' I ask Sasha, as she fumbles with her backpack.

'Nearly,' she replies. 'You got a spare facemask? I can't find mine.'

'Yeah, sure.' I reach into my coat and pull out an old disposable one. 'Here.'

She puts it to her nose and sniffs. 'Eurgh, that does not smell good. How old is that? Is that all you've got?'

'Sorry, I don't have anything else. Where's your issue one?'

'Not sure, must have left it somewhere again.' She takes another sniff and then wipes off the mask with her hand. 'This'll have to do. If we get stopped, I'll just say mine's in the wash or something. Alright, I think we are ready.'

She pulls the bag onto her back before continuing. 'I'm excited,' she says with a smile. 'I haven't been to Zone 2 for ages!'

'I've got it all planned out,' I say, opening the door.

'You always do,' she replies.

20|

'What's our route in?' she asks, adjusting the straps on her shoulders as we walk out into a cloud covered night.

'We are going through Kwame's place,' I reply.

'Oh, I love Kwame,' she smiles, 'he's the best. Can we pick up some supplies on the way through?'

'We won't have time.'

She always does this. If we stop to get supplies then she'll hang around chatting for ages and then not be able to decide what to take. I don't say this to her because she gets annoyed when I read her right. She used to like it, because I *know* her, but I guess everyone hates being predictable at some point. She is now giving me a look like I'm her parent; I hate it when she does this.

'Okay, if we just stop for a couple of minutes, we should be able to adjust our schedule,' I say, caving in. Again.

She sighs deliberately.

'I just don't want us…'

'…to get caught. I know,' she says dismissively. 'Neither do I, but I'm sure we can spare five minutes. Come on.'

21|

The door of Kwame's place buzzes as we enter, two minutes before curfew begins, as I planned. The white strip lights hum just above our heads as my eyes follow the chequered tiled flooring of an aisle that leads to a man at the end.

He looks up from the counter and smiles.

'Wagwan! You're here!' he says, looking at his watch. 'And right on time as always, my brother. Let me close the shutters on you *fine* people.'

He carries his heavy frame round the counter and down one of the aisles, his sliders slapping on the floor with each step. Stopping at the end, he presses a button and a metal grill instantly fires across the shop front from either side.

'What's the trip this time? Anyting good?' he asks, stretching his neck from side to side and sucking on a lolly.

'Just another mayhem mission,' Sasha replies, fist bumping Kwame in the process. 'If we can get hold of any decent tech then we will, but we are only really going to disrupt on this one.'

'Nice, nice,' he nods, curling the sides of his mouth down. 'Mayhem missions are dope. I had mad love for them back in the day, when I was a bit...leaner, you could say!' He rubs his belly and laughs. 'What's the target?'

'They're putting up new surveillance cameras in Morden, replacing the old ones and adding more.'

'So you're gonna bang 'em up, innit?!' he says with his face beaming.

'You know it, fam!' Sasha beams back. She always talks differently when she's around Kwame. Her accent changes slightly, more Jamaican than usual, and she starts to mirror the way he speaks, using words she doesn't use with me. It kind of annoys me that she does it, because I don't know if she sounds more like her real self when she's with him or me.

'Yes, my sister! You show 'em what's what! You're a bad girl!' Kwame licks his lips. 'You want anything before you go? A lickle something to keep you going? Girl's gonna get hungry out there!'

'You always hook me up, Kwames,' Sasha leans in for a hug before moving off down the aisle.

'You want something too, my man?' Kwame points at me with one eye half-closed.

'I'll grab a quick drink, thanks. We can't stay long – got to get out there whilst the time is good.'

'Sure, sure. I hear ya. Take what you like and just shout when you're done. You can get through the back whenever, bruv.'

I look around but can't spot Sasha, until her voice gives her away.

'Damn, it's so hard to choose,' she says to herself.

22|

Kwame rolls the wheelie bins to one side to reveal the tiny, crawl-size hole in the wall. When they built the border wall across the bottom of the back yard of his dad's shop without asking permission, his Dad was outraged like everyone else. Kwame was barely old enough at the time to remember it happening, but ever since the virus got his dad, he made it his personal mission to dig out a hole for trippers. He talks about how he hates having to run the shop, and how he wishes his dad hadn't left it for him to take on. But I feel jealous of him – at least he has something that he can call his, something of his own.

'How long?' he asks, arms folded across his barrel stomach.

'We've got three hours,' I reply.

'No problem,' he says, nodding. 'I'll let you back through later. Peace and love. Smash it up, sister!'

Sasha grins and hugs him as she goes towards the wall.

'Thanks, Kwame,' I say.

'Easy,' he says, grabbing hold of the bins again to wheel them back into position.

The gap is so tight it feels like I could get stuck there and my body wriggles ferociously to try and make some space. Once I have wrestled my way through, I crouch inside the crate that covers our arrival. Looking through the spy hole, the road looks deserted so I move myself and the crate to one side to allow Sasha the room. Grabbing her

65

hands with mine, I pull her through and she rolls out onto the pavement. I put the crate back and we duck behind another pile of boxes, as we agreed.

'Okay,' I say. 'We just have to wait here for two minutes to check the quarter past patrol has been and gone. We are a bit behind the plan.'

We stay where we are and the silence feels unbearable. I can't keep it a secret anymore.

'I've got a surprise for you,' I say.

She twists to look at me, her face looking perplexed. 'What do you mean?'

'I mean I've got a surprise for you. You'll see. Just follow me.'

'What about the new cameras?'

'There aren't any. I needed a distraction to get you out. This one isn't for Thaw. Or anyone else. I've got something planned, just for us.'

She smiles and leans into me. 'Well aren't you quite the surprise? Okay, Mr. Dark Horse, impress me.'

23|

She throws herself back on the bed, grasping the white sheets and pushing them into her face. The wood of the four posts creaks as she rolls over into the thick duvet, splaying herself out into a star shape. I want to jump on too, but I'm so happy watching her that I wait.

'This place is amazing,' she says. 'How did you find it?'

'Let's just say I asked around. One of the guys found it by accident a while back and gave me the directions.'

I pull the pack from my back and empty out its contents.

'I can't believe how much great stuff they've got,' I say, unzipping the bag.

I sort the contents on the bed – a block of cheese, a bunch of grapes, crusty bread, bars of real chocolate, fresh tomatoes and apples. Everything I could hurriedly fit in whilst Sasha waited in here.

'What?!' she says, looking at the loot. 'Oh my god – where is this from?'

'The kitchen,' I reply. 'This is a kind of second home place that belongs to some rich guy who must be from Zone 1. The guy I spoke to said it looked like he never used it, but that it must be stocked by a maid or something in case he visits.'

Sasha has torn off a handful of the bread and is chewing on it loudly. 'This is so good,' she says. 'You have to try some.'

I pick up an apple and crunch into it. It is crisp and sweet and juicy and it tastes delicious.

'Sit with me,' she says, patting the bed.

I sit down onto the soft bedding and check my watch. 'We only have an hour left,' I say, taking another bite. 'The patrols will be round this area soon.'

'Just relax,' she sighs. 'Come on, enjoy it for a little bit – be in the moment with me. Don't think about leaving already.'

I slump back onto the bed and she shifts up next to me. She starts stroking my hair as I lie there and my eyes close.

'Thanks for doing this,' she whispers. 'It's really nice of you.' She takes another bite of something and goes quiet for a minute. 'I don't deserve you,' she continues.

'Don't be silly,' I say.

'No, I don't,' she replies quietly.

I lean up onto one elbow. 'What do you mean?'

She rubs her nose and looks down at the bread in her hand. 'Never mind, forget it. Come on, let's have some chocolate. This looks like some expensive stuff.'

She bends over to pick up the bar and then kisses me on the forehead. 'Thank you,' she says, her brown eyes sharing mine.

And then, just for a second, there is something terribly sad in her face and if I wasn't paying attention I wouldn't have caught it. It's new; I haven't seen that look before. It flickers for the briefest of times and then it is gone.

24|

Sasha's dad is out again. He works two jobs so he's hardly ever around. She says she doesn't care, but I know she does. She told me that he hasn't been the same since her mum left. Even when he is there, he's pretty much silent. They live together but barely communicate. She never wants to talk about it though, I've tried. I've only met him a couple of times and he didn't say much to me either – it was usually as he was heading out the door to work. He speaks very softly and with a bit of a Jamaican accent, which comes out in Sasha sometimes, especially when she is with him, or Kwame.

Sasha told me the story once about how her great great grandma came across from Jamaica to the UK as a teenager on a boat called the Windrush. Apparently it was a big deal at the time, the second world war had just finished and she was offered a new life in London. She met Sasha's great great grandpa on the boat coming over and when they got married later that year, they decided to change their name to Shiverstone. They weren't getting any work and thought an English sounding name might help with applications. Her great great grandma picked the name because that was how she described England – a freezing cold rock that was windy and wet most of the time – a Shiverstone.

Sasha told me about the "No blacks! No dogs! No Irish!" signs that started popping up in London soon after her great great grandma had arrived and how her dad always used to remind her of this whenever she got in trouble. *You've got to remember*, he would say, *that they never wanted us here in the first place so if you go around causing trouble, that just gives them reason to think they were right.* He used to tell her that they have to be better than everyone else just to make it level, and it's not fair and it's not right but that's just the way it is. Sasha never used to get in trouble. She used to be a straight A student. But after her mum disappeared, she didn't care about any of that anymore.

The good news with her dad working so much is that her place is free most of the time. I love the nights we spend just the two of us when the rest of Thaw aren't around. It's great not to have my brother here too; since they first met, he's been hanging out with us a lot and for a month or so now it's been harder and harder to get our own space. The last few weeks since the surprise trip I planned for us have been weird; I can't put my finger on what it is, but she's been more distant. Still, I'm sure she feels the same as me: a chance to have a night on our own is like gold dust.

Having raided her dad's secret beer stash, we are both on it and after a few bottles I'm already feeling the buzz.

'Do you still wonder about the strangeness of it all?' I ask, examining the label on my bottle. 'I think about it a lot. Time used to pass in silence, without anyone even noticing it. I was thinking last night: what did people used to care about before all this? Before the freeze and countdown clocks and zones and time stoppages? Before Thaw?'

She takes a swig of warm beer and replies. 'Probably the same things they care about now just minus the freeze stuff: being young and getting old; the virus; the vaccines; wars; making money; families, friends and survival. Love and all that.' She takes another swig, staring up at the wall. 'They cared, or didn't care, for the Republic when it began, I guess,' she continues. 'Oh, and Brexit. People really used to care about that, apparently,' she laughed.

She is missing my point. 'But the arrow of time itself didn't used to be an issue; it was…a background assumption. It simply ticked by unnoticed, making sense of people's lives. Everyone cares about time now. It's all anyone at Thaw talks about. It feels like it's all any of us talk about anymore. We're so obsessed with it that we forget all the other stuff.'

'You say that like it's a bad thing,' she replies, curtly. 'There's a reason why we talk about it so much: because we've got no answers – the government gives nothing. Literally, *nothing*. Why don't they explain what's going on? If time is alterable, then what the hell else is? And why is this happening now, after everything else in the last few years? What are they covering up?

'That's why we need Thaw. People are angry, Thaw gives us a name and a reason to be so. It's all we talk about because it's the only thing important enough to talk about. I thought you got that?' She sits up on her elbows and looks at me. 'Don't you want to know *why?*'

'Of course I do, you know that. Only, it's…don't you ever just want to live your life? Get out of here and stop worrying about it?'

She tilts her head, scrunching up her eyes. I press on, but I can sense I'm losing her; she's going to that dark place again.

'The Freeze only happens in the EPRL, right? I mean that's what people at Thaw say. Don't you ever think about getting out? Going somewhere else and just…living?'

'As far as we *know* this only happens here.' She lifts the bottle to her mouth once more, but I wish she would stop drinking. 'The government says it's happening in other places in the world too, remember. But that's bullshit and we both know it.

'You really want to go somewhere else? The whole world is already screwed – you think people aren't pissed out there, too?' She points at the window. 'People were angry enough before the freeze; it just galvanised us. The Republic was supposed to be the *answer* to all our problems; the last bastion of hope on this god-forsaken island. The holy project of democracy in the face of demagogues and fascists. The fact-based liberal wet dream of tolerance and respect. And look how that turned out. There's been so many waves of infection God knows what's even left out there.'

I sit up and take her hand. 'But isn't that an opportunity, though? A chance to make something of our own without any old people telling us what to do?'

'So it's good that all these people died?' Sasha asks, looking at me in that way I can't bear.

'No, no...that's not what I mean. It's a chance for us to do something right in the world. Something good. Make something for ourselves away from all these mistakes.'

She stands up and her hand moves from mine. 'Only,' she says casually, 'it turns out that history is just people making the same mistakes in different ways.' She sighs. 'I'm getting another beer.'

Sasha's shutting down again. I try quickly to change tack. 'I was talking to one of the new guys who's just joined. He said that he knew a guy who met a Brit once who'd come in from out there beyond the wall. He told me about this place he described outside called Cornwall. He said time doesn't freeze there. It's nowhere near any of the coast where the holiday corridors are set up. Apparently, it has fields and sea and moorlands and beaches. There's wind and blue sky and fresh air that smells like spring. He told me about these things called crofter's houses there: tiny old stone cottages sitting empty with no one to fill them. You can be self-sufficient, he said. Live off the land and sea and rely on no one else. Catch your own fish. Grow your own fresh vegetables – none of this processed nutrition crap we get. No grown-ups, no police, no government. Just us.'

'What about the virus?'

'Pretty much only middle-aged or sick people die from the virus, right? So we'd be just fine.'

'Maybe for now, sure. But what if we got ill? Who would look after us, James? The only slim chance of getting a vaccine that works is in the EPRL, you know that. Hardly anyone ever leaves the Republic because you can't come back in if you do. And what about anyone else outside the city? I'm not sure they're going to be friendly. We've talked about setting something up outside already – you were at the meetings – it's a good idea but it's going to take time to put everything in place. We need a proper community out there. And we need to figure out a way to get in and out of the city without getting caught.' She twists the lid off another bottle and takes a gulp then looks at the floor. 'We can't just leave. I can't. And…I don't want to.'

She stops talking and for a moment it is so quiet, it is as if we are frozen. I went too far; I shouldn't have said anything. She's in that place again and I need to pull her back.

I stand up and wrap my arms around her.

'I know, I know,' I mutter quietly. 'I'm sorry, it was a silly idea, you're right. I just want us to be together, that's all. I kind of pictured us like your great great grandma and grandad, taking a risk and leaving home for somewhere new with something exciting to try and build for ourselves.'

'Yeah, and look how that turned out for them!' she says, rolling her eyes. 'Look,' she sighs, 'I'm tired. Let's go to bed.'

She stands up and steps over me.

25|

I am sitting at the dinner table. It's the usual frozen ready meal crap topped up with a cheap synthetic filler that tastes a bit like everything and a lot like nothing. Foster dad is flicking through his interzoner as he shovels food into his mouth. Bits of the gelatinous gloop stick to his scraggly beard and sit there. Every time he puts more of it in, he starts chewing for a few seconds before his mouth closes. It creates this wet crunching sound that sounds like a cockroach getting squashed. It's so noticeable now that I can't help but listen out for it. I hear him swallow, before the sound of scraping the bowl for another spoonful and then I wait for it. I swear it's a form of torture.

He puts another mouthful in and I picture standing up, leaning over and stabbing my fork through his hand, pinning it to the table so he can't shovel any more of this shit into his fat face.

My brother bursts in. He's in one of his highs again today and I'm not in the mood for it. It's exhausting. Sasha and I just had a big fight and I don't want to have to listen to him spouting shit for the next half an hour.

'Foster father!' he bellows, pulling a chair out and sitting down. 'How goes it?'

Foster dad raises his eyes and sighs, before returning to his bowl and scraping around again. I'm waiting for that sound and as he dumps another mouthful, I imagine smashing my glass over his head and then stabbing him with the shards left behind.

'Oh, why so glum?!' continues my brother, undeterred. 'How about some facts to cheer you up? Yes?' Foster dad keeps scrolling and ignores him. 'It's fun fact Friday! Entertaining and educational!' One of his favourite games. 'Here we go – did you know that Zone 4 has a six hundred per cent higher mortality rate than any other zone? Even Zone 3 – great, huh?! How about this one – did you know that in Zone 1 all babies are vaccinated against the virus at birth, even though infants are statistically the least at-risk group? All this while the government says they don't have the resources to vaccinate those in Zone 4 anymore where basically no one survives beyond middle age! What a fun fact!'

He'll keep doing this for hours if no one stops him.

'I can tell you're eager for more!' The toes on his left foot are tapping the floor in the way that they do. 'Here's another – did you know that Zone 1 accounts for over seventy-five per cent of the government's spending and investment, in spite of the majority of the taxes coming from the other three zones! Hilarious!'

Foster dad stirs from his screen-induced coma. 'Where are you getting these facts from, genius? There's no way the government releases that kind of data.'

'Ah, well, wouldn't you like to know? I have my sources.'

I know exactly where he got them: from the guys at Thaw. They have a whole archive of facts about zonal inequality. It's enough to make anyone question the point of their existence. Apparently, they have some new government insiders who leak documents and info to them. People who are part of the new wave who are working to challenge the system. Thaw's at the front of it all; people are starting to reach out to them, and as far as they're concerned we are going to have a revolution. Turns out that in the very act of making Thaw out to be a big concern, the government might actually be turning them into one. I've got no idea if any of these facts are true, but they *feel* believable and that seems more important to everyone at Thaw. I guess they're right.

'Want another?' he asks.

'I think we've had enough,' replies foster dad, but we both know it won't make any difference.

'Okay, okay, grumplestiltskin! Last one – the funnest fact of all – did you know that the freeze is just a cover for the fact that the government can't keep running this city anymore? They're using it as a smokescreen to divide up the city and reduce the population size!'

Foster dad puts his phone down and scrapes his chair backwards to stand up. 'Not this again! Enough with the conspiracy theory nonsense, okay? I'm tired of hearing it. It's just a bunch of crackpots and extremists. You'll be talking about Thaw next as if they aren't simply disgruntled unemployed wasters and wackos trying to get everyone else more into the shit.'

'Foster father! Less of the foul language, please!' My brother mocks shock by placing his hands on his cheeks.

Foster dad looks skywards before walking away and saying, 'Don't bring that conspiracy bollocks into this house, okay?'

'It's not a conspiracy if it's true.'

'Yes, but you have no idea if it is true, do you?!'

My brother stands now too. 'Yes, I do actually.'

'Right, sure! Where's the proof if you're so sure?'

He pauses for a moment and I can see in his eyes his brain is trying to filter what he'll say next. He knows he can't tell them about being part of Thaw because they'd probably report us faster than you can squash a cockroach. But he hates losing arguments. 'I'm sure there's plenty out there, you'll see.'

Foster dad laughs and a piece of gloop drops from his beard. 'In other words, you have none!' He raises his meaty hand and points at my brother. 'Listen, and you listen good: Shut up about this stuff. I don't care if you think it's true or not. If the wrong person hears you chatting that shit you're going to get arrested or worse. For your own good, and mine, keep it zipped, Einstein. Understand?'

His face is stern and taught. He really means it. I've not seen him like this before. He holds his outstretched sausage finger in the air for long enough that everyone goes silent, and then walks off.

My brother pulls his chair out again, sits down and digs his fork into the slop. 'What's his problem?' he asks.

'He's got a point,' I say quietly into my bowl.

He spins to face me, his mouth full. 'So you're on his side now, are you?'

'No, don't be stupid. I'm not on his side, I'm just saying he's got a point, that's all.'

'And what point is that exactly?' He's not going to let this one go.

'Forget it.'

'Oh, that's helpful. I'll just forget the fact that my brother's backing some random foster over me.' His knee is bouncing now too. 'Jesus! What's your problem at the moment? You've been such a prick recently. You're the one who got us into Thaw, remember?'

He's trying to make it my fault again. We always used to back each other no matter what. Something went missing from foster's wallet: neither of us knew. One of us wasn't at school: don't know who it was. Living room got trashed: neither of us saw anything. We always had each other. Us against the world. But he's different now and I guess he thinks I am too. I would have backed him to foster dad's face, but I don't say that.

'Yes,' I reply. 'I know I did. But I'm not the one who's got all messed up by it. All this Thaw stuff has got you like a broken record. It's always Thaw this and Thaw that.'

'Maybe,' he says with gritted teeth, 'that's because it's important. I thought you got that? I thought you were one of us?'

'Do you hear yourself? *One of us*…what does that even mean?' My fork is playing with food in front of me. 'I thought *we* were the us.'

'Come on, we aren't kids anymore. This stuff is important. I know Sasha agrees with me.'

My fork drops. 'Leave her out of it,' I snarl. 'You understand?'

'You know,' he says casually, his mouth full of food as he stands up and walks away, 'I hear you two arguing. You need to do a better job or you're going to lose her.'

The door slams and I'm left at the table on my own.

26|

'Hey, have you seen Sasha?' I ask.

A couple of the guys turn around. The room is buzzing with activity as it always is before a big trip. Hand drawn maps and screen-shot composites sprawl out across the table, markers placed strategically at various points. Sticky notes are spread like tiles in a mosaic across a giant noticeboard. Pulse guns hang from their straps off the back of the door and backpacks are being filled with supplies. The guys are holding handwritten instructions in my familiar scrawl. This one has taken weeks to prep and now, only hours before we are supposed to go, Sasha has disappeared. She helped with the planning, but, as has been happening more and more, I took the lead. The trips have been getting more and more ambitious these last few months. More people, longer timeframes, bigger locations. We've got to be meticulous; we've got to get it right.

'Not seen her,' says one of the guys.

'I think she was with your bro somewhere,' says another. 'Do you want me to go look?'

'No, it's fine,' I reply. 'I'll look for her. You carry on going over the plan – commit it to memory, okay? You can't take those in with you, remember? We can't risk getting caught with them. We can't mess this up.'

'That's what we are doing,' one of the guys replies, testily.

I had taken a step away but turn back quickly. 'You don't need to take that tone. Do you want to be part of Thaw or not? They put me on point for this one, so just do as I ask, okay?'

'Yes, *sir*!' he says, before giving a mock salute and turning back to the table. My fist clenches by my side, but I turn and walk away. I don't have time to get involved.

Where is Sasha?

27|

'Where have you been?' I ask. I finally find her in one of the bedrooms.

'Nowhere,' she says. 'Just getting ready for the trip.'

'Where? What were you doing? The prep room is right here.'

'I've been around, getting things sorted,' she answers, brushing past me and out of the door. I spin as she passes and grab her by the arm.

'What things? I want to know where you've been.'

She shakes my hand off her arm. 'Let go of me! Stop being a creep.'

'Why won't you tell me where you were?'

'Because it's none of your business.' Her voice is rising now but she won't look at me.

'It *is* my business,' I shout. 'You're my girlfriend, I have a right to know where you were!'

'Well, we can change that if you like! Stop suffocating me, it's too much. I'm allowed my own space,' she starts to walk away but I follow her.

'Yes, but having space isn't the same as keeping secrets. You're not telling me something – I want to know what it is!' The darkness is starting to creep its way forward and I can't control it.

'Stop yelling at me! Just leave me alone, before we both say things we'll regret.'

'You mean like telling me the truth about what the hell is going on with you?' My hands open up in front of her and it all spills out. 'You're distant. We hardly spend any time alone together anymore. You're always out and when you're back you barely come near me. We don't…I've had enough: something's going on. Am I crazy? Tell me I'm crazy and I'll forget all about this.'

She closes her eyes and leans against the wall.

'Tell me I'm crazy,' I repeat, my eyes welling up and my heart racing. Darkness is all muddled up with sadness and there's this giant mess where my mind should be. 'Please, tell me this is all in my head. Tell me I'm imagining it.'

She stands there for a moment, as if frozen. Tears fall from my eyes and I can't take how much it hurts. She reaches for the door handle and walks out. I sink to the floor with my head in my hands.

The door opens again, and footsteps enter the room.

'I'm sorry,' I say, rubbing my eyes and looking up, but it's not Sasha.

It's my brother.

28|

He looks down at me with something in his eyes that I don't recognise.

'We have to talk. It's time you knew,' he says, and the world skips a frame. Something is very wrong. I can't see what it is for a moment; his expression is new, something between pity and guilt. But it soon changes once I realise what's going on.

My knees hunch up further. He didn't do this to me. He couldn't have. I must be reading him wrong.

'It just happened,' he says, his shoulders hunched. 'It wasn't anything either of us planned.'

And there it is. I feel so angry I can hardly hear.

'Are you serious? You and Sasha? Really? You can't mean it,' I say in a voice that rasps and cracks.

'I'm sorry, mate. Like I said, it just happened.'

'That kind of thing doesn't just happen! It doesn't! Do you really expect me to believe that?'

'Well, yes. It is the truth, after all.' He traces his toes in semi-circles across the floor.

'Sure, sure it is. The truth.' Everything is rushing to crumble away. I need to know before it's all gone. 'How long has it been going on for?'

'Does it matter?'

'Yes,' I half shout. 'It matters to me.'

The howl inside me is heartless and whole. It wants to tear my brother apart and rip up the entire fabric of existence along with him.

'About a month or so.'

'A month?!'

He crouches down to my level and tries to look at me. 'Look, you're my brother. You're my best friend. I wanted to tell you before, but the right moment didn't come up.' He sighs. 'You're not exactly the easiest person to talk to sometimes.'

'So this is my fault?'

'No, I'm not saying that.' He rises from his haunches and moves back, looking at his feet in the way that he does when he wants to change the subject. 'I want us to be okay about this. She's helping me, you know? I'm back on the meds and I'm feeling more…centred. I want to be in control. She's making me better. I think you need to talk to Sasha.'

'Why?'

'She'll explain things better than me.'

'Oh really?! You're trying to get out of any responsibility, is that it? What a surprise.'

'Look, I've tried to do this as best I can. This isn't easy.'

'Oh yeah, you're a real hero.'

'Well, maybe you need to take a look at yourself. Have you considered that? You're no hero either, you know. I think Sasha had her reasons.'

I jump to my feet and feel the anger raging through me. 'What do you mean?'

'Look…Just talk to Sasha about it, okay? Take a minute. Have a think. I've got to go.'

He doesn't have to go. He wants to, though. He always goes when he thinks I'm being too difficult. After everything I've done for him. The times I pulled him out of the pit; the times I covered for him; the times I held him when he needed to cry. I thought it was us against the world. And this is how he treats me: he rips the one good thing out of my life without even a second thought.

I push him in the back and he stumbles forwards.

'Leave it,' he says.

I push him again. 'Come on, I say. You fucking thief.'

'I'm not doing this,' he says as he carries on walking.

'Fine. Go off to her. You deserve each other,' I say. 'She's one more thing I got first, remember. You didn't find her, I did. You're not special. You're not unique. You're not even first out of two. You had to settle for second place. My seconds…'

He turns and swings before I can even see it coming. My head hits the floor and the pain goes away for the shortest of moments.

29|

Sorting my handful of gravel, I throw the pieces off the roof one by one. They fall, disappearing into the shade that lies below. The dull sun is setting over grey concrete silhouettes that stretch out across the horizon.

It is cold.

As I watch one of the tiny fragments of rock fall to earth, I can see people beginning to board up beneath me. It's Zone 4's turn to freeze tonight. People are worried about trippers; about what they'll do with another thirty days in a frozen zone that police don't give a shit about. They should be. No matter what they say, trippers aren't principled freedom fighters. They pretend to care about getting answers, but they don't. Not really. They're just people: complicated, messed-up and self-centred, same as everyone. They just want to trash stuff and steal things and break the rules. They're angry and they don't care about anyone but themselves. Living off their entitled sense of self-righteousness as if they are somehow better than everyone else.

I should know; I was one.

It's been twenty four hours since I stopped being a tripper. Twenty four hours since I found out. I did the trip after Jake told me, not that I remember it. I went through the motions in a daze, not able to process what had just happened. As soon as we were back through the wall, I left. I haven't been home since, and I haven't seen Sasha or my brother. My brother. I thought that word used to mean something; I guess I was wrong.

I throw another eroded rock off the edge, leaning right over to watch it fall. As I peer into the void, for a fraction of a second my foot slides in the shingle and with a slight, heightened wobble I get the rush of what it might be like to fall. I always have the desire to jump whenever I'm standing on something high – what is that about? Maybe this time I will; it's not like anyone would care. I thought someone might, but they don't.

In front of me, grey clouds haunt the sky. It's going to rain again soon. A man below busies himself with a series of padlocks on the grill that spans the front of his shop. A woman is shouting into her interzoner, asking *why* over and over again before hanging up and thrusting it back into her pocket. A pile of bin bags sits torn beside her on the pavement as a dog picks through its contents with his teeth.

After my brother spoke to me, and everything came out, nobody even asked if I was okay. They all knew already. Of course they did. They were all on his side. I was the idiot who was the last to find out. The trip happened as planned and as I was leaving, they all thanked me and acted as if nothing were wrong. As if the whole world hadn't just fallen apart.

And this afternoon they messaged me to ask me to plan the next trip. To carry on with everything just the same as before.

Well, screw them. I'm not doing it.

They think I'm only in this for answers and I'm not. They think what I care most about is their stupid cause and the one percent of the one percent and all their other bullshit, but it's not. The only thing I care about isn't talking to me. And every time I see her with him, it's like looking at a messed-up reflection. As if he stole my life and is living it without my permission.

I know Sasha and I argued but I never thought it had gotten that bad. It was like she enjoyed fighting. At least, after enough fights I got to thinking that she did. She would build and build and then it would all come out and afterwards she would be calm again, as if she needed the explosion. It's like she needs some disaster, it's woven into her being. But she was trying to escape that with me. To get out of herself. To remove the catastrophe that is inked into her skin.

I think she wanted that at the start. To change who she was and have me be the one to do it. I was her safety net, her plain beige airbag. She wanted security and stability. But she couldn't get free of it. There is no laser removal for pain. She couldn't un-pick the darkness. And when the black holes that are in both her and I materialised, they sucked the good out of both of us and just made everything worse. It turns out two people's darkness can't cancel each other out and become light, although I really wish they could.

She thinks I can't save her. She must do. That's why she's with him, my twin brother. It's like she gave up on herself. He won't help her escape the black hole, he'll just drag her further down into it. If I'm plain beige, then he is neon red. He explodes in volcanic eruptions that shatter and consume everything, and then tries to rebuild in the ashes every time. But he needs help. He needs saving, or he'll take you down into the ashes with him.

I don't know which one Sasha wants from him, whether she wants to build or burn. Sometimes she wants to get buried in the dark. But I know that's not really her. And I know that I can get her back; I just have to help her get free of the disaster. Get free of all the negativity and the loss. Get out of this god-awful place. Escape the city and she can escape that part of herself too. I know I can help her. I just need a way to get her back.

I filter through the gravel and dust in my hand to throw again when I hear the stairwell door open. I expect to see my brother's molten face ready to spew, but instead, a man in a mustard V-neck sweater with clean shoes steps onto the roof. He looks almost middle-aged.

He doesn't belong here.

30|

Watching him carefully, I reach behind and under my shirt for the gun Sasha gave me but curse myself because it's not there. She would never have forgotten hers.

'Hey, don't be alarmed,' he says, hands raised in the air, 'Easy. Easy. I just want to talk. Okay?' He keeps his arms up and stops a few yards away.

'Who are you? What are you doing here?' I eye a route to the stairwell but if he has a sting stick or worse, there really is no way past.

'I'm FPD. But that's not important. What's more important is what I can do for you.'

A rush of adrenaline fires through my body and I pivot from the ledge, making a break for the stairwell. Everything rushes and just as I think I might be free, with a wave of his arm the sting stick lashes out and wraps around my leg. My body hits the shingle hard and my calf burns and blisters until he retracts the heated coil. He walks next to me and kneels, looking straight into my eyes.

'Like I said, I just want to talk,' he says. 'Please don't try and run. If I just wanted to arrest you, I'd have done it by now. Running from an FPD officer in Zone 4 is a shoot to kill offence anyway – if I wanted you dead, you would be.'

He reaches a hand out to me and pulls me off my back. I sit up, nursing the marks on my shin that continue to burn as the heat passes from cell to cell like a house on fire.

'I think we can help each other. We've been keeping tabs on this location for a little while now, waiting for you to come back. But you haven't been up here for quite some time, have you? You and your brother. And the girl. What's her name?'

'Like I'm going to tell you,' I reply with all the contempt I can muster.

'Ah, so you like her...' he raises a smile that makes me feel stupid. I shouldn't have shown him my feelings. 'I'm not surprised,' he continues, 'I've only seen her on the footage from downstairs, but there's something about her, isn't there?' He pauses and rubs his thumb into the meat of his palm. 'You really shouldn't meet girls on the roof of an ex-London gang hideout.'

Smiling, he looks at my face and I obviously give away my surprise. 'Oh yes,' he continues, 'most unfortunate for you. This was once a real den of iniquity in the twenty thirties. A gang of weapons runners worked out of here. Interzone crime when it was still a new thing, before some parts of the walls were even finished. It took years to pin them down, but pin them we did.'

He looks across the skyline and then back at me. 'We always do...right?' There's a pause and we both know what he means. 'I assumed they would have removed all the old surveillance technology when they condemned the building, but no – they left something behind, by accident I would surmise. But you never know these days, everyone's so paranoid.' He clears his throat. 'Anyway, once the old motion cameras picked something up and the voice-pattern algorithm got to work and identified the word '*thaw*' we got the flag. We didn't believe it to start with – this place has been out of action for years. But, as you know, the footage was correct. A lucky catch, you might say. I'll be honest: after the flag, I forgot about this place. I didn't think you were ever coming back. But, hey. Here we are! Lucky us! And now I'm here, I think it's lucky for you.'

90

The sting still clings to my leg. 'How could this possibly be lucky for me?' I reply, fighting back tears from the pain. 'I'm stuck on a roof with some FPD agent who talks too much. Can't you just arrest me and get it over with?'

I've had enough. Of everything. I'm tired and I'm angry, and at least if they arrest me, it might be a distraction from the need for revenge that's eating away at my insides.

'I could arrest you, yes. But what will that do for either of us? I could take you into the station right now for trying to run from an officer. We could book you and you'd have at least a few nights in a cell. With some demonstrable connection to Thaw, you'll probably be interrogated. It won't be pleasant. And even if you don't say anything and get out, you'll be surveilled within an inch of your life for the foreseeable. No more tripping, if that's what you're up to. And no more seeing that girl…what's her name?'

'Screw you.'

'Yes, well. You won't be screwing her again, will you? You see her and she's immediately in the same boat as you are now. And I don't think you want that for either of you, do you?

'Or…you give me something. Something I can use. You trippers are all remarkably good at covering your tracks. We know you change your planning and meeting locations every operation, and use different entrance points each time you trip. It's remarkably hard to track you all down to one place. You're actually quite organised…for a bunch of kids.

'If you're in Thaw, I need some intel. Names, locations, slipways, details of a trip. Better yet, give me some of Thaw's big guns and I'll let you and that girl go free, out of the city. I'll even give you a place to get you started, a disused house with a front door and a lock. Even some money, provisions and a gun to get you up and running. It might not be so bad. You can be free: free from surveillance, free from the

EPRL, free from your shitty life in this,' he waves his hand through the air, 'depressing hole of a zone. I've got a feeling about you – and with twenty years of police work my gut is pretty good – I know you want to get out of here, I can see it all over your face. Stay here and have us monitor your every move for the rest of your life or leave here with her and start fresh. Isn't that what you want?'

I want a lot of things right now. I want to grab a handful of this gravel, hold him by his mustard sweater and shove it down his throat until he stops breathing. I want to run and jump off the roof so that I disappear into the darkness below. I want to hack a hole into this backwards reality and climb through to the other side where everything is light and perfect. I want to curl up into a ball and disappear into nothingness. I want to be free and clean and clear and beautiful. I want to be new again. I want to find my brother and tell him to run before I can punch his nose inside his skull. I want to hate and hate and hate. I want to release the pull for revenge that's trapped in my bones and crumbling them from the inside.

And I want to love.

And the memory of the feeling of Sasha's hair falling over my shoulders brushes away everything else.

I want her. This whole big disaster is about her. There really isn't anything left that isn't.

How do I even try to make any of this right?

I stand and brush the dust off my top, grabbing a last handful of shingle and throwing it over the ledge. As I look out across the bleak horizon, the rectangular shadows from the tower blocks grow long, inching their darkness over the city below. The sun has almost set; the freeze is about to begin.

'Okay, alright,' he exhales, 'we don't have much time left here. What's it going to be?'

PART 2:
AFTER

31|

The white mist sticks to my fingers. It hangs between the spaces in thin, syrupy strings. More than usual, but it was a bad night. My eyes might have waited to clear naturally on another day. Blinked it all out and woken slowly in the sheets until the dawn filled the room. But today isn't normal. Today is the day after the freeze and, as usual, anything could have happened.

Sitting up, the covers slide off. Under the pillow, my gun is cold. Its metal chassis is scratched and bare and the rotating cylinders show its age.

When Sasha had given it to me, she was lying in bed in the early sunshine. Her breath warm against my neck and her head resting on my shoulder. The sheets made a silhouette of our bodies with our heartbeats still fast and one.

'Happy birthday, James,' she said. 'I knew that you always wanted one of the classics. A beautiful way to kill someone, no?'

She laughed and we kissed the way that people kiss when that moment is everything and nothing else matters.

My eyes scan the room. The clock is showing six thirty four. Its tiny green spaced bars provide a dim glow on the bedside table. The orange tablet bottle reflects this in a sickly puce colour. An electronic countdown calendar shows *day zero*. Except that it isn't. How many cycles has it been now since it happened? Familiar routine resets it to thirty and picks up the tablets. Popping the white cap, one tips into my mouth and goes down.

Swallowing these always used to require water. Without it they would sit on my tongue, their foul-tasting chemical burn spreading across my mouth. My throat would swallow and swallow and swallow, but it wouldn't go away, each attempt only making it worse. Water had to wash it down. A spider down a plughole.

Only, that was in the beginning. Now they go down like anything else. Mundane. Common. The *status quo*. My brain doesn't know when the beginning became now. When what I used to be wasn't what I am.

A picture of my face next to my brother sits beside the clock. No memory remains of it being taken. Stories have to be invented now to connect to the child in that image and feel that fragment of recorded time. That piece of my continuous self that my mind can no longer recollect. The younger me that now isn't me.

Over enough time, invented truths become true and there's no longer any difference.

A long time ago, Sasha told me that I looked exactly like my brother. That we were almost impossible to tell apart. Not precisely identical, nothing ever is, but alike in so many ways. Same eyes. Same smile. Same frown. Ever since, there has been a wish that she hadn't said that. A hope that it wasn't true. Perhaps if it weren't, things might have been different.

Holding the gun with both hands, my legs stand up and walk to the bathroom. There is a slim chance that somebody might not have left yet. Some kid zone tripper on drugs or a couple of first timers who got lost or left behind. Sometimes the organised ones got something wrong and needed to hide out until the searches were over. Average households. Nothing bathrooms. Greenhouses. Empty attics. Walk-in wardrobes. Cupboards under the stairs. These were the places to do it. Old warehouses and factories were the first places to get hit these days.

Everyone knew that the FPD squads only did random searches outside the common hiding places. The trippers might get lucky.

I used to be a tripper. Before everything went wrong.

My knees go down onto the carpet outside of my bathroom door. It is ajar. Can't remember whether it was left open or closed. In the old days that would have been second nature. Always record a room before a freeze. Know your surroundings. Preparation was everything back then.

Eyes blink out some more white as the tip of my gun eases the door open. The curved cylinder shines and there is a feeling of Sasha's head resting on my shoulder. Her hands around my waist. The sense of her smell inside me.

The creak of the door meets with silence on the other side. Imagination pictures my body hiding in the bath. Balled up behind the shower curtain and trying not to laugh. Wondering whose house this is and how they will react. Waiting to explode out of the door with Sasha next to me holding my hand.

There are no explosions. There is no shower curtain. The bath is empty as empty. No trippers this time. My knees crack as they lift off the ground. Checking behind the door happens as a matter of habit. Nothing. Another cycle been and gone. How many has it been now since it happened?

Gun clinks on porcelain and the taps squeak as they turn. Water washes my face and cleans out its foul eyes. They look at me bloodshot in a dirty mirror.

Towels are lying bunched up on the floor. My nose examines the nearest one. The smell is wet, like rotting carpet. Mould and decomposition. After picking it up, days old bacteria begin crawling and creeping and smearing all over my face.

The towel returns to the floor and my legs to the bedroom. Clothes that had been on my body yesterday dress me. Only it wasn't really yesterday. The interzoner raises in my hand and my index finger flicks it on. The screen illuminates in the same way it always does. As if nothing ever changes. The welcome tones accompany me down the stairs.

GOOD MORNING! INTERZONER 5.2 YOUR GUIDE TO KEEPING UP WITH FREEZE NEWS THE INSTANT IT HAPPENS.

My brain already knows it does this but the machine reminds me every day. The screen moves down and then clicks on NEW CYCLE ZONE 4 FREEZE NEWS. Words and images begin scrolling across where the palm of my hand would be.

ONE OF THE BIGGEST FREEZE THEFTS IN RECORDED HISTORY! TWENTY MURDERED IN FREEZE STATE! MILLIONS MISSING FROM BANK OF THE REPUBLIC! VACCINES STOLEN FROM COLD STORAGE! VIOLENT KILLERS STILL AT LARGE! COULD STILL BE IN ZONE 4! CAUTION!

Capitals tell people to care. A finger reaches for the television and switches it on so it can crackle with static and begin its latest efforts to distract me. The kettle begins to heat up when my tap fills it. The toaster filament alights at the touch of a hand. Stale crumbs brush off of a dirty plate. A knife pulls from a drawer.

I am the master of my tiny world. This is not what the dream was supposed to look like.

The larder contains jam and so my hands open it. Behind the door, her face is staring straight at me. My mind is panicked and starts to feel too fast. Things start fading around the edges. Is she really there?

'Don't freak out,' she says. 'Don't. Please don't. I know what you are thinking. Stay with me. Just listen. I need your help.'

32|

The chair is solid under the weight of me. My interzoner is on the table still scrolling news about the freeze theft. Twenty dead. Cold blooded murders. The television is providing BREAKING NEWS! in big letters. A reporter is standing outside a large building. Important people are milling around and he is pointing to the inside and putting on his sombre expression. It must appear as if he is moved, otherwise we don't know if we should be upset. He is now telling me to be vigilant and report anything strange.

What does strange even mean?

She is explaining to me about today's mess. She's still tripping, even after what happened. Even after what they did. I thought that would be the final trip; I was wrong. I got a lot wrong about that day.

My ears detect her voice, but I am not able to hear. She looks just like she used to, only different. She doesn't smell the same anymore. Her hair has changed. It used to be long and, when it wasn't in dreads, it floated like a cloud. Now it is short and curt. Expressionless. Slicked flat. Her cheeks are empty and her face is filled with something that my eyes haven't seen before. My brain thinks it might be fear.

Something had gone wrong on this trip.

'This was supposed to be the big one,' she says. 'The one with the answers. The one where we find out. The one where we blow this government apart and reveal the truth about their lies. But they knew we were coming. How did they know? Drake and Sara didn't make it. God knows what happened to all the others. I didn't know where else to go. I know I hurt you but I'm really in the shit here. I think they have my photo. I think they know I'm a tripper.'

'Then you have no choice,' my voice tells her. 'Known trippers don't live, you know that. At least, not past the next cycle. You can't leave this zone and once it's frozen they'll kill you in Freeze state.'

'Not if they don't find me,' she says.

My eyes blink and a little white mist creeps in. Her face gives away what we both already know.

They always find you eventually.

33|

She has been talking at me for half an hour. Repeating the same lines and still stuck on the same theory. The one that her and Drake and Sara had been on for years now. The one that changed her. The one that got in the way of her loving me.

'I can't believe they're still getting away with this,' she says. The burnt wiring in my brain already stores this about her, but she carries on anyway. She sounds worse now, like a fanatic blindly holding onto an idea that can't be falsified. As bad as the religious ones who keep preparing for the rapture. The Freeze is the beginning of the end, they say. The time for stewardship is over. Raise your hearts up to the heavens. God's taking it all back. Join us or face eternal damnation. That was the kind of person we used to laugh about.

'You can't still think there's even a possibility that all this happened by chance, can you? By natural events? You haven't gone back to any of that, have you? You don't believe any of their lies now, do you?'

I don't believe in anything anymore. But my voice doesn't say this.

She is waiting for a response. The look she has for me is different now. My mind remembers holding hands and running. Gliding through a frozen zone with everything static around us. Complete freedom pushing through our veins. We could go anywhere and do anything and it was only ever us. Us, the rulers of a frozen world. Together and complete. Excitement forcing love into our hearts.

'Anyway,' she carries on. 'I need to get back to Zone 1. That's where we were supposed to meet, but our exit route got blocked. God, how did they know where we were getting out?'

'What happened?'

She leans forwards. 'We planned it meticulously,' she says. 'We were going to break into the Zone 4 Federal Building. That's one of the biggest ones. Intelligence told us it is the one with some of the secrets. Drake had the blueprints – an insider joined the cause and gave them to him.'

She talks like a crazy person. There is no cause. There are angry people. There is a need for answers. There is fear and frustration. A lack of *meaning*. But no cause.

'We knew the layout and were going to get into the main vault. We only wanted to prove that we could do it. Get them worried about us. We weren't after the money, we've changed now. We're organised. Principled.'

They weren't principled when Jake died.

'I don't know how twenty million was stolen or by who,' she claims. 'I'm not even sure if it was taken. They probably just made it up to make us look like common criminals. When we got inside there was an FPD squad waiting for us. They opened fire and we had no choice but to fire back. We didn't hit any frozens though, so I don't know how that became part of the news. They're trying to frame us, they must be.

'We were massively outnumbered and scattered anywhere out of there. I ran to our exit point but there were troops all over it. We only dug it out yesterday, so how they knew I don't know. That wall is kilometres long; they can't have simply got lucky. Someone must have informed them, but I can't think of anyone who would have done it. God, it's all a mess.'

The television makes its most significant contribution to my life so far. An image begins blazing brightly on the screen. Tiny electronic pixels. Bold and precise. Blinking out some white, my eyes can see it clearly. Sasha looks at me and then follows my gaze. She experiences something that most people never do. She is looking at herself on live television.

HAVE YOU SEEN THIS WOMAN? SASHA SHIVERSTONE. TERRORIST WANTED IN CONNECTION WITH ZONE CRIME! RESPONSIBLE FOR THEFT AND MURDER. MULTIPLE FELON! CONSIDERED ARMED AND DANGEROUS! REPORT ANY SIGHTINGS TO FREEZE POLICE DEPT IMMEDIATELY!

'They've got my photo,' she says. 'Oh God. They know who I am.'

This is the first time for a long time that my mind can remember being sure of something. It knows that she won't survive the cycle.

34|

The window is stained yellow and brown. Condensation drops slide slowly down the pane. There are patches of clear glass and nothing unusual is to be seen on the other side. The familiar view. Concrete and bricks. Litter and grey.

'How are your eyes?' she asks. 'Can you still feel it? Is it getting any better?'

My hand rubs my left eye. Yes, I can still feel it. No, it's not getting any better.

The outside is clear. If the FPD knew where she was, they would be here by now. We have some time.

'You have to leave,' my voice says. 'If they come here and find you with me then we will both be killed. I can't get found. I'm supposed to be dead, remember?'

After it happened, I had to go into hiding. They didn't know who got out, and I couldn't face the others, so I went into exile. I had to pretend to be dead, and in all the messy fallout, it must have worked despite the fact that my body remains here, squatting in this derelict house. Sometimes I'm not sure if I'm already dead. Maybe I died when it happened and this is my hell. I've thought about it and I really don't know how I could tell if it weren't.

'I know, I know,' she says, waiting for a moment. 'How long has it been now? Almost a year?'

'More than a year.'

'How are you coping?' she asks. 'You don't look well.'

'I am fine. You have to go. I can't help you.'

'You don't seem fine.' She pauses again. 'Don't you miss it? The freedom. The thrill. The adrenaline. The *rush*. You should re-join the cause – we are so much more than before. You were one of the best trippers I ever knew, you know that? The way you would put a trip together, it was special. We could use you.'

'I can't help you.'

My legs walk back to the stairs. She grabs my arm and a memory remembers holding her. Her hands running through my hair. Her tracing the outlines of my shoulders.

Her waving me away, my brother's dead body at her side.

'Please,' she says. 'Just help me get to the border. I won't ask any-more of you than that. When we get there, you can leave me and never look back if that's what you want. Please, a little help? Doesn't what we had count for anything? You know I won't make it on my own.'

She's right. Out there, she won't make it alone. Most people don't. My bitterness and resentment don't want her too. But some part of me feels stronger. The part that remembers her beside me. The chest-nut brown of her eyes. The softness of her breath when she slept.

'I'll help you get to the border,' that part of me says, 'but that is it.'

Moving up the stairs, my brain tells me what she needs to do next. 'Come up here,' it tells her. 'We need to change the way you look.'

'Thank you,' she says. 'Really, I mean it.'

35|

The bathroom grows cultures on the floor. The door opens and a pale light bulb illuminates patches of mould. Sasha looks at it and frowns.

'When did you last clean in here?' she says.

'Do you want my help or not?'

'You know I do. I'm sorry, I didn't mean anything by it. This is not like you, that's all. You used to be so...organised. So careful.'

My mind can barely remember that being the case.

'We need to cut your hair. And I have bleach in the cupboard. We should make you blond. That will help if someone only catches you at a glance. Do you still have any colour contacts?'

'No, I ran out.'

'I may have a set or two left somewhere.' My legs take me to the cabinet to look.

'You used to look so good with green eyes,' she says. 'Forest-like.' She scratches at something on her shoulder. 'I remember that time we tripped in Zone 1 in your green contacts. Do you remember? When we were inside that football stadium, and the guys came too. You all played a match. It was so much fun! I can't say that the standard was too high, but it was a match nonetheless. How many people can say they've done that, huh? That was hilarious!'

A vague memory spurts and stutters into my mind. The perfect blades of synthetic grass brushing against my knees as I fell. The rows and rows of empty seats looking down upon us. The beaming glare of the spotlights. Sasha's cheers on the touchline. Her hug as we celebrate scoring a goal. The warmth of her body next to mine.

And then it's gone.

'I need to go look for the contacts next door,' my voice says.

She carries on talking in the bathroom. 'You've missed out on a lot this last year,' she says. 'We tripped in the Royal Palace a few months ago. Did you hear about it? Now that was something! That took some real planning. Once we were in, we spray painted the main reception room, turned the furniture upside down and burnt all the artwork. Grace moved some frozen butler next to the fire and hung a board around his neck saying *this will all burn*. It was genius. A real starting point for the revolution. Lots of people joined us after they saw that and realised that tripping in even the most secure places really was possible. It got our message across more than anything else we've done so far. It was incredible in there.'

So that was her. It was impressive that they had managed to break into the palace. That used to be a tripper's mecca. The Shangri-la. The mythical place you'd like to trip the most but knew you never could. It was a shame that they used it as a stunt. If it were me, I would have done it differently.

'What's the easiest route out of here?' she asks. 'I mean, to somewhere safe.'

'There's nowhere safe now; they know who you are.'

36|

Memory. It glitters. Until it is gone.

She once was there. Bright burns of her beauty blistering my brain. Every trip we took. When they were over she hung in the air around me, like smoke from a chemical reaction.

I was bravery for her. I was freedom for her. I was disaster for her. I am ruin for her.

For a time, I loved the trips. But I always loved her more.

The stairs are descended. Our bodies are in the kitchen. My arms are folded. Hers are leaning on the chair.

'Can I eat something?' she says. 'I've not had a meal since yesterday morning.'

She opens the refrigerator before there is time to reply. Her eyes shine deceiving green in the fake light. The chemical cold reflects off her peroxide blond and makes the hairs on my arms rise as one.

'What do you eat these days? There's nothing in here,' she slams the door shut.

'There's a loaf on the side.'

White blinks into the corner of my eye and stays there, partially obscuring the interzoner on the table. My thumb scrolls around an electronic zone map trying to identify a route. A way out. Hope in a pixelated, high-definition graphic.

She picks up the baked, homogenised salt, flour and yeast and peers into its cellophane wrapping.

'I think it's gone off,' she sniffs.

This is no surprise. It has to happen.

'You got anything at all I can eat? I'm starving.'

'I've got jam.'

She takes the jam from the larder, unscrews the lid and dips her fingers into it. She pulls them out all sticky and dripping in red, boiled sugar. She puts this into her mouth and swallows.

The blood red ooze dribbles down the side of the jar.

37|

'What's the best way to get to the border?' she asks. 'Can we use one of the old slip routes?' Cold water gushes over her fingers and remnants of preserved strawberries are lost forever. 'The sooner I get there, the better.'

'I don't know. There isn't an easy route. Do they know about Carlisle St?'

'Oh yeah, that was busted months ago.' She wipes her hands on the tablecloth.

My fingers trace the digital picture of reality.

'Oldham St might be a possibility.'

'Where's that?'

'Off Cheade Avenue.'

'Oh, I remember it,' she says. 'Didn't we slip a trip down there once?'

We did. She is right. She can't remember what happened or why we slipped there, otherwise she wouldn't have brought it up.

'When was that?' she asks.

'Maybe we should try Blackacre. That might be okay.'

She is not listening to me. Her eyes squint as she searches space for the story. 'Was it the time with Geri and Soraya? You know the docks trip?'

'I don't remember. I think Blackacre is our only choice,' my voice continues.

She grips the seat with her damp hands. 'Oh,' she says. 'Was that the time with…?'

It was.

'I don't know,' my mouth says. 'We should go.'

'I'm sorry. I forgot.' She rubs her nose and looks at me. 'It feels like so long ago.'

It doesn't. Not to me.

'Get your things, we should go. We haven't got any time to waste.'

38|

The tattered coat from my cupboard smells of dust and stale air. Empty pockets but for year old receipts. Feet wriggle to find familiarity in old shoes. Opening the front door and the white mist crawls further in. It's settling now, crowding in the corner of my eye. An opaque globe that will only get bigger. No time to get the drops. Blinking quickly, my eyes scan the street. Still nothing.

The keys feel cold and conflicted against the palm of my hand. One turns in the lock and each shaft of rusty metal slides perfectly into line. It clicks. An empty space securely sealed.

She is leaning against the rough, crumbling plaster, her head hiding in a hood. Knees bent, cat-like. Briefly, her eyes flash to mine. Green like a leaf lost.

'Where now?' she asks.

'This way,' points my hand. 'Follow me and keep a little distance. You're less visible on your own. They may see me too if you're spotted. That can't happen. I need to stay dead.'

My lungs cough in the cold air as clouds of breath desperately escape, the insides of me condensing as they enter the world. Legs begin to move. The pavement is hard. My shoulders hunch. It has been a week since this skin has felt daylight and attempted to draw vitamins from the grey.

Sasha has started to move. A quietish shuffle. Too deliberate. Conspicuous. She isn't used to subtlety. For her, it was adventure. Excitement. Extroversion.

Not this.

39|

The morning is quiet. Still early. People are inside. Children wrapped in blankets. Curled up in their beds. Cuddled next to fathers and mothers who sleep soundly. Safe. Better not to come across an FPD squad the first day after a freeze. No matter who you are. Stop and search laws justify active engagement. The freeze zone riots enabled new police powers for our protection. Physical mobility between zones became tightly restricted. Since before I died this restricted mobility had become social too. Now it was financial. Educational. Institutional. Racial. Prejudicial.

Zone 1 achieves in ways Zone 4 does not. Visas protect the prosperity of the powerful. Zonal property prices shift and slide with the quiet rehousing of the socially undesirable. Middle classes flock together for mutual appreciation. Those with no choice watch passively as their world gentrifies or decays. Zone 4 becomes the hole for the less 'fiscally dynamic'. Vaccine supply continues to become scarcer and scarcer, and it doesn't take long to realise how rich you have to be to get the latest doses. Petty crime rises. Tripper gangs spring up to break the monotony. Schools lose influence. Employment levels fall. Parents disengage.

This was when the riots flared again. *Operation Pay Yourself*, they called it. We have nothing and are nothing: what can we possibly lose?

The government blamed society. Society blamed the government. Nobody thought that they might be the same thing.

Usually these truths have no impact on my life. After all, I'm dead. Today, however, this changes like everything else.

My existence is in Zone 4. My shadow. My carbon dioxide. Sasha needs to slip back to Zone 1. Zone 4 is a shit heap of depression and despair. Zone 1 is the playground for the chosen few. Pomp and preening. Pedestals and perfume. Pretensions and puke.

It's the hardest zone to trip into when it's in freeze. It has the fewest unguarded slipways through which to escape.

My mind searches its synaptic connections. As far as it can recall, no one has tried to break in during normal time. And now a wanted woman and a dead man are attempting it the day after a major catastrophe. This is not part of the plan.

40|

My legs round the corner onto Eagle Avenue. The local convenience store is boarded up; no longer convenient. The blocks of flats that continue either side are obelisk-like. Towers of mundanity. Regulation, identically designed, factory-built housing. Temporary solutions to permanent problems. Piles upon piles of places in which to pass the time.

A few squares dot the uniform exterior, glowing yellow. Lives seeping out in tiny, suspicious slivers. Continuing out of the hope for something better. Half an eye remains on these lights. Too early for most, but we don't want to be spotted out on the street.

My feet keep moving, eyes keep darting. Hands clench into fists in my coat pockets. Still no sign of the FPD.

The road soon begins to open up. Stale white paint has worn away on its surface. Directions for people with somewhere to go. My legs walk past a burnt ergonomic shell that sits silently. No longer a vehicle, now simply a metal cage. Full of holes and rusting and peeling. Another product of destruction. The fruit of frustration. Giving meaning to someone's life for the short time that it took to watch it burn.

Weeds push out and up through the cracks in the ground. My mind runs over the time and distance until the old slipway. Twenty minutes if we walk fast. Two visible flashpoints. Maybe three.

'Psst. Hey! Get off the road!'

My head snaps around to see Sasha running from the pavement. She moves quickly and jumps over a low wall. She disappears.

I am frozen.

Fight. Flight. Or freeze. Make a decision. My ears hear the crunch of tires on concrete, gravel and broken glass. Then there is the unmistakable rumble of an FPD van. A loudspeaker emits sound waves in the form of words.

'STAY INDOORS. DO NOT VENTURE OUT. ANYONE FOUND ON THE ROAD WILL BE QUESTIONED. CONTACT THE FPD TO REPORT ANYTHING SUSPICIOUS. STAY INDOORS. DO NOT VENTURE OUT. ANYONE...'

Flight.

My arms and legs pump and sprint towards the wall, leaping over it. Briefly in the air, gravity traps this collection of atoms and returns it to the floor. Skin scrapes on asphalt as the world tumbles and rolls. Momentum stops. My hands and knees scramble to stability. Sasha scowls at me as she crouches and monitors.

'Shit! Did they see you?' She returns her eyes to the road. My lungs are burning. Oxygen is not transferring quickly enough. Coughing annoys her. 'I said, did they see you?' she repeats.

'No.' Breath. 'I don't know.' Breath. Cough.

'Stop coughing!'

Swallow. 'I think I made it.' Breath. Cough.

'Oh God, oh God. I hope so.'

The van draws near.

'STAY INDOORS. DO NOT VENTURE OUT. ANYONE FOUND ON THE ROAD WILL BE QUESTIONED...'

41|

'They don't usually do this,' says my mouth in a whisper.

'Shh!' she hisses, flashing me her fake eyes and putting a finger over her lips.

Her stare says don't move. My memory flickers and remembers that this is not the first time that I have been in a situation like this. Experience dictates our behaviour. FPD squads are not well-adjusted, caring individuals; they don't enjoy interacting with civilians. The squad troopers receive special training. Elite. The best of the best. Time shift response drills. How to react in freeze conditions. Arrest and suppress. Improved reaction times. Ingrained patriotism and allegiance. Behavioural therapy treatments. Operant conditioning. Love for the cause. Lessons on ways to stop people living.

Their pulse guns box out your lungs. The electric net lines of their snare sticks sting as they cling. Burn marks that never descend below their pink ridge scars. My leg still bears the edges of one. A close call when I used to be alive.

Decisive action of an FPD agent involves temporary paralysis and potential abolition of the insurgent. Criminal. Victim. Rebel. Freedom fighter. Friend. Soul mate.

Brother.

42|

A rotary whir whines as the door of the FPD van lifts open. From our position we can see one of the troopers climb out. His hi-tech body shield uniform accentuates his figure. Superhero shaped. He stands looking out across the junction up ahead. A visual display visor scrolls the latest freeze news across in front of his eyes. Its black tint hides his humanity. Stretching out his back, the pulse gun is positioned at the pinnacle of his arcing frame. He grunts as he twists his torso.

'STAY INDOORS. DO NOT VENTURE OUT. ANYONE FOUND ON THE ROAD WILL BE QUESTIONED…'

His feet crunch the gravel and begin a slow walk towards the curb.

'Hey Miller!' he shouts.

'Yeah?' grunts a voice from inside the van.

'I'm gonna check the perimeter. Stay hot on the radio, don't think we're gonna get much from round here. People living in this shit hole are too dumb to be the kind of trippers we're after.'

'Maybe so, but keep them peeled, Randle. You never know with these losers.'

'Yeah, yeah. I know.'

He looks at an instrument on his wrist and briefly walks out of sight.

Sasha turns to face me.

'What should we do?' she whispers.

'We can't run now. They'll see us. If not, one of their motion scanners will pick us up. We have to stay still. Just don't move.'

'Oh God. I'm scared,' she says.

'Stay still, it will be okay,' my mouth lies.

Our bodies sink down as low as they can go behind the wall.

The footsteps reappear. Getting louder and more clear. Sasha's body is shaking next to mine. Still louder. One heavy rhythmic thump after another. Staccato. A body weighed down by equipment. Movement restricted. They approach and stop. The electronic clicks of an FPD freeze scroller being utilised are filling my ears. The live feed on his device linking it to central FPD, and now making them aware of its newly activated motion sensor. He is standing on the other side of the wall.

'STAY INDOORS. DO NOT VENTURE OUT. ANYONE FOUND ON THE ROAD WILL BE QUESTIONED...'

Sasha is looking at me like she is going to run for it. My eyes tell her not to. At least that is what they try to do. White mist is thickening in the corners and clouding their vision. Everything is obfuscated. Milky and unclear. My hands instinctively want to wipe it away, but for Sasha they don't move.

The sound of his feet turning on the concrete. His heavy breathing as if it were inside my head.

Sasha readies herself to run. She is gripping my knee and poised to push off. My hand puts itself on hers. It feels soft. Warm. Like the past.

'Hey, Randle!' comes a shout from the grunter inside the van.

'Yeah?' he yells back, close enough to make my ears vibrate.

'They think they've got something. Near the border. Oldham St slipway. Potential sighting of one of the trippers.'

'Christ! They went down Oldham St.? How stupid are these people?'

'Never mind that. Let's get going. There's nothing moving here on the motion scanners.'

'Okay, okay.'

The feet turn and start to move off towards the van. Slowly fading. The voices start again, only quieter this time. Partially contained by the van.

'Plug in the route. We can be there in fifteen.'

'FPD thirty-two en route. Maintain visual on suspect until we arrive.'

The engine starts up and the mechanical whir shuts the discussion away. A roar from the turbines chews up the air around them and spits it out. The recorded message stops, and the road becomes quiet once more.

Sasha's body relaxes next to mine and she takes a deep breath.

'Thank God,' she says.

'Thank the radio,' my mouth says as my hands furiously rub my eyes. The stinging and itching and prickling take over. If there is a God and he had anything to do with any of this, then he doesn't deserve thanks. None at all.

43|

The sky is passing above our heads. The earth continues to rotate. Round and round and round. Gravity persists in preventing my body from floating into the acres of empty space that surrounds me. Dark matter continues to conceal mine and the universe's reality.

The stelliferous era is a blip in the history of time. The sun and the solar system are a blip in the stelliferous era. Complex life is a blip in the solar system. Humans are a blip in the existence of complex life. My life is a blip in the human race. This moment is a blip in my life. I am a carbon-based life-form that crawls through a cancerous corner of contingent space/time.

My mind is not sure if something inside it wanted to get my lungs punched out by a superhero shaped bringer of destiny. If only that meant that there was a destiny. A fate. A meaning to any of this. If my death could have been for some kind of purpose. A gesture of significance.

A sense of use escapes my very being. Elusive. Invisible. Imaginary.

Everything is everything and there is nothing more. These were the last words that my brother said to me before he died. It was probably bullshit. He was full of that. But it was what helped me to block everything out. There is nothing more.

Nothing feels like anything anymore. Nothing except a sense of waiting. Waiting for something to happen. Waiting in limbo not knowing what's coming next. Waiting for the FPD to come and arrest me.

Waiting.
For.
The.
End.
Whatever that is.

44|

'Are we safe to move, do you think?' asks Sasha.

'I think so,' says my mouth, based on little other than the disappearance of the van.

She stands up and stretches out her arms behind her back. 'Are we okay to carry on on this route?' she continues. 'Is there another way that is further off the road?'

My fingers click on the scroller and glide the pixels around.

'This is the only route towards the slipway on Blackacre,' my mind replies. 'It's the closest slipway now by far. There is only one other main flashpoint at a junction about ten minutes from here. We can stay on the quiet roads until then.'

'Okay,' she says. 'Okay. I guess we just carry on then.'

'Follow me. Same distance as before,' comes my advice. 'Try to look less suspicious.'

'Suspicious?' she snaps.

'Yes, suspicious.'

Feet move again and take us away from the junction. The side street is narrow and bland and quiet as the previous one was before this. Change is an illusion.

45|

My legs warm as they move more regularly. Five minutes pass with no contact apart from the concrete and the cold air. Silent streets.

Sasha is still shuffling. Stinging eyes spot her. The bottle of drops that stops the itch sits in the cabinet in the bathroom. It should have been used by now today. This will only get worse.

The scrapes on my retina have never healed properly. Shards of glass from the explosion never completely removed. It was too late, the doctor at the clinic said. You should have come earlier. You should have gone to the hospital. Except, I was supposed to be dead. Dead people don't go to the hospital. By the time I had the confidence to venture out and visit an open clinic, the damage had been done. I pretended to be my brother in case they came after me. No one did. We can treat the symptoms, said the doctor, but no more.

He then asked me how my mood was. I seemed down. It says on my brother's record that I take tablets. Prescribed medication. Mood regulators. Chemicals to curb and repress highs and lows into a singular state of *okay*. Keep me on an even keel. 'Do you need any more?' he asked, thinking I was him. 'This must be a difficult time for you, damaging one's eyesight and appearance in this way can be distressing.'

'Why not?' was the response. Maybe they'll stop life getting any worse. I don't know if this has happened or not. Feelings aren't the same as they used to be. Everything is disconnected and pulled apart.

The tablets just smudge everything into a background blur so I can't tell what's really there.

46|

The junction approaches. My hand waves to Sasha to hide by the side of the road. The world stops moving around me. Scanning the road up ahead and crouching behind a collection of bins, rotting smells fill my nostrils.

She catches me up.

'How does it look?' she asks.

'It seems clear. Let's wait a minute and see if anything happens. There may be undercovers around; this is usually a busy junction.'

Today the junction is quiet as death. It is early still. However, not as early as before. More people will be awake. And awake people can follow the news. Television tells people to stay indoors the day after the freeze. *For your own safety.* Fear is easy to spread. It clings to people like the virus. This means more danger for us. We have to look out for waving curtains. Sliding blinds. Eyes upon the world. This road is a visible interchange, not a quiet side street. High rise cuboids surround it. Watchful, intentional looks could come from anywhere.

'What do you think?' she says. 'Is it safe? Shall we make a run for it? It's just straight across from here, isn't it?'

She points to the road that continues ahead of us. Leading between two blocks and then bending away to the left. The line of sight ahead is clear. However, the view left or right is not. This makes things difficult.

My brain clunks and makes a decision. 'I will go ahead to the junction and look. You stay here. I'll wave you over if it's clear.'

'Are you sure? What if someone sees you?'

'Then I will run and you will stay perfectly still here and do nothing. I'll distract them and then run away from the slipway.'

My finger awakens the interzoner in my hand and points to the exit point on the map.

'If I don't come back, you wait for five minutes and then head for here. There always used to be a hole hidden under a heap of old road signs.' A memory flashes briefly, but gets moved out of the way.

'But what about you?' she asks.

'Don't worry about me.'

My legs straighten to a half bend and scurry out following along the edge of the building, hands feeling the imaginary curves of the walls. My body is now only a metre or so from the junction and it stops in a crouch. Everything seems quiet. Adjusting to a crawl, my hands and knees control momentum. Inch by inch, the space opens up. Looking around the corner to the left, there is nothing but an empty street. Another inch forward and my neck cranes around to the right. A gust of cold air. Litter floating and turning and skittering as it blows. Dust particles scatter onto my face. But still nothing more.

We are lucky.

My body raises to the hunched over position of an old man and moves to wave in the direction of Sasha.

But the corner of my eye. In the mist. Was it?

On the side of one of the buildings, high on the left. A sliver of life. Did it move? Blinking to get some clarity. Time slows down to the speed of a heartbeat. The clock ticking over with every pump of an artery. A life that is slowly ending one contraction at a time. My eyes are fixed. Sasha hasn't moved yet. She must sense something is wrong.

Did my mind imagine it? My eyes aren't as they should be. Sensory perception lacks the integrity of before.

In another hesitant flicker the curtain proves my senses correct.

Everything in my body starts firing. Time begins to race. This feels unusual. My eyes move to Sasha's hiding spot. She is still behind the bins. Nothing from her yet. The curtains may think it's only me.

If they find her, they'll catch her and they'll hurt her and then they'll kill her.

Her smell briefly tingles somewhere in my brain before an image of her face in pulse gun agony takes over. The image makes me feel hurt. It makes me feel upset. It makes me *feel*.

It's time to run.

47|

Thoughts pan across in conscious layers. Now it is most likely that my body has been reported in a location. An FPD squad with full tracker equipment will be here in two minutes. This is their post-freeze response time. Regular as machines.

All I am is a choice of few options.

Continued running will inevitably lead to motion sensor detection. And then take-down by sting stick. Or worse, destruction by pulse gun. These options are worthy of consideration, but not highly productive.

Ceasing to run and electing to hide outside will mean a lock down of the area perimeter. This will be followed with a metre-by-metre search using motion and heat sensing technology should my body not be found immediately. This scenario buys time, but no escape.

There is a minimal chance that if they found me, they wouldn't connect me to who I really am. However, my mind knows that if the trooper performs the standard protocol instant DNA identity check, which they almost certainly will, then this is extremely unlikely.

Legs keep moving. They are running off the main road now and down a narrow alley. One minute and ten seconds left until superhero shaped destiny. My breathing is heavy and tight. More choices.

Breaking into an apartment building and entering a home. This could enable me to disappear if it is done quickly enough before the FPD sensors arrive. However, this is a risk. Murder in defence of private property is no longer an offence in Zone 4. An attempt to put off the gangs. Meet guns with guns. Let the poor people kill each other. It could work if done within a minute and if nobody kills me in the process.

Suicide. My mind knows that this is always an option. The best existence is one in which one never existed at all. It also knows that cowardice is a strong emotion. And this may not gain Sasha the time to escape.

Sixty seconds.

A decision makes itself. My legs change angle. Running is slowing down. I see my hands reach out and grab a graffitied backdoor communal entrance. It opens and creaks, then slams behind. The noise echoes in a dark corner of an empty concrete car park. My eyes turn left then right then straight ahead. Another door appears through the white mist and I am moving towards it. Breathing becomes wheezing. Sweating forms a salty shine that drips down my shoulders. The handle is wrenched open and legs approach the stairs. Lactic acid builds and builds and builds.

Forty seconds.

First floor. Through the entrance, there is a corridor ahead. A balcony. Four doors in a row on the right-hand side. Pick one. Pick one.

Twenty seconds.

My mind elects, sending my shoulder charging into a wooden door. Its frame shudders and my body repels backwards. Blood vessels and muscle tissue swell and damage and bruise. Vibrations move through bone and cartilage. The brain ricochets into its skull casing in a tide of cerebrospinal fluid.

Ten seconds.

My shoulder charges again. A large bang and the door opens. Arms, hips and palms hit the floor. My body rolls inside the home and feet attempt to kick the door closed. The latch is broken and the door swings ajar. Looking up, four eyes meet mine. Conscious penetration. Two children staring from a sofa.

Time.

'Who the fuck are you?'

48|

'I'm no one.'

The air is forcing a path in and out of my lungs. Everywhere hurts.

'What you doing here?' asks one of the boys. He has blond hair.

'I'm.' Breath. Cough. Sweat. 'Lost.' Cough. Sweat.

Their eyes turn to the television which is blazing FREEZE ZONE THEFT NEWS in ticker tape across its screen. The bright lights colour their faces in a changing blur. Their eyes turn back.

'Are you one of them trippers?' A joint intake of breath follows this realisation.

'Shit! I bet he is!' says the boy with blond hair.

'No, I'm not.' Cough. 'I'm a person who's lost, that's all.'

A look on their faces tells me this will not pass as an excuse. The childish fat in their cheeks rises with smiles and pushes my words out as a lie. The grey whites of their eyes glisten with a sheen of contempt.

In this uncertain silence the community alarms start ringing. It is now exactly the wrong time for this to happen. This block, like all others in Zone 4, is fitted with FPD community alarms *for our safety*. Every corridor on every floor has one. The sound waves they emit are at a specific number of decibels to cause distress, but no permanent damage. With the ringing follows the familiar message.

'THIS IS THE FREEZE POLICE DEPARTMENT. STAY IN YOUR HOMES. WE HAVE REASON TO BELIEVE THAT THERE IS A FUGITIVE IN YOUR MIDST. A ROUTINE

RANDOM SEARCH OF LOCAL RESIDENCES IS NOW IN PROGRESS. REPEAT. DO NOT LEAVE YOUR HOMES…'

Now it will definitely not pass as an excuse.

'Shit! He is one as well!' Lurid desire and destruction steal their expressions. 'Hell yes! Awesome!'

The brown-haired boy sits up in his seat. 'How much did you steal? Holy crap! Hold on a minute…Did you kill someone?' He points to the television in garish glee. 'What was it like? I bet you have!'

'Yeah, I bet he has,' adds the blond haired one, certainty in every pore of his pallor. 'Probably squished 'em up good.' His arms hold an imaginary rifle in the air and fires. 'Pulse gunned out his face or something. Peaow! My friend Jonny saw a trooper flatten someone with a pulse gun once. He said it was the grossest thing he ever saw.' These words are said with tribal excitement and thrill, life yet to peel that from their bones.

'Who did you kill? Hope it was the police. I'd kill one of 'em if I had the chance!'

The blond boy waves his hands in the air in some kind of martial art movement. They stare at me with blue irises and deep red, burning amazement.

They cannot be any more than eight or nine years old.

49|

My body rises onto its feet. Hands lean against the wall and mouth begins to talk. Feign authority. We had done this before after a freeze. In a tight spot. People are only projections.

'Listen boys. I just need to hide here until the search is over. I won't cause you any harm. When the FPD have gone, then I'll go too.'

It feels as though being an authority has disappeared with everything else. More than as if it has just gone though. As if the authority and charisma were never really there in the first place. Sweat continues to drip. My throat swallows and needs water.

'Hide?'

'He wants to hide?' Scrumples form on a brow too used to confusion.

'What about squishing the troopers? Get out your semi-automatic and rub them out? Why don't you do that?'

'Yeah, why don't you do that?'

'I'm not after trouble. I need to stay unnoticed, that's all.'

'What? Hey! No!' A crackle of suppressed indignation wrestles its way out of the blond boy. 'You can't stay here unless you're gonna do something cool.'

'I'll go get my dad, you'll see.'

'No, no. There's no need to do that. Where is your dad?' My mind had not yet considered this question. A touch of panic. A sensation.

'Two floors up. With Wendy from 3g. They're screwing.'

'But they don't love each other,' adds the brown haired one.

'No. We know they don't. Dad still loves Mum, you see. But she's dead.'

'Hey, you don't know that!' The brown haired one sits up straight in his seat.

'Well, what do you think, dummy? Night before the freeze she was here. Night after, she wasn't.'

'Which freeze cycle was this? Yesterday's?' my voice interrupts. If it was last night, this could be bad news for me. This could be a marked site.

'No, no. Stupid. Three cycles ago. Dad says that kind of shit happens all the time now. People go missing in freeze state. He says it's FPD. They take people.'

'You don't know they do...' says brown hair.

'They take 'em for experimenting on and shit.' A secret scar of intrigue reveals itself in his lips. 'Or messing with. Or something. Either way. She's dead as dead now.'

'You don't know that!' shouts the brown haired one. He runs into the next room and slams the door.

'Do too!' shouts back the blond hair.

His face turns back to mine. It is crumpled and complicated. His eyes deep set. His hair is thin and messy, the strands stuck together like glue. He stands up as a middle-aged man.

'I guess you can hide here if you like. Even if you won't kill anybody, you're on our side. Dad says troopers still can't cross doorways yet without warrants. Dad sometimes hides Wendy under the sofa when we come home from school, so I suppose you could hide there.'

He walks up close to me and looks at my face. 'You don't look like a tripper. Your eyes look funny. I thought trippers were supposed to be cool.'

'Well, I'm sorry,' my mouth says while my body is crawling under the sofa. 'Thank you,' it adds.

'Yeah, yeah. If Dad catches you though, he won't be happy. I'll tell him you made us do it, just so you know.'

My eyes watch small sideways feet turn to point back at the television. A noise comes from the balcony. It is the corridor door opening. Heavy footsteps are approaching the entrance.

50|

Hiding between the beer cans, the body hair and the broken glass, the conversation begins.

Knock. Knock.

'This is the Freeze Police Department. Please would the owner of the household come to the front door with relevant ownership documentation.'

'Hey! Who are you?' say the affronted small shoes. They move away from the sofa towards the front door.

'I am a member of the FPD. I need to see your mother or father please.'

'Well you can't.'

'Can you please explain to me why not, young man?'

'They ain't in.'

'Where are they?'

'My Dad's out and my Mum's dead.'

'I am sorry to hear about your mother.' He speaks in flat line tones. 'Where is your father?'

'Dunno. Was it you who killed my Mum?'

'I'm sorry?'

'Was it you? It probably was. You've probably killed so many people you've forgotten by now.'

'Where is your father likely to be?'

'Bet it was you. Do you always steal people when they're frozen and kill them? Is that your job?'

'Answer my question. Where is he likely to be?'

'I. Don't. Know. Maybe you killed him already?'

'Listen, kid. You are pushing my patience.' He rises to the bait. 'I'm coming in to look for him.'

'No you're not. You can't come in without a particular permit. Or warrant. Or whatever you losers call it.'

'How do you know that?'

'My dad told me. I know it's true. You can't lie to me.'

'Oh really? Did he tell you anything else?'

'Yeah. He told me FPD stands for flaccid police dick. He says that's true too.'

There is a shuffle of armoured boots. A moment of quiet at the door. Only the sounds of faint knocking on doors and echoed voices. There is a rustle of paper. The barcode scanning noise of an FPD inter-zoner begins. This means that he is preparing a return notice. The kid has pissed him off, so they'll come back and arrest his dad.

The voice continues. 'Tell your father that he needs to contact the FPD the minute he gets home. Due to absence and lack of valid ownership documentation, under Section 24 of the Freeze Police Department this residence is now marked for investigation. Please hand this document to your father on his return. We will be back later in the day to speak to him personally.'

'Okay, if you say so. Try not to kill anyone in the meantime, FPD.'

The boots sound out again and the trooper moves away from the open door.

'You can come out now, tripper wimp.'

51|

The sleeve of my coat is now damp with stale beer. It has gradually seeped through the fibres, one by one, leading to an unpleasantly moist, cold feeling that won't go away.

My limbs scrabble and crawl out from under the sofa. The boy stands and watches as my hands brush off the grey clouds of dust and dark hairs. When they stop moving, he walks towards me and kicks me in the shin.

'Shithead!' he says. 'Dad's gonna freak at me now.'

He paces from side to side. His feet slightly sliding on the lino floor with each turn. The scrumples return. Rubbing the back of his neck, he ignores me.

'I only need to stay here until the search is over and then I can leave,' my mouth says.

'Well I never wanted you here in the first place.' His fists are clenched together into a tight bundle in front of him. The knuckles are white. 'I hate moving,' he says. His voice explodes into steam. 'This is all your fault!'

The bedroom door opens.

'What's going on?' says brown hair.

'Shut up,' says blond hair. 'Go back and cry in the pillows like a baby. You're no help at all.'

'Hey! I'm not a baby! Tell me what's going on!'

The pacing stops. 'What's going on is we are going to be in big trouble with Dad.'

Brown haired pupils dilate. 'How much trouble?'

'You remember that time with mum?'

'Yes.'

'That much trouble.'

Brown hair breathes in. 'But why?'

'The FPD turds are coming back with a paper thing.'

'Oh no. Are we going to move again?'

'I don't know. Probably. Use your head stupid, that's what's happened every other time.'

'Don't call me stupid!' he yells.

'Why not? Stupid stupid stupid stupid. You're stupid.'

Blond haired boy pushes the other one to the floor. He starts crying.

'Why are you such a baby?'

'I'm not a baby.'

He is curled up on the floor like an overgrown foetus.

The front door slams open. A new voice bangs. 'What the hell is going on?' His stare raises and notices my body. There is an empty moment before his eyes narrow. 'Holy shit,' he says. 'Are you...? Crap! It really is you! James! What's going on? You? Here? I thought you were dead.'

52|

'Do I know you?'

His face is a front line of trenches and war. His hair a greasy, thick explosion of curls. My mind thinks it would remember such features.

'No. But I know you. Shit. Everyone in the rebellion knows who you are! You're a bloody hero. Boys, stand up straight! You're in the presence of greatness.'

My mind darts. The boys' backs straighten like starch.

He continues. 'Christ! You're still alive. So the whole thing was a cover? It was planned?…Ah! Of course it was! You went underground. Only by faking your own death could you really escape surveillance. Genius. You had to pretend to die in order to be invisible. It's the only way.'

'It's the only way to what?' my mouth questions. 'How do you know who I am?'

The boys are staring at my face with open mouths.

'The incident. You and Sasha Shiverstone tripping into the federal reserve with the founders of Thaw. The fire fight. Your death. I mean, your supposed death. The spark for the rebellion.'

'The spark?'

'Yes. For Thaw. You know. The people in charge of the rebellion.' His eyes flash with panic. 'Wait. Is this a test? Are you here to check on our cell's progress? We are on track I assure you. I don't know who sparked off the search here, but they won't find anything. We are pre-pared for the second strike. I can't believe the first trip got busted.

There's got to be somebody who's telling the FPD our plans. If I find them, I'll kill them. In your name, sir.'

'Yeah! Peaow, peaow! Pulse gun the fuckers!' says blond hair, aiming his invisible sight.

'Language!' shouts the man. He hits blond hair on the back of his head. The boy scowls and retreats.

'So what is the plan now?' he asks, the words dripping with gravity. His face is expectant.

My mind doesn't know what is happening.

'What do you think happened at the Federal Reserve?' my mouth asks.

'Only the shitting incredible! You, Sasha and some of the majors planned it out and tripped into the Reserve to get funds and prove anything could be tripped. You tripped to redress the balance. You know, put some of the money back into the zones who need it. Who deserve it. Instead of everything getting sunk into Zone 1's bloody pockets. To fund the next projects and zone riots. You got in and out but caught in the slipway back into this zone. They ambushed you and the fight ensued. You and the majors took down half a battalion of the FPD pricks, but they had heavy artillery and specialist units. They rocket launched you into the next world. Except, it turns out that they didn't. Unbelievable.'

Elements of truth twist into my mind with myth and exaggeration.

'How do you know about all this?'

'Everyone knows about it. It's the first thing the majors tell you when you become part of the rebellion. It is the story that finally got people moving. That finally got us organised. That started to make people *believe*. How many are there now sir? Are we ready for the next riot?'

My teeth clench. The white mist is crawling back in. My fist is in a ball.

'Stop calling me sir. I don't know anything about the plans you are referring to. I'm not in charge of anything. I never was.'

'What? What do you mean?'

'I mean you've been lied to. I'm not what you just said.'

'Then why the hell are you here? Wait. Is this part of the cover? What's really going on? Give it to me straight. I'm on your side.'

My fist reaches up to scratch the itch, but stops inches away.

'I was helping Sasha get to the slipway on Blackacre and we got spotted. We got separated. I tried to find somewhere to hide. Now I'm here. That's the truth.'

'Sasha Shiverstone?'

'Yes, Sasha Shiverstone.'

'Holy shit! So you are still in contact!' His eyebrows raise. 'I've never met her myself. Only seen the pictures. Heard the stories. She's an incredible woman. Flippin' stunner! That kind of woman doesn't exist in real life. Oh, God. I can't believe you're here. I can't believe this is happening.' His face crinkles into a smile. 'I need a beer,' he says. 'Do you want a beer? I'm having a beer.'

His feet take him to the kitchen and his hands open the fridge.

'Shit, we're out.' His neck turns. 'Boys! Go up to Wendy's and grab some drinks.'

'Aw Dad! Can't we stay here and speak to the tripper?' says the blond one.

'Yeah, can we?' asks brown.

'Do as you're told,' shouts Dad.

The boys slink out of the door.

'Right,' says Dad. 'Tell me what the plan is.'

53|

What has been created in my absence? Thaw had been more obvious in the last year. Even dead, I was aware of this. More overground. More brave. The television had told me so. Shown me so.

Faces of arrested insurgents. Reports of criminal court cases resulting in cast iron convictions. Community service orders. *Hard* time. Agitated reporters and images of vandalism. Interviews with well-dressed outraged innocents who can't understand the pointless aggression of it all. The mindless disturbances. The need to not simply live as a law-abiding citizen like the rest of us. The fear that they now have for the safety of their children. The lack of humanity in these rebellious thugs. Where has the common human decency gone? The question of when the world came to *this*.

Zone 1 had raised security. Their lives are too valuable to be caught up in the cause. But it seems that what had only been the paranoid insecurities of a few had now become something of a movement. A few people can be ignored. Ridiculed. Rejected. But movements are dangerous. Once something becomes bigger than the people involved it takes on a new existence. Becomes a substance in its own right. That strange category of being a thing that doesn't exist. A social black hole. The gravitational lure of the mysterious sucking in people who get too close. People who are curious. Who want an answer. Who long to be carved from a mould. To have a maker and model to live up to. Who are willing to falsify life for a single piece of certainty.

The only certainty that my mind finds in this kitchen with the boys' dad is that movements have a habit of forgetting why they started once they carry enough weight to actually move anywhere.

'Where to?' he asks again. 'What do you want me to do?'

A sickly desire to follow shines in his eyes.

My mind is outside the building. On the road with Sasha. Crouching and creeping to Blackacre. Darting from alley to alley. She is touching my hand again. Holding my head in her palms as we hide. Telling me she is sorry. That she wants things back the way they were.

This kind of woman doesn't exist in real life.

The tablets are beginning to wear off. The ache is coming back. My body can never place the ache. It moves as it is searched for. Always everywhere except the place you are looking for it. The doctor said that it might be in my mind. But my mind knows that it is in my bones. Buried in the calcium and the marrow. Deep inside my very atoms. Filling the vast spaces between the protons and electrons and neutrons and quarks. It is my Higgs Boson. My God particle. It gives my body such unbearable mass.

'What now, sir? Sir?'

Even after all that happened, she controls me. Apart from her, the ache is all I have.

'I need to get to Blackacre slipway,' my mouth says. 'I have to make sure that Sasha has slipped it through okay.'

'Well, I can help there,' he says smiling. 'We've got a passage that'll get you to Zone 1 and you can check it from there. No FPD monitoring it on the other side of the fence. You should have asked earlier. I'll take you if you like?'

'Thank you.'

'It would be my honour, sir. Wait 'til the guys hear about this!'

'When can we go?'

147

'Once we've had our beer, we'll be right on our way. Where are those flaming boys? They are the bane of my life, I'm telling you.'

54|

The beer that was forced into my hand is being drunk. Six eyes follow every sip. It is being poured quickly and the bubbles rush up into my nostrils. Coughing, some liquid spatters from my lips. Blond and brown hair laugh.

'We need to leave,' my mouth fumbles through a splutter. Time is being wasted here.

'Okay,' he says. 'I'll just finish my beer. It's a celebratory moment.'

My eyes glare. As if they believe the myth about this all being part of the *plan*. Truth is like poetry. You can interpret it in many different ways.

He looks down and says 'okay', before tipping the beer bottle vertically and sinking its contents. 'Aah,' he grunts. 'Right. Boys, you need to wait here. I'll be back this evening. If you get hungry, go and ask Wendy.'

'Aw, Dad! We want to come with you,' says Blond.

'Yes, yes, can we?' Brown hair is jumping up and down on the spot.

'No,' he barks. 'You stay here. This is serious and we can't risk having any silly kids ruining anything.'

'We ain't silly kids,' yells Blond before running to the bedroom. Brown follows and slams the door.

'Right,' he says, walking over to the rotten sink and reaching into the cupboard underneath. His hands reveal themselves again with a shiny symbol of my past.

'I keep this for emergencies. Take it. You might need it.'

A pulse gun.

Its shiny cylinder passes into my hands.

55|

The entrance is beneath a wrecked van in the car park. My legs move quickly, one after the other, and follow Dad's lead down the steep descent. His building is far away from our subterranean world now. The tunnel is dank and dark and only half my height.

Our necessary crouching is pushing the ache. Teasing and testing it. Its presence creeping out of my bones and starting to fill the empty space within me.

A circle of light begins to grow in front of our heads. He talks and talks. About the work of his cell. The preparations that have been made for the next big hit. What he would do if he got his hands on the president. His words sink like stones in the cold air and fall on the soil beneath my feet. Inert pieces of the earth.

The light is big and reveals a green bush in front of us. Healthy natural green. Lifelike. Dad turns to me and now I listen.

'We have to move very quickly as soon as we are out in the open,' he says. 'This spot is quiet but we both don't look like we belong here. Zone 1s are different. Pigs. Remember, they don't dress like us. There's a shed about a hundred yards to the left with some clothes where we can get some cover and figure out what to do next. He hesitates for a moment. Is that okay, sir?'

'Yes. Let's just go,' my false truth replies.

He darts out into the light and my legs follow. Three steps forward and…

'Freeze!'

56|

My eyebrows tighten and the lids beneath squint. Pupils contract and shrink as photons hit the retina and cast an inverted image which transmits to my brain. An FPD squad van. Two superhero shapes. The glint of metal casings. Dad opening his mouth and pointing before scrabbling his legs in the dirt. Dad moving his arms and raging his brow. Dad drawing his gun. The fingers of destiny moving. Pieces of Dad's body disintegrating as it flies towards the zone wall. Guns repositioning on my body.

'Don't you move! Freeze, insurgent!'

Fight. Flight. Or Freeze. My body is now several feet away from the tunnel. Behind the blank black visors the glinting guns hold their focus.

'Don't move! On your knees!'

A noise comes from my right. My head turns and the healthy green of the bush's leaves moves again. Another body appears out of the dark. It hesitates. The guns turn and bring destiny once more. The pulses emit and shatter the air and everything else around the chloroplasts. My eyes look down. Cells and structures are ruptured. A body is in pieces. Blond hair is lying on the floor.

My hands move instantly and reach for the pulse gun. It feels like a reflex. Inbuilt. Innate. My arm swings around and unleashes. Trigger slides back twice with perfectly designed ease. Matter is manipulated at the request of man.

Visors shatter and bounce off the van. What's left of limbs lie on the ground. Superhero shaped no more.

Destiny.

57|

The gun tumbles to the floor and my legs move quickly to the left. The shed is in view on the other side of a low fence that runs parallel to a house. Jumping over and into the garden, my body tumbles forward through soft, green grass until it hits the wooden door. Scrambling to get up, my hands grasp the globe shaped, black Perspex handle and twist it. The door opens and then slams shut. Breathing and breathing and coughing and breathing. The concrete floor of the shed feels cool underneath my feet. Tiny particles of dust dance in the sunlight as it shines through the window. One more change that has resulted from my actions. One more thing that is my fault.

Hands wipe my eyes and forehead, the sweat and mist smearing across sleeves into one substance. Standing up, my brain reacts and leaves the world outside for a moment in order to look around the shed. There are dusty tarpaulins covering a pile of objects in the far corner. The material is removed and underneath there is a singular, bulky package wrapped in clear plastic. Whilst unwrapping, my ears are drawn to the outside again. Screams. Loud voices. Running around. Panic.

My brain remembers that this is Zone 1.

People don't die here.

My body just committed murder in luxury suburbia. It killed two FPD policemen with an illegal pulse gun. And will be blamed for the death of an innocent child. That means that I am *evil*. An enemy of the people. A disgusting monster of a human being. And it is punishable by death. Luckily, my mind remembers that they can't kill me. What's already dead can't die.

58|

Inside the package there is a change of clothes. These are clean clothes. They feel strange in my fingers. The style is smart – a high buttoned, collared shirt and fine, pressed cotton trousers. This is the uniform of the average Zone 1 aristocrat. Conformity is cultural. There is also some water, an energy capsule, a new design interzoner and a pop gun. The pop gun is hand sized and light, like a toy. It is a younger brother of the pulse rifle. My brain can't remember holding one before. It was only invented recently and was quickly made illegal in all zones. Only specially trained, *righteous* state agents are allowed to carry them. Their effectiveness is limited to close range, but it can disintegrate a face without concern. Too easy to conceal, that was the reason given for making them illegal.

Holding it somehow feels right.

The energy fluid oozes out of the capsule. It contains all the vital nutrients and vitamins that my metabolism needs to keep going for 24 hours. This should be long enough. It is thick and viscous as it runs down my throat. It brings with it an unpleasantly fast feeling of fullness that unsettles my stomach. Water washes it down and then pours over my face. Sweat and dirt and dust run off into a puddle on the floor. Hands rub my eyes with fury and the framework of my retina flashes up as white mist stretches across my field of vision.

BEEP. Bzzzzz. BEEP. Bzzzzz. BEEP.

BEEP. Bzzzzz. BEEP. Bzzzzz. BEEP.

The interzoner in my hand is signalling a desire to connect. Brain fires up and thoughts emerge. There's no chance of making it to the Blackacre slipway on my own, not now. And even if I do, if Sasha isn't there then someone will need to know what's happened to her. Help is needed. My finger slides across the connect button and a representation of a man's face appears in tiny, coloured light.

'Who the hell is this?' the tiny representation says. 'And why the hell are you killing FPD men in the very broad daylight of Zone 1? This is not part of the plan.'

Part of the plan, it says. Supposedly there's a plan.

My eyes look down at the interzoner. The face is round and red. It has a greying goatee beard which has been sculpted with absurd precision. It has tight, dark curly hair and thick eyebrows. It's nose is small with tiny, flared nostrils.

'Hold on,' it says. 'Is that?' It squints and leans in to become an even bigger collection of pixels. 'No! You're dead!'

Only I'm not. Apparently.

59|

'We need to come get you. How did you get there? No, don't worry, you can tell me later. There's no time. Search and interrogate units are minutes away from the slipway exit. Everything is on heightened alert because of the bust this morning – this was not a good time to cross a border. Look, you stay there. You should be safe in the shed until we arrive. Someone will knock for you in five minutes. Just hold tight until then. Are you okay?'

'No, not really.'

'Never mind. We can talk about this when you arrive here. God! This is very exciting! Got to go – sometimes they monitor interzoner use in hotspot areas. Sit tight. Someone will be with you soon.'

My body sits tight. However that is supposed to occur. The itch is back. And so is the dark feeling. The middle nowhere is fading away as the tablets do.

I don't want to feel anymore.

60|

Sirens and talking and engines are sounding outside. Five minutes they said. It has now been ten, and there has been no knock on the door.

The roof of the shed is arced in shape and there is a cross pinned to the space above the doorway. It brings back memories of being in a chapel as a child. A small, grey stoned building that smelt of wood chips and soil. The feel of the cold wind on my cheeks as my legs walk through the park wild grass and inside the four small walls. The sense of reverence, of the other. The feeling of the sacred and the profane. The sense that somewhere amidst the stone and the rotting wood and the dirt there was something perfect to be found. Something *better than this*. There had to be, because this couldn't be all there is. Nothing could be this inert. My brain remembers those feelings like fallen trees washed away by a thunderstorm. The bodies of them are no longer there. All that is left are the dead stumps that sit like scars on the landscapes.

KNOCK. KNOCK.

'I'm coming in,' the voice says. The door opens and now there are two human beings shut inside a small wooden structure built at the end of a private garden. 'We need to get out of here, fast,' it says.

61|

'I'm Edmundsen. I know, I know. I'm late. I'm sorry. Listen, if you knew what I had to get through to be here, you'd forgive me. Not that I expect you to forgive me, sir. I mean, that's your decision.'

He scratched a patch of his sharp stubble.

'You obviously don't have to forgive me. Hell, you don't have to forgive anyone anything *ever* considering the things you've done for the cause.'

My eyes get caught again on the tiny particles dancing in the sunlight.

'I'm sorry. I'm talking too much. I always do that when I'm nervous. Hey, at least I know why I'm doing it, right? Knowledge of self and all that. Anyway, we have to go. Right now.'

'Where are we going?'

'I have a car waiting out the front. We own this house so we can get through to the front drive no problem. The tricky part will be getting out of this suburb. It's under almost complete lockdown and that means they'll check every car that leaves the area.'

A smirk stretches across his face.

'But they don't know about our new shit yet. You are gonna love it, seriously!'

'Just tell me how we are going to leave this place and where we are going to go.'

'We got secret compartments built into a couple of cars. It's next level, trust me. The seats and other bits can organise and reorganise to keep you hidden from anything but a really thorough search.'

Our legs are walking now, hurrying out of the shed and towards the backdoor of the house. The garden is immaculately presented. Neat rows of petunias and chrysanthemums and rose bushes. Rocks ordered to look unordered. Millimetres long grass soft as our feet bounce over it. Through the side-return of the house and up to a wooden gate that leads to the road. Exaggerated, Edmundsen holds out his palm indicating for me to stop as if he's in an action war movie. As if this is all oh so very important. His eyes peer out through a crack in a wooden panel.

He lifts his sleeve to his mouth.

'Snowman, come in Snowman. We are in position by the front gate. Repeat, we are by the front gate. Say again, over. Okay, preparing to exit the property. Exiting the property. Get ready now, sir. Follow me and go straight into the car. Exiting in three, two, one. Sir, time to go.'

62|

Our bodies race through the front garden and onto the pavement on the other side. A door opens automatically and Edmundsen pulls my arm into the car before the black interior closes back in. For a moment all there is is darkness and my mind thinks it wouldn't be so bad if this were all over.

'Please lie flat across the seat, sir.'

'What?'

'Do it, now. Otherwise we might be too late.'

Edmundsen pulls my shoulders down towards the fake cow skin covers.

'Lie still. This won't hurt, but it will feel pretty weird.'

He climbs into the front seat as the car pulls away slowly. My shoulders and back rest against the seat for a moment before a mechanism quickly swallows my body whole.

Everything is black and feels like leather. My body has sunken into the seat and is pinned entirely. There is an uncompromising pressure. A sense of complete enclosure. It is a burial. Has this whole episode been the dream of a dead man who is now waking? These thoughts breed a sense of panic until it is interrupted by the faint sounds of a conversation.

'Good afternoon, sir. I apologise for stopping you here but you may be aware that there are some dangerous individuals on the loose. Your's and the wonderful people of Zone 1's safety is our top priority so we are stopping everyone as a matter of routine.'

'That's no problem, officer.' This is the voice of Edmundsen. 'You're just doing your job. Please feel free to check the car.'

'Thank you, sir.'

My body feels the vibrations of a car door open. Something leans on my buried body.

'I do hope that this won't take too long, officer. I'm sure you understand that I have important business to attend to.'

'Yes, sir.' A door closes. 'Everything seems to be in order. I apologise again for the inconvenience. Have an enjoyable day.'

My body senses movement as the car rolls away.

'You can come out now,' says Edmundsen. 'I'll switch it off.'

The world is distorted. Fragmented and pulled apart. My body is regurgitated onto the backseat once more. The car is driving down a busy road in the centre of Zone 1. I am resurrected.

'What just happened?'

'A quick inspection,' says Edmundsen. 'Not to worry, I sorted it all out.'

'How do they know who you are?'

'Because I'm an elected representative of the people, sir. I have been for a year now. I was fed into the system as a plant. We've got people in all sorts of places. It's all part of the plan.'

'You're an elected representative of the people?'

'Only in a junior position, but I'm a member of the Zone 1 council. First rung. Not policy worthy yet, but known enough to get away from an FPD inspection during a lockdown. I'm not a big deal or anything, just trying to do my bit for the cause. I'm nothing like you, of course. What you've done is unparalleled.'

What I've done, my mind thinks. *What have I done?*

'We're only a few minutes away now,' he says as he turns his head. 'There's a safe house entry just up the road which then leads into our main headquarters.'

'There's a headquarters?'

'You didn't know about the headquarters? Jesus, you were deep undercover. You've made such a sacrifice, sir. It is truly remarkable. I can't wait to bring you in. Just you wait!'

I am waiting. Waiting is all I ever do.

63|

The car pulls up onto the pavement of a deserted side street. Edmundsen hops out and looks around him carefully before touching a hidden button that must have been embedded in the wall. There is a pause before a section of smooth, artisan dead stone façade moves and the car lurches through to the other side before stopping. It is dark and Edmundsen turns on a flashlight.

'This way, follow me.' Edmundsen starts off away from the front of the car and towards another golden beam of light. 'It's not far now. I'm excited for you; there's so much for you to see!'

The golden beam of light emits from a torch held by a man with serious eyes. He flashes the light on our faces and then stares at a space in the wall. A blue light shines and pans the serious eyes. A moment after, another door slides open. As it does so, light first slivers its way into existence before widening and establishing itself upon the whole width of the pathway.

The view on the other side is busy. My eyes see people walking from one place to another with purpose. None of them pay us any attention as we step through the gate and into the moving collection of living things. The space looks like a community. Humans working together using made up rules to achieve pretend goals.

I don't want this. I shouldn't be here.

I can't beat the ache.

64|

'Sir, come this way. Come, come. People are incredibly excited to see you.'

My legs move in measured steps towards a doorway. My mind is a preoccupied mess of unchosen questions. It chooses what it chooses.

The door is sheet steel and, in perfect circles, fiercely reflects the lights that dot the open courtyard. Edmundsen reaches towards it, grabs a handle and pushes it down. There is a screech that shudders my neck before the click of release and pull. Warm, bright air escapes the room and my body moves inside. The light makes our eyes tighten. Memories of sunshine and a lake blow into place. Sasha and the clean beauty of dancing spots of sunlight on the water. Footprints sunk into the silt two by two. The removal of the world as my head submerged into frozen water; its strange stillness unchanging as we moved through it.

'Sir? Sir? Please, follow me.' A different voice interrupted this time. 'Edmundsen, what took you so long? She has been waiting. Sir, this way.'

Edmundsen's young face is disgruntled as he bows out.

This next room is warmer than the last. Not in temperature but in ambience. There is a mahogany wooden desk at one end and bookshelves set to its left. On the shelves there is a collection of vintage antiques: a pile of CDs next to a hi-fi, a digital alarm clock, a brightly coloured coffee pot, a sheathed samurai sword and an old double-barrelled shotgun. The floor is carpeted and an orange, domed light shade that looks like something from the mid twentieth century hangs from the ceiling. The light emitting from it is dim and distorts the colour of everything else. My eyes move to the right and standing in this orange light is a woman. She has one of those faces that is hard to age. It has some lines, but her eyes look young and alive. Her frame is slight, but she stands with a certain power in her body. She has hair that is tied tight in a ponytail which frays at the ends.

'We finally meet,' she says.

65|

'Finally?'

'I have been waiting a long time for this to happen. You are the last important piece of the puzzle. I knew she would get you out of whatever state you put yourself in.'

'What do you mean?'

'Sasha knew just as I did that we needed you for the plan. If what happens next is going to work, we need a living saint. A prophet for the people. A new Jesus for our times if you will. A sacrificial lamb who gave his life for the cause in order that we might all be redeemed. All we needed was our resurrection. You can't convince them all without a touch of the miraculous.'

'What?'

'We need you. You complete us.'

She laughs. A raucous, powerful laugh that rings in my ears.

'We sent Sasha to you to bring you back to life. I'm sorry that we had to do it this way, but I don't think you would have come any other way. She wanted to tell you the whole story, but I asked her not to. Not until we could get you on site.'

'Sasha was at my house deliberately? What about the incident? The trip that went wrong? It was all over the news.'

'Yes, yes. Well, we can't figure out what went wrong there. Someone must have tipped off the FPD. Always a risk now in this fight. The pressure that the FPD are willing to apply to get what they want is extraordinary. Still, it ended up with you being here now, so we must focus on the positives. Every cloud, as they say.

'Excuse me, where are my manners? You don't even know who I am. Here is me knowing everything about you and yet you don't even know my name. My name is Grace.'

Grace reaches out a hand to shake mine. My hand moves forwards and takes hers. Her skin feels rough and dry.

'I am now what I suppose you would call the leader of Thaw. I joined just after the terrible events with your brother and we have really gone from strength to strength since then. You and your brother's actions that night provided the perfect story to motivate new members. To spread our message of strength and courage in the face of pitiless power and indifference. We created and cultivated the story of your death. You have no idea how powerful your actions have become. And now you are back, the power will be a hundred times, a thousand times more significant. Now is the time. I have everything prepared for you; a whole story of your life undercover.'

'No,' my voice says. 'I shouldn't be here. None of what you are saying is true.'

'But is that relevant? The question to my mind is not what is true, but what is useful. Untruth can be much more useful than truth. Especially in a battle filled with lies, maybe more lies are what we need to level the playing field a little. We need you to play a part. No more than that.' Her eyes look directly at mine, and she continues. 'Aren't we all playing parts? This is simply another role. I play the leader. You play the returning hero.'

'But I have nothing to say. I'm not a part of Thaw anymore. I'm not a part of anything. There are no feelings left.'

Eyes itch and hands rub.

'What you think is irrelevant; you are a part of this. You don't get to opt out of the human race. Come with me and meet some of these people. See how we have grown. Then you will know what it is to feel something.'

66|

Grace leads me. Our bodies descend some steps and enter a covered walkway under some tattered tarpaulin sheets that stretch out like giant hammocks between the buildings. She hands me a tissue as we walk.

'I knew about your eyes,' she says. 'I didn't realise they were quite so bad. We might have someone who can take a look at them, if you would like? Some of this new nanotech is quite astounding. You saw our new nano-gate at the entrance? That's cutting-edge technology which we've only just got our hands on in the last couple of months. We are hoping to start rolling those out to use in the border walls if we can, but it takes a long time to install them so we're not there yet. If the government knew we had it there would be another cull of employees at their research headquarters. We can't afford to lose our contacts in there, it took the whole time you were away to get them to this point. Don't answer me now about your eyes. Just look around, if you can, and see people who clearly need your help.'

Groups of people are talking to each other in small circles. They stop as their eyes meet mine. Nods and smiles.

'Why don't you get help from outside?' is the obvious question. 'There must be people who are willing to get involved outside the EPRL?'

'We are trying different options, but it's not as straightforward as you might think. Our limited intel from the few people who have managed to make it in from beyond the walls suggests there are not many people left out there. Since the uprisings, there's been no official form of government in England outside of the EPRL, and without the vaccines the virus got most of them. If the virus didn't, then it seems they killed each other in a struggle for power and survival. I think there are other organisations set up in a few other cities – we've heard of some kind of cartel running Liverpool, but we have no idea who is in charge and how they work. The rumours we hear about them suggest they're not exactly sympathetic to outsiders either. Life is not pretty – I'm not sure if we really want them involved. If we invited them into the city, I have no idea if it would ameliorate our situation or make it worse.

'Regardless, any communication lines we try to set up aren't working. We've tried using tampered tech, modified interzoners, even old radios to make contact but nothing so far. They're still saying that the temporal anomaly blocks radio waves and satellite links, but we'll figure it out. We have yet to get the breakthrough with our equipment, but we will.

'And when we do, we need a hero to represent us.'

67|

Many eyes stare at my body as it walks. One pair drops to the ground the moment that my gaze catches it. A young girl who tucks her hair behind her ear as she looks away.

'This is our main production area. Here, we grow a number of vegetables to supplement the lab synthetics that keep us going. Everyone has a job, a place and a role. There is no money and no private property. We live by a common law that we impose upon ourselves. We all contribute and no one is treated differently to anyone else. In here, we can be ourselves. We can be free from FPD intervention, even in freeze state.'

'How do you know that? You can't know what happens when you're frozen.'

'No, I can't. But we know that the FPD has no idea that this place exists. If they did, do you think that we would still be here? Also, on a reconnaissance mission we managed to trip here a couple of cycles ago and the security features remained intact. The FPD doesn't know about it and we are working as hard as we can to keep it that way. The whole place is covered by an adaptable roof and every entrance hidden with the latest encryption coding technology. Nanotech doors seal over into brick walls once closed. We are safe here. For now. But you've seen the way the world is out there. You've been in Zone 4. It's time we revealed the government's secrets. We can't keep living in a world of such inequality. People used to talk about the one percent.

You know that's old news. It's a percentage of a percentage of a percentage now. And it's got to stop.'

68|

We carry on walking into an open courtyard. Plants grow over on one side and there are chickens in a coop on another. Two dogs bowl into each other and roll over in a scrap. A man is sitting at a table next to a pile of pulse rifles, cleaning parts meticulously. Some women are washing clothes next to a running tap. Their eyes follow me as my body walks past. Grace introduces some people and they say hello politely. One man with long grey hair and a beard drops to his knees and grabs my hand. I've never seen anyone this old before. His skin has deep wrinkles and the worn texture of leather. The lines around his eyes give him a weary look.

'Sir,' he says. 'This is a joyous day. Such a joyous day. We knew someone would come to save us. I am so happy that you decided to come back now. I knew I'd been spared for a reason. The time for reckoning is here!'

He raises his hands to the roof and smiles.

A bright light catches my eye and a pain starts to grow in my forehead. A ball of pressure pushing its way forwards. My hand reaches towards my temple but something piercing spears it inside and my head shakes.

Knees give way and my body falls to the floor.

'Sir, are you okay?'

Jagged, searing thoughts of an FPD squad and a home raid. I am there with them. They smash the door down and search each room. I am pointing to a bedroom door. My hand pushes it open and in the light a body is half hidden under the bed. Not quite crawled underneath. Out of time before he could complete the task. The frozen body has that strange, ghostly look they have. Static and stiff. No heartbeat. No breath. Technically dead. Timeless. My thoughts throb as they show the frozen body being taken out the house. Sparks of lightning flash. My eyes sting and itch and as hands begin to rub my mind jumps back.

Looking up from the floor, my eyes open and people are crowded around me with shock in their faces.

The middle has fallen away. Nowhere is becoming somewhere again.

'Are you okay, James? It's time to get up,' says Grace. 'Come on. We need to get you up.'

69|

In her office, Grace searches me with her eyes. Her features are concerned. For what, it is unclear. It does not seem that she had accounted for this. In all her certainty, a flash of doubt has stolen its way in. She breathes in through her nose and then speaks.

'What just happened?'

There is an uncertainty in what to say. Answers create and eliminate and recreate. Some are hardly even heard; faint echoes somewhere in the dark depths.

'I don't know,' answers my mouth.

'Are you unwell?'

'I don't think so.' No more than anyone else.

'You don't look well,' she replies. 'Are you taking anything? Are you on any drugs?'

'Only my brother's old medication.'

'What was that?'

'I don't remember.'

'What do you mean you don't remember?'

'I can't remember,' my mouth repeats. In recollection, the face of the pill bottle is blank. The sickly colour of the label in the bedroom light is all that remains. 'I just took them, that's all. They helped to even me out.'

'Even you out?' she sighs. 'I'll see if I can get hold of something to help. For the moment, you need to rest.' A pause and then a smile slowly spreads itself over the bottom half of her face. 'We need you on top form for tomorrow.'

'Why?'

'That is when we give our talk. When we introduce you to Thaw and reveal our plan to the people. Such an exciting day. You must rest.'

Grace walks to the door and ushers me out. 'Come on, please. Someone will take you to a place where you can have a lie down.'

She puts her hands on my shoulders and looks into my sticky, stinging eyes.

'You are safe here,' she says. 'You don't need to worry anymore.'

70|

A knock sounds on the door. Eyes peel open. So much mist. Lashes crusted together in tangled triangles. Knuckles dig in and rub. My hand reaches under the pillow for my gun. Memories of blond and brown hair surface and need to be erased.

Memories can be forgotten. I have tried. If there are enough layers on top of each other then the memory changes ever so slightly each time. Like changing one letter of a word over and over again, it doesn't take long before it has nothing of the original left. Attach a different feeling to the new word and it's all good to go. Green light. But I can't remember which memories I have deleted. Sometimes the silhouettes of the original words stand out in the shadows. That is when the darkness confuses me. When I have to say goodbye. It's when my mind doesn't know what is dark and what is just a shadow that I need to even out. Drinking enough until the lights shut off used to work. It's the light that makes the dark seem so much darker. After the drinking, the pills kept everything in twilight. But I don't have any left and now light is peering in to create more shadows.

71|

'Come in.'

'Good morning, sir.'

'Good morning, Grace.'

'Are you feeling better?'

My mind tries to remember the last time that it was feeling *better*.

'Yes, thank you.'

'Excellent. Here.'

She hands me a glass of water and two tiny, perfectly smooth red and white capsules.

'These should help you to feel a little more comfortable.'

The tablets go into my mouth and the water washes them down. They taste of nothing.

'I have arranged for you to see our doctor this afternoon. He is going to take a look at your eyes and has a potential solution to your problem. But for now, I need you to shower, shave and get dressed. You look like shit and the saviour of the city has to look the part. You'll find some new clothes in the top drawer of the cupboard over there. I'll see you in half an hour.'

My body moves itself to the edge of the bed. It feels achy and tired and feet are heavy on the floor.

'I don't know if I can do this. I don't think I'm really the person for whatever you have planned. As I tried to say before, I don't know if I even believe in the cause anymore.'

Her face straightens out. She tries to look into my eyes, but averts her gaze when she catches sight of them. They repulse her.

'Listen to me,' she says, looking at my mouth. 'They have Sasha.'

The light shines in too bright and makes the darkness cower.

'They have her? What do you mean? How do you know?'

'We have contacts in the FPD. They captured her somewhere not that far from your place in Zone 4. After you lost her, apparently she tried out of an old slipway which they had been monitoring. So now we have to get her out. Last time I checked, she took a massive risk trying to get you back over here. And you led her into trouble. So you owe her. The only way we are going to get her out is if we execute the break-in that we've been planning into the central FPD headquarters. And for that to work, I need you to be the man everyone thinks you are. You owe us. So don't give me this non-believer crap. I don't care whether you *believe* or not right now. I care about Sasha, finding out about the truth and taking down as many of those FPD agents as I can in the process.

'You know what will happen to Sasha once they have finished with her. You don't want that on your conscience, do you? So get up, get in the shower and get dressed. You are coming to meet everyone in half an hour, and you are going to be on our side when you do it.'

Grace walks out of the door.

My hands push on the bed and then things move into the shower.

72|

Walking through the doorway and onto the raised platform, there is a thick, sticky silence in the air. It's all over everything. It's inside everybody. Grace looks to me, smiles and begins to applaud. This interruption releases the air, as if it were opening a prison door, and suddenly it is gone. It disappears and is replaced by raucous applause and cheering. My eyes scan the room through the mist. There's a milky crowd of several hundred people packed into a tight space, all clapping and waving their arms in the air. The lights at the back of the room create silhouettes of their faces, and, without any windows or natural light, it feels claustrophobic and cramped. My hands dig themselves further into pockets.

I am floating above my body and the crowd.

Grace gestures for the crowd to calm down by raising and lowering her hands.

'Okay, okay. Thank you everyone for being here this morning on such an important day. Please, settle down.'

She speaks in a clean, calm manner. The people listen as she commands.

'He is not dead! He is back! He is back!'

She grabs my hand and raises it into the air. There is another cheer that hurts my ears.

'He is here to complete the revolution!'

Applause. Screams. Cheers.

'You all know how he sparked Thaw at the very beginning; well now he is back to finish the job! Some of you may be wondering where he has been and why we kept it a secret. Well, I can finally tell you that during his months and months of recovery he was hidden away in Zone 4. We couldn't risk the FPD tracking him down because of his importance to the cause. But rest assured, he has been in contact with me throughout his absence and has been a big part of the plans which we will execute in two days' time. I have been promising you this moment for many months and now, finally, we can actualise our preparations for Operation Truth!'

Applause. Cheers.

I am floating over their heads and trying to find a quiet space away from everything. But a heavy bright light keeps pulling me down. It's pulling and pulling until it feels as though it is tearing at my soul. Clawing at my thoughts and trying to rip them in two. My brother is shouting at me. He is yelling some words that only appear as noises but each one gives me a sharp pain. My body buckles over onto the ground. The noises come into focus and he is yelling at me, asking why I did it. Why I couldn't let it go. Why I had to put him second and why I should leave her out of it. If I loved her, I wouldn't have done it, he is saying. My eyes blink and blink and blink. Then they are looking sideways at the floor.

The cheering stops.

'Take him away, take him away,' a voice says.

My body is moving through the air.

'You're not going to ruin this for us again,' says a voice faintly. 'It's not fucking happening.'

The brightness spreads to everything and I'm gone.

73|

'Come on, sir. Come on.'

A smell shoots up my nose and my head shakes awake.

'There we go. He's awake. He's awake. Someone get him a glass of water.'

The smell again and my body bolts upright.

'It's okay, sir. It's just some strong-smelling salts. Grace? Grace? He's conscious.'

Grace glides in through a door and kneels over me. She doesn't look concerned this time. She looks cross.

'You listen to me. We need you present. Present. *Now.* There's a large crowd of very concerned people out there. Just hold it together for the next ten minutes and then we can have a conversation about what the fuck is going on with you. You understand? Give him another hit of the salts.'

The smell forces its way in to fire up my synapses.

'We are going out there. You are going to say how this is all because of your exhausting journey escaping Zone 4 and the threats to your life. You will reassure them how much you are looking forward to changing the face of this world with them. Sasha needs you. Got it?'

'Okay.'

Up and out through the door. Expectant faces all stare at once. Grace talks and then looks at me. My mouth says some things and the crowd cheers. My hands wave and then Grace talks some more. Something about another meeting.

Then we are out through the door again and heading back towards the room where my body slept before.

'You are going to pull yourself together,' she says. 'This is too important. You hear me?'

My ears hear but the words fall into the twilight.

Lying down on the bed, she closes the door. My eyes lock tight. Something feels very wrong.

But I cannot remember what it is.

74|

Light creeps across my face in a stranger's bedroom. Thick burgundy curtains that are impossible to draw properly hang over the window. Dusty books line a shelf and cracks climb up the paint that covers the walls. My body stirs and the dusty wooden bed-frame creaks as my thoughts begin again. How many days has it been now since the last freeze? Two? Three? More? The new medication seems to have brought back some balance. The red and white capsules are returning me to twilight, but in a slightly different way. Something is trying to claw its way out of the dark. Time is hard to place now. If it isn't the changing of events, then what is it? Its arrow always seems to point in one direction, but can I even guarantee that is happening anymore? What if it were propelling me forward only to then send me back again? Would anyone even know if it had? Would I know? Sitting up, the room remains the same as before. At least it appears to.

Shirt and trousers clothe me and water washes over my face. The reflection of a mirror shows the fine, raised scars across my eyes and the wet, weeping shine of their corners. It is a worn, tired visage. Surely these things are the product of time?

The door knocks.

'May I come in?'

This is not a question, and the door opens. A man enters with a bulky briefcase and a white coat.

'Have we met?'

Something flickers in the shadows.

'No, sir. I have not yet had the honour. How are you this morning? Grace sent me. I am the resident physician and nano-physician on site.'

My head nods as if it recognises what this means.

'I am here to look at your eyes.'

My hands rub them as a reaction. The feeling of absolute satisfaction as the itch is rubbed. So pure in the moment; so sullied once it is done.

The physician places his briefcase on the dresser and scans his thumb in order to release the catch. It pops open and he spreads the two wings flat side by side.

'Where is my interzoner?'

He doesn't look up. 'You don't need that here,' he replies. 'No one keeps one on site. In case of FPD tracking. They are all held securely by the entrance. You can retrieve it when you leave.'

'When will that be?'

He picks up an instrument. 'Right. Let's take a look at these peepers then, shall we?'

75|

The tiny dot of bright light brings faint pink veins into my field of vision. His breath smells of something that my brain can't define. Something ersatz. Something fake. His breathing is deep and intentional and distracting.

'Uh huh. I see.'

The light moves to the other eye. Ghosts of patterns filter my vision.

'Well, well.'

He flicks off the light and leans back.

'Okay. Would you like the good news?' he asks as he scratches his elbow.

'Is there other news?'

'Yes and no. I'll be straight with you. No use sugar-coating this. Your eyes are good candidates for the latest nano-tech surgery procedure.'

He pauses and slaps his hands on his thighs.

'But, well, this is brand new medical technology and, therefore, there will be some risks. The benefits would mean healing over the eyes and gaining improved visual capabilities. However, there is a small chance you could lose your sight if something were to go wrong. I should let you know that Grace thinks that we should take the risk. If it goes according to plan, then you could be back to your best in no time at all. Which would, all things considered, be something of an outstanding improvement for your quality of life, sir.'

If it doesn't work then everything will always be dark, and there will be no need to worry about the light getting in anymore. It if doesn't work, I can go back to being dead.

If it does work, it means I can help Sasha and then get back to being dead.

'Do it.'

'Oh. Sorry? Are you sure? Would you like more time to think it over?'

'No, I'm sure.'

'Well, I'll be! Okay, then! Yes sir, right away. If you lie back, I will clean up, ready the equipment and fire up the implants.'

76|

My head is held in a padded, vice-like tool. The physician is leaning over me with the third bottle of drops that he then squeezes into my eyes. The metal forks keeping my eyelids open feel thick and blunt because of the anaesthetic. All of the light is flooding into my dilated pupils. My eyes no longer feel itchy as the viscous fluid rolls out of them and down my cheeks.

'This may feel a little unusual,' he says. 'Tell me if it hurts.'

The smooth blade begins to scrape over the cornea and remove its top layer. It moves with precision from side to side. Each drag across my field of vision is numbed but still feels like the ripping off of semi-formed skin from a recent cut. He puts down the blade and picks up the tweezers. Sight goes blurry as the layer is peeled off of the first eye and then the second. They feel so raw and delicate that they would fold in on themselves at the slightest touch. Purple, rotating bars of flashing light pulse into both eyes. He squeezes in more drops and waits a few minutes. The physician then turns to collect the implants and leans in close to my forehead.

'I must be honest; this will be painful,' he says.

Something is inserted into the corner of my eyes. It digs in and a blistering pain races across my eyeballs. It is as if he stuck a sharp stick into them, but the pain repeats itself over and over again. Tiny movements of something, like ants or lice, crawl across, through and inside my eyes. There is no control of my eyeballs as they are taken over by the foreign bodies and begin to eat themselves. There is a pain, an intense, unforgiving pain, which brings out silhouettes of Sasha from the deep. The tears in her eyes as mine feel like they are disappearing. The way she looks at me in complete horror before screaming and running away.

Is this pain real?

The world becomes a white tunnel of blinding light. The light seems to want me to travel towards it. I raise and watch as my body convulses in the vice. My consciousness begins to expand into something beyond perception. An indescribable transformation in which it feels as though death might only be a moment of transition from a temporal consciousness to a timeless experience. Let the angels take me away. Let them breathe over my wounds and heal my imperfections. Let me fail to transform into the likeness of God and watch as the gates close and I fall backwards staring at my brother's face the whole way down. Let me descend to the place I deserve to be.

Everything switches off.

77|

I am in the living room. I look into the square mirror with the dark, sea-beaten wooden frame and the reflection of my brother walks in.

'What're you doing?'

'Trying to get this picture finished,' I say.

'Oh, cool. Can I help?'

'Um, I suppose so. But don't mess it up, okay?'

'Okay.'

He sees the plastic paint palette and sits down. Rummaging through the box of brushes, he picks one out and dunks it in blue paint. He holds it dripping in the air, before reaching over.

'No, no. That's the wrong colour,' I say.

'It's fine.'

He daubs it across the top of the picture in one thick, gloopy stroke.

'See?'

'No, no. That's not how it's supposed to look.'

I take the brush off him and put it back into the box.

'Hey! Give that back!'

'No! I told you not to mess it up! Blue doesn't go there. This is my picture; I decide which colours go where!'

'You don't get to decide all of that!'

He smears another slab of blue across the paper.

'Yes, yes I do!'

I rip off the part that he painted on, scrunch it up into a ball and throw it at him.

'Hey!' he yells.

'You two! Shut the hell up! For one damn minute, just shut up! You hear me?'

We both freeze by the paint palette.

If mum were here, she'd be on my side.

'Wake up,' he whispers.

'What? I've got to finish the picture, and Foster Dad's angry, no thanks to you. This is going to take ages.'

'No. It's time to wake up.'

'Why?'

'You've got to find her. She needs your help.'

78|

My body aches.

Everything is black. But my eyeballs move in the darkness, so they must be somewhere.

Where am I?

Voices talk quietly. Their words float in the emptiness. In a place between somewhere and nowhere.

'How long will he be out for?'

'It should only be for another twelve hours or so. He's on the drip to keep him sedated.'

'Did the operation go okay?'

'Yes, as well as could be expected.'

'Did he agree to it, or did you have to use the drugs?'

'He agreed right away. Gees, it was immediate. He's nothing like I remember at all. If I had to diagnose it, I'd say he's displaying many of the symptoms of PTSD.'

'I know.'

'That mixed with taking Jake's medication – he's really messed up. Does he even remember anything?'

'Doesn't seem like it.'

'None of it?'

'I don't think so. He's got a lot of it confused. And we have to keep it that way. You understand?'

'Absolutely.'

'Call me when he wakes?'

'Of course.'

What are they talking about? What don't I remember? I can't even remember what PTSD stands for. A horrible feeling of not being able to remember what I don't remember comes over me and, as I try to pull apart my confusion, I look down in horror to see tentacles reaching up through the bed around me. I try to wriggle free but am paralysed with fear and can only watch as they wrap around my body and pull me down. From here, my body sinks into the ground, the cold, damp earth crumbling into my face and mouth. The voices are muffled now. One of them sounds like my mother. She's singing something and I fall asleep deep compressed in the suffocating soil.

79|

Sitting up, the nano-physician is unwrapping my bandages. He does so precisely and with his fingers pressing into one side of my forehead and temple.

How much time passed in the darkness?

'Almost there. Um hmmm. Just another moment. Very exciting all this, isn't it?! Ah, almost time for the big reveal!'

There is an effort to remember what it feels like to be excited.

The last of the bandages come off and my eyelids free themselves, blinking instinctively. Instantly, my whole face squints. Tightening itself up into furrows, wrinkles and trenches. Blinking and blinking and blinking. After a few moments, they begin to open tentatively.

Sharp, clean lines. Colours and shapes. Precision and perfect aperture. Brightness and brilliance slowly move into focus as the blinking stops.

My eyes scan the room.

'Look at me,' he says. 'Straight into here. Just follow the red dot. Oh, that's marvellous. Yes. Okay. Great. Just wonderful! They look as good as new! Well, technically they are exactly that – brand new! This is great news! You must be thrilled!'

Everything looks wrong. Reality isn't supposed to be like this.

80|

There is a knock at the door.

My fingers are examining the threads of the cotton shirt that clothes me. The raised fibres interweaving and revealing every individual textured strand. The colour is something that doesn't exist in my conceptual scheme. A red that could only be described as vibrant. Remarkable. This new world startles me with its brightness. All of my perceptions feel as though they are attacking me at once.

I want my own eyes back.

'How is the patient?'

'When do we get Sasha?'

'Don't you worry about that right now. Very soon, sir. Very soon. We just need to be sure that you are ready for what's ahead. Okay?'

'My eyes feel gritty, as if they still have something in them.'

'Well, that's probably just the implants. They stay in now in order to regulate the health of your eyes. If any further damage or infections are picked up by the implants, then they will repair your eyes automatically. You'll get used to it. People say they hardly notice it's there after a short while.'

He places two more red and white tablets on the table next to the glass of water.

'You take these and then come out into the mews when you're ready. Grace is holding a meeting in the discussion room – someone will point you in the right direction. It would be wonderful if you could join us.'

He opens the door and leaves.

It is daytime and the sound of people living their lives tumbles in before being shut off again.

The tablets wash down and there is a pause as my body stands and hesitates, before it exits out into the world.

My lungs take a deep breath. The world here is hyper-visible; there is a cobbled, covered courtyard that looks like it was once a cul-de-sac, and small, run down two-storey buildings that line it on each side. The wall at the far end has a mural saying 'The Mews' swirling across it in multi-coloured paint. People are moving in and out of the doors on either side of the courtyard and talking, laughing and walking, living together in unison. But this new reality feels even more detached than before. There is nothing here of the quiet of my old life in the derelict house; the silence of a year spent in solitude. It's all happening in front of me and my senses are observing it, but it's as if my mind is a theatre of perceptual performances – sounds, visuals, smells, feels – and I'm stuck watching them from the stalls. It seems impossible to engage with this world, to actually move into it and become a part of it.

But I am an attempt to get out of the stalls and back on stage, because Sasha needs me.

A man approaches and ushers to follow him. He looks at me strangely.

'This way, sir.'

He shows me to another door and puts his hand to a scanner. The entrance opens and four faces look towards me. They are sitting around a large wooden table in what looks like it used to be someone's living room. Tired, flowery wallpaper is peeling off the walls and there is a beige carpet covered in stains on the floor. The table is covered in laptops and interzoners.

'So good of you to join us. We were just reviewing our plans for Operation Truth. Come in. Sit. Peter, fetch us something to eat. You must be starving!'

81|

Grace introduces the other three people around the table. My eyes get lost in the vivid detail of their faces. The sunken, black pores on their skin. The fine, blond hairs on Grace's cheeks. The sheen on the tight curls on Bridges' head. The crinkled lines on Maddox's nose. The furry, dark hairs on the edges of Meloy's ears.

They introduce themselves one by one as if we are all first-time members of a cancer support group. My name is Grace. I have been a diagnosed conspiracy theory sufferer for three years now. I am in the final stages and the disease has spread to all parts of my body. There is no known cure for someone in my condition. As a result of my illness, I like to spend time planning pointless missions that only get people killed. I draw a sense of self-esteem from trying to rescue people who were only captured because I inspired them to believe in a lie. Still, there is some comfort in knowing that it will all be over soon. The end is near.

They self-identify as Thaw's lead discussion group. Bridges is the one who spoke to me over the interzoner in the shed. His air of assumed authority betters anything my pretence has attempted before. His body leans forward as he speaks and it is clear that he considers himself to be very important.

Nobody is important, not really.

'We want to go over the plans with you, sir. Grace suggested that we revisit them for one last time today so that nothing will be left to chance. I must say, I think that you and Grace have done an excellent job putting them together. Quite brilliant, really.'

Grace looks at me and her eyes say don't ruin this in high definition.

'Thank you,' my mouth replies.

'Maddox, you start us off with the morning preparations and then Meloy can you begin the briefing on the operation itself?'

'Certainly, Grace,' reply Maddox and Meloy together. They are both eager to please. Maddox starts to talk.

'So, at 0700 tomorrow morning we will convene in the discussion room to go over final checks. It will be you, me, Grace, Meloy, Bridges and Edmundsen. We need Edmundsen to get us over the first hurdle on the approach to the FPD headquarters. It's a small team because the operation requires stealth and subtlety. We cannot afford to get caught at any point. They won't be expecting an operation this early in the cycle, especially after the recent failed trip and the length of time until the next freeze. This is our moment. Once we have got all of our gear, we will get the troops together and give a final speech. They will all be needed if this job goes well, so we need to keep them motivated. Morale is low after the failure of the last trip, so we need a win on this. I cannot stress how important this is, sir.'

'You ought to tell him about the sub-atomic slider, Maddox. He needs to know.'

'Well, this is something that Grace tells me she kept from you because she couldn't guarantee we would get it in time. But it turns out that our contact at the FPD pulled through. Look, this confuses some people at first, but I'm told it is completely safe, so I'll just cut to the chase.'

Maddox produces a small box the size of something in which you might keep a wedding ring. It is black and matte and has two ports on the side. There is a pulsing, circular white light surrounding a button on the top. A tiny visual display occupies the rest of the top surface. He passes it to my hand, and it weighs almost nothing. My fingers rotate the cube between them. It feels smooth, as if it could be a toy.

'This,' Maddox continues, 'is nick-named the subatomic slider. There are only a few of these on the entire planet as far as we understand. No one in the general population even knows that they exist yet. So, needless to say, this is something that we keep between us. Our plan is to use this in order to get you into the FPD headquarters.'

'What is it?'

'Let me answer that,' says Meloy. His face is excited and eager to explain. 'As I'm sure you know, sir, the vast majority of you, as with everything else, is empty space.' His hands wave around my body. 'What the sub-atomic slider does is remove that empty space. What we are able to do with this is remove the space within your atoms and reduce you to less than the size of a pin-head. You will not be a tiny version of you, but merely the appropriate collection of sub-atomic particles collected in such a way that all the relevant information is stored in the slider so that when we release you, you will return to your original state. Edmundsen will gain access to the FPD headquarters, deposit the slider in the designated location and then activate it remotely once he has left the building. You won't be conscious during this time, just like you aren't in freeze state, and to you it will seem as if no time has passed between you entering and exiting the slider.'

'Rest assured,' says Maddox, 'as far as we know, this has been tested successfully by the FPD and there are no known side effects.'

'It makes you wonder what they are using it for, right?' Grace leans into the discussion table. 'Where are they sneaking people into? Also, if they can do this with subatomic particles, what else can they do? If there was ever any doubt before, this proves to me that all this bullshit about the freeze being down to quantum mechanics and random behaviour is just that: bullshit.'

'So,' continues Maddox, 'Edmundsen will secrete you and the team inside. From there our plans of the headquarters will take us to the unidentified rooms at the centre.'

Meloy rolls out a blueprint onto the table.

'You can see, here,' he points, 'that there are unidentified, classified rooms at the centre of the FPD headquarters. We believe that this is where they are keeping the machines that are causing the freeze. We are bringing some more nano-tech with us which should help us to get into that room. Once inside we can finally get some evidence to reveal the truth about this corrupt government.'

'When do we rescue Sasha?'

'We will pick her up on the way out, sir. Once we have collected her we will return to the designated location and the subatomic slider and Edmundsen will come and collect us the next day.'

'How are you expecting to walk around inside the headquarters without being noticed?'

They don't know what they are doing. They are evangelists, protestors and campaigners, not soldiers.

'We have FPD uniforms and badges. They should work well enough to give us the time to do what we need to. Remember,' says Maddox, 'nobody has ever tried this before so they won't be expecting it.'

There's a reason no one has ever tried it before: because they are always expecting it.

Grace leans over and touches my arm. 'This is your chance to rescue Sasha and make things *right*. Isn't that what you want?'

My mind searches for things that it wants. It flits through the numb, dark emptiness and finds little to land on. It discovers an empty cabinet where my desires used to be. In the shadows, the only image that carries something of a feeling is that of Sasha's face. Her hand holding mine and her eyes looking down to the floor.

There is no way to make things right, but I want to know that she will be okay. I want to see her face again before the end.

'Yes, I say. That's what I want.'

82|

The food arrives. There are plates of sandwiches and some bowls of synthetic filler. The sandwiches contain some of the fresh vegetables from inside the compound and they taste natural and healthy, and there is no memory of the last time that plants entered my body. It feels good.

The final remnants of the sandwich enter my mouth and then my hand reaches for the bowl. Synthetic filler spoons itself inside me. A distinctive taste that is a bit like everything but also a lot like nothing. The spoon moves quickly as it scrapes up the last of the glutinous substance. The bowl returns to the table and my stomach feels instantly full.

My eyes look up to see everyone else staring at me. They have barely begun their sandwiches.

'Well,' says Grace. 'We have some time after we have eaten to get all of the equipment together for the final checks. You don't need to do much more tonight, sir. You may as well return to your room to let your eyes rest some more after the operation. How are they feeling?'

'Strange.'

'I can only imagine.' Grace smiles and turns to the others who then realise that they should smile too. They all do so quickly before returning their attention to their food.

'Peters, please escort our guest back to his room. We will wake you in the morning when it is time to speak to the people and make our final arrangements. Peters will be on hand if you need anything. I will pop in to check on you later. Rest well, sir. It's a big day tomorrow!'

Peters shows my body back to its room. There are two more pills on the bedside table and they are swallowed before my head hits the pillow.

Everything is so tired. The ache is there momentarily, down deep, before my mind starts to scatter its thoughts into sleep. A picture of the jam oozing off of Sasha's fingers morphs into her face staring at me from across a crowded dance floor. Her eyes are looking right through me. She sees me, but not for who I really am.

83|

'Sir? It's time to wake up, sir. Please shower and get dressed.'

Hands reach up to rub my eyes but then stop themselves. No tingling or stickiness. Nothing to peel off them. They simply open and are immediately in sharp focus. It thrusts my mind into overdrive.

'What time is it?'

'It's 0600, sir. We have the final assembly at 0630 and then the briefing at 0700. Your FPD uniform is on the chair over there. If you have any issues putting it on, please don't hesitate to give me a call.'

'Thank you.'

'No problem. Excited to be a part of such a big day. Long live the revolution!'

Peters walks to the door and leaves. The tablets from the table go down, as does the filler, and then my eyes cast themselves over the superhero shaped costume. The matt metallic body armour reflects no light. The display on the panel on the right forearm flickers on at my touch but remains blank. The heavy helmet with black visor fits perfectly as if it has been on my head before. Pushing the button on the side of the armoured temple fires the internal display into life. An image of reality appears in front of my eyes along with an array of different numbers, measurements and menu settings. Looking in different directions activates the menu and the computer simulated voice inside my ear. The gloves are snug and comfortable with additional grip tight features. My hand picks up the gun from the bedside table and the glove seals itself around it.

I stand in front of the mirror and see a bringer of destiny staring back at me.

Somehow, wearing this uniform feels right.

It quickly comes off and my body tries to scrub this feeling out of itself in the shower. Wash it away with the bacteria and dirt. Get it out of my bones. Remove the stench of it. Dispose of its filthy reek. Destroy the unplaceable feeling that I have worn something like this before. I cannot be a bringer of destiny.

Because there is no such thing.

84|

'Do I really have to wear this?'

'Yes. We won't be able to complete the mission without it. Don't worry; you look good in it.'

My jaw clenches.

'Are you ready for the people? Are you feeling okay?'

'Do you mean am I going to pass out again?'

'Yes,' she nods, pointedly.

'I don't think so.'

'Have you taken your tablets?'

'Yes.'

'Then you should be fine. Don't say anything until I say so. Stay by my side and wave or clap whenever anyone else is.'

'Wave or clap? Am I really the right person for this? I still don't really understand why I'm here. I've not been involved in the planning and build up. I don't…believe. You've invented this insane story of me that just isn't true. I have no experience of leadership. I'm not a hero. All I do is hurt the people around me. I'm only going to slow this operation down.'

'That's not true. Your presence on the mission is absolutely vital. Without you, we wouldn't have the belief of the people. All you need to do is follow orders and that will be enough. When we come home with proof of the government's part in the freeze, you'll be a hero regardless of what you did on the operation. Don't you see? All they need is someone to believe in. You must see the importance of having something to believe in in this world?'

My mind did see this but ripped out the heart of it.

'What if there isn't anything to believe in in this world?'

'Then you make someone to believe in,' she says before turning towards the door and opening it on to the stage.

'The moment has finally arrived,' she announces. 'We have been waiting so long to see this government exposed for what it is. Too long have we been silent and sat as our rights have been gradually stripped away. Too long have we watched our lives and the lives of our families and friends damaged and broken. The never-ending segregation. The hurtful disappearances. The lack of distribution of wealth. The lack of free health care and quality educational services for those in the lower zones. The greed and power of the few who run this place like an oligarchy. All of that stops today. Today we take the power back and return it to the people who rightfully own it. By destroying the myth of the freeze, we can galvanise all those oppressed by this regime to stand up and overthrow it. Today, the future begins! Long live the rebellion!'

Uproarious applause. Invisible energy somehow passing through the air as electricity and forking like lightning into people, before erupting out of them in claps of thunder. Voices punctuate this solid mass of noise with high pitched hollers, shrieks and cheers. There is a tingle of euphoria on the back of everyone's necks.

As she stands in silence on the steps of the street, she steers their souls. The power of personality. She sucks in a mouthful of the silence and then continues to speak.

'Why does all life endeavour to overcome? The need to vent its strength, to express itself is not unique to human beings. All matter is simply engaged in a competition. A competition to survive and fulfil its basic functions. You are matter. You exist and you *matter*. You are

210

part of that competition. What will you do to compete? To vent your strength? To fulfil your function? To make your life count? To express yourself in a meaningful way that makes your life significant?

'All of history has led us to this moment right now, nothing beyond this has ever been achieved. If you had to live your life over forever, knowing that what you did now, you would have to repeat for eternity, how would you act? Would you hide from the FPD for the rest of your life? Would you cower away in a lack of certainty, in a position of fear and not knowing? Or would you seize your truth, affirm your life and shoulder the burden of humanity with us by bending the world to our perspective? You can be masterful. Powerful. Sublime. You can make this piece of existence yours. Now is the time to be great. Now is the time to matter. There is no greater moment than now.'

The men roar. It is a guttural cry. An evolved, animalistic, tribal chant. In mustered fever they cling to each other and beam and shout. A sense of belonging. A sense of purpose.

She is so good I almost believe her.

Only right now, belief doesn't feel like a choice. There is no choice involved in what my mind believes; it thinks what it thinks. But then, how does anyone change their mind? Is that even possible? Did I ever do it? Did I never believe?

My mind tries but can't picture a time in which it did believe. Scattered images like part exposed polaroids shake their way into semi-existence. Always something missing. Always incomplete. It is as if the pictures are reversing out of focus and disappearing into nothing. Memories seem more like feelings than visual perceptions.

In front of me, there is now a mass of expectant faces beginning to quiet.

As Grace sends her eyes towards mine all of theirs follow. Her look lies. It is a look of admiration and companionship and respect. And it is a lie. Her hand raises with an open palm and angles towards my body.

'Speak, please,' she says softly.

My heart races to use up more of its allocated number of beats. Everything quickens and heightens and tightens at once.

My mouth opens to talk.

85|

'That was incredible,' she says. 'Incredible. Where the hell did that come from?'

We are walking off the stage.

'I don't know.' There is no knowledge of what she is talking about. Everything is a blur.

'Well, wherever that came from you had them in the palm of your hand. They hung on your every word; they loved it! We might just have ourselves a saviour after all!'

She leads us both into the discussion room and pours out two mugs of black coffee.

'Okay, we have ten minutes before the final briefing. Here, drink your coffee and go and put on the last parts of your FPD suit.'

She puts her hands on my arms and squeezes them tightly.

'Whatever has helped get you into this state of mind, stick with it. We need you fully functional and awake on this now. No more fainting, okay?'

The coffee touches my lips and it is hot. Its earthy, dirty smell makes me picture an office with a desk and a screen. They are inside a tiny, box cubicle with scraps of note paper pinned to it in precise patterns. The handwriting looks familiar. There is a plastic pot plant with pretend leaves drooping in the corner. This feels like a memory, but I can't be sure. There are people walking past in a hurry. One of them flicks me a glance as they approach, holding two cups with steam rising off them. In a mustard-coloured sweater, he sits down inside the cubicle and hands me one, saying let's get started. Looking up, I think I can see a face in the black mirror of the screen. Before it flickers on, the face looks at me like I'm a foreigner and I can't tell if it's me or someone else.

'Okay?' She repeats herself whilst leaning into the blank middle distance that occupies my stare.

'Okay…I don't like the way that the suit feels.'

'We don't have any other sizes, I'm afraid.'

'No, it's not the size. It's something else. It feels…I don't know. It's as if I've worn it before. It feels strange.'

'Don't worry about that now. It's only natural for it to feel strange. They are the people who killed your brother. It's bound to bring up some emotions and the human being is a complicated thing. Who knows why it feels the way it does sometimes, right? Just forget about it. Go and get ready and I'll see you back here in five minutes. Keep hold of that energy,' she says whilst patting me on the back. 'Think of Sasha.'

86|

My body re-enters the discussion room with a superhero shaped FPD helmet under one arm.

'Welcome back,' she says. 'Right. Now, let's get started. Time for the final briefing before departure. Maddox, please begin.'

Edmundsen is in the far corner of the room rocking from heel to toe to heel. His arms are crossed around his middle and he is staring at the floor.

'Okay, everyone gather in. We don't have much time. Once you are inside the compound, you will all be placed inside the sub-atomic slider. We don't know if it's stable enough yet to travel long distances so we will need to get you inside the gates using the switch seats first before we deconstruct you. Edmundsen will drive you inside the compound and then you will be reconstituted in a disused service cupboard on the second floor.'

'I'm still not comfortable about getting there,' says Edmundsen. 'What if someone stops me?'

'Yes, well, you will have to charm your way out of any other possibilities, won't you? You've done this kind of thing before; you'll think of something. Be unique!'

'Very funny.'

'Come on, that's why we chose you. I'm sorry for being flippant. Just keep your head down, only divert from your stated destination at the last moment and pretend you're lost if anyone asks. You'll be fine, Edmundsen. We believe in you.'

Grace puts her hand on his cheek and looks into his eyes.

'We can't do this without you. When the revolution happens, your name will go down in history as one of the vital pieces of this plan. You are a hero,' she says. 'Don't forget that.'

Edmundsen looks down at his shoes and smiles. Grace turns to Maddox and beckons him to continue.

'I will lead the way to the location specified and then we will need to be combat ready once we are in range. Make no mistake, if we are caught they will torture us and then kill us. We don't know exactly what to expect once we are inside, but if we make it out of the secret room then we must ensure that we immediately head to the jails in order to grab Sasha. From there, we return to the slider and reconvene with Edmundsen so that he can drive us all out of there.

'If there is going to be any chance to rescue Sasha, we need to complete the first objective smoothly. Her safety depends upon our success.'

My mind remembers something it thought not so long ago.

Sasha won't make it past the next cycle.

87|

We are in the car and my body is swallowed by the switch seat once more. Everything looks black and I am somehow part of it. The sound of the car rumbling is consuming the empty somewhere in which I find myself.

The engine begins to slow and quieten. The smooth sound of tyres on tarmac turns into the bite and crunch of tyres on gravel.

'We are approaching the front gates,' Edmundsen says.

'Good morning, identification please.'

'Oh yes, of course. Here. Lovely day today, isn't it officer?'

'Yes, sir. Please wait a moment whilst we verify your card. What is the purpose of your visit today?'

'I have an appointment with Councillor Tremaine. We are discussing the police distribution in my district.'

'Thank you, this won't take a moment.'

A suspenseful silence secretes itself into the empty somewhere.

I am the feeling of anxiety. It is not only somewhere but everywhere.

'Is there any reason for the hold up, officer? I have a very important meeting, you see, and I don't want to be late. This zone doesn't run itself!'

'No reason to worry, sir. Please remain calm in your vehicle and my colleague will be with us shortly.'

'Of course. Sorry.'

Boots shift gravel. Fingers drum on a steering wheel.

'Sorry to keep you, sir. Please head on through. The main car park is straight ahead and on your left. Have a nice day.'

'You too, officer. Thank you. Enjoy the sun.'

'Yes sir.'

The wheels move on and a sense of vibration passes through the spaces in between my atoms.

'We are through the front gates,' says Edmundsen. 'In a moment I will pull into the underground car park. Be ready for re-materialisation and deconstruction in thirty seconds.'

Engine noises stop and buttons are pressed.

'Okay, ready in three, two, one. Now.'

My body is regurgitated by the seat. There is a brief moment where my eyes can see the car with its full complement of passengers before a bright white light no bigger than a pinhead pierces into my skull. Before my mind can work out where it is coming from, the light grows in disc shaped spurts and swallows me up whole. For the shortest of milliseconds everything feels light and free and infinite and perfect.

88|

'GO! GO! NOW! Get the fuck out of here!'

Edmundsen is shouting as loudly as someone who is trying to whisper can. His face is a frenzy of fear and urgency.

Where am I? Nothing is perfect anymore and I'm not in the car. It feels as though my body has just been hauled out of the ocean. Everything is numb. Drenched and freezing and disconnected. Queasy with no point on the horizon upon which to fix. Limbs are not in contact with their control centres. Arms and legs sacrificed as extremities in order to protect the core. Suddenly, it is not possible to understand how to stand. Almost nothing appears to be working. It all collapses down onto the floor.

I am a shivering, jellied corpse.

Luckily, my perfect, laser-edged vision still works and treats my eyes to the sight of a body that is lying a foot away on the floor. It is Maddox. It is definitely his body, but something looks wrong. It isn't obvious initially, but it only takes a few seconds to realise. Curled up in the fetal position on his side, Maddox's left leg is not where it should be. It is protruding from his stomach and in the position near his hip where his leg should be is a blood soaked, torn section of his trousers. There is only a slight gap in the seam of the trouser where the stitching has been pulled apart, but it reveals a red mush of sinew and tendons.

'Shit! What happened to Maddox?' yells Meloy.

My head can now lift itself an inch or two and it turns to see horror in Meloy's face. A kind of terrified horror that paints his insides onto the world. My mind remembers Jake lying on the floor.

'He didn't reconfigure properly,' says Grace. 'He's dead.' Her voice sounds as though it is coming from somewhere near Edmundsen. 'Shit,' she carries on, 'what is going on, Edmundsen? Who the hell is that?'

Continuing to scan the room, my eyes fall upon another human form crumpled up on the ceramic magnolia tiles. This one doesn't seem recognisable. His chest has been opened up by a pulse rifle and is an empty cavity. It is an absence of ribs and lungs and pectorals and heart. A thin trail of blood is trickling towards me along the narrow geometric lines of grey grouting. Its metallic smell seems to push my mind into taking back control of my upper body as the world raises up to a seated position.

'He was following me,' rushes Edmundsen. 'He was behind me the whole time I was going up the stairs. When I reached the cupboard, I couldn't just stop. I either had to keep going or deal with it. So I dealt with it.'

'By shooting him?!' Grace's face is visible now. It is contorted and something is burning in her eyes.

'I dealt with it. This was too important to risk anything, Grace. You said so yourself. I had to. I had to. He had a look on him…He was onto us, I'm sure.'

'Tell me you didn't pulse him in the main corridor. Tell me you brought him in here first.'

'I only brought him in here to tie him up. But he kept on talking and you can't know with these FPD uniforms. What the hell was he recording? He kept on trying to look at me and talking. I told him to shut up, but he just kept on. It's not my fault. I had to do it. I warned him. If he had only listened,' he said to the body, 'then he wouldn't

220

be dead. I pulsed him and then flicked on the slider. I can't believe what's happened to Maddox. Everything is messed up. Oh God, we are all going to get caught.'

The cupboard suddenly feels very small. Meloy is now raising himself to his feet, but stumbling as if he were punch drunk. Grace is propping herself up against the door with one leg locked straight and the other stamping on the ground. She is holding her hand to her head and teasing her eyebrows. Edmunsen is near her, running his hands through his hair and pacing up and down. Maddox is still in the same position. Mutated. Sub-atomically rearranged for a made-up cause.

Pins and needles begin shooting up my legs in splintering daggers. Feet start stamping themselves on the floor in unison with Grace. Meloy's legs begin too as everyone's feeling and circulation begin to return. It's as though the process disconnected everything and our dead legs are only just coming back to life. Edmundsen is breathing heavily and talking to himself. The marble of blood on the tiles extends its veins.

What could be made of this sight? Four terrified mad creations maniacally moving their limbs, one dead creation with nothing left of his torso and another piece of dead matter altered on the most fundamental level that man has never before managed. God's greatest triumph. Such beauty and exquisite majesty. Unending love and craft on show. Such a magnificent example of the fruits of his work. The pinnacle of existence.

What beauty lies here. Man made in the image of God.

89|

'We have to get moving,' says Grace.

'I can barely stand,' mutters Meloy.

'Well, you've got to pull yourself together. We can't stay here. The longer this goes on the more likely someone is to realise that this guy has gone missing. Edmundsen, hide the bodies behind those boxes in the corner and clear up this mess.'

'How am I supposed to do that?'

'I don't know. Figure something out. It's your mess; you deal with it.'

The numbness is starting to fade. The ache is coming back.

'Come on, come on! We need to go! Nothing has changed; we need to follow the plans and get into that room. Helmets on. Hurry up!'

Grace gives her legs a final stamp and then slides the helmet over her head. The indicator light on the side switches on with a brief, high-pitched whine. My helmet does the same. The room looks different now it is mediated via the visor. Augmented reality. As if I am a character in one of the latest computer games. The ones that offer lifetime membership and a way out of this world. Simulated consciousness that is indistinguishable from the real thing.

'Okay. Stay close behind me and don't say anything,' she hisses. 'If we get asked any questions let me do the talking. Remember, the line is that we are taking inventory items back out to Zone 1. Edmundsen?'

Edmundsen pauses with the dead body halfway across the floor. There is a thick, textured smear of blood and innards trailing him. His face tells me that he won't be able to come back from this.

'Yes?'

'You can do this.' She touches him on the shoulder. 'Sort out the bodies. Go to your meetings, have lunch as normal and then come back here. We will need to get out of here today; we can't wait anymore for you to pick up the slider tomorrow. If we aren't back here by fourteen hundred hours, then leave and take the slider with you. They can't know that we have one.'

'But what will you do if you can't get back here in time?'

'Leave that to me. Now get this cleaned up and be on your way. You mustn't be too late or give anyone any reason to doubt that this is a normal day for you.' She lets go of his shoulder. 'Right, you two, with me. Let's do this.'

Edmundsen returns to dragging the body towards a pile of cardboard boxes. Grace pushes off from the door and opens it a crack. Her eyes peer out onto the corridor with a look of intense concentration.

'It's clear. Let's go.'

90|

The harsh, cold lighting of the corridor is tempered by my visor. The climate controlled FPD suit provides optimum conditions for performance on all basic accounts. Within the suit, light levels, body temperature, humidity, oxygen and PH balance are all monitored for efficiency. The digital display that circumscribes the view of the corridor tells me my heart and breathing rate in two tiny icons. It tells me at what percentage I am currently performing. This is important if there are any insurgents nearby that may need to be eradicated. The power assisted bodysuit gives support where needed. Encased inside the boots, it feels as though nothing is touching the floor. The world is simply *out there*. None of it makes it through to me without some kind of deliberate filter. Every interpretation and perception is by design. A controlled perspective in order to enact control.

My mind wonders if it can remember what being in control feels like. At this moment, in the corridor behind Grace and Meloy, the world that my body is engaging with is not under my control at all.

Uniform windows, doors and tiles pass by each other. Everything is homogenous. The rectangular walls and ceilings frame Grace's figure as she strides forwards. A beep sounds and a bright yellow sign flashes up on screen indicating that her voice will now be transmitted into my earpiece.

'Can you both hear me okay?'

'Yes.'

'There is a left turn coming up in ten yards.'

Two FPD troopers walk past to our right. They are not wearing their helmets and look like ordinary people. Two human beings finding ways to pass the time like the rest of us. They are conversing and ignoring us. This means that the news of the cupboard body has not spread yet. Maybe it won't be an instant capture.

A red warning light is flashing in front of my right high-definition eye. Heart rate is above optimal level. *Consider using mindfulness training technique to regulate*, says the computer-generated voice in my ear.

Mindfulness. My mind is already full, it doesn't need any more.

'Turn right now,' says Grace.

All three of us turn, one after the other, and enter another identikit corridor. Clean lines, spotless walls and absolutely nothing remarkable. A standardised version of space.

We follow this corridor for another twenty metres and then get into a lift.

'I will press the correct floor. Stay close to me and avoid any difficult conversations.'

We walk down the corridor and the lift approaches. Polished stainless steel sliding doors. There is an electronic push panel and Grace touches the button with her gloved finger. A man appears and proceeds to wait next to my suit. He stares straight ahead, as is lift protocol, but my red warning light begins to flash again. *Consider using mindfulness training technique…*

A voice in my ear tells me to stay calm. It sounds a bit like Sasha. You owe me, it says.

'Sasha?'

'I'm sorry?' The man next to me turns in my direction. He is stale looking. 'Did you say something?'

'Oh no, nothing. Sorry.' My thoughts are racing too fast.

'You guys must be headed out somewhere urgently,' says the stale man. His hair is combed over in thin, greasy lines of grey and he has

225

a gaunt, pale face. In the middle of this is a pair of sunken blue eyes that look dead.

'I'm sorry?'

'It's just, you're wearing your combat uniform. It's unusual, is all. The only guys I see leaving from this floor in full suit are usually needed *pretty* urgently.'

There is a hint of a smile on his face as he accentuates the pretty urgently part, as though he is somehow part of some special secret.

'Oh, yes. Of course. We are…'

'We're heading up to sixth for an urgent briefing,' interrupted Grace. 'I'm sure you'll understand that we can't say any more than that.'

'Sixth? Gosh! Well, say no more, Captain.'

There is a pause and my visor display continues to flash red. *Consider using mindfulness training technique…*

A lift arrives and we walk in. The automatic doors slide to a cushioned close and everyone stares at the empty space in front of them. Meloy's heavy breathing is filling my ears. He is continually tapping the toe of his left boot on the ground. It isn't loud but everyone can feel it. The stale man looks down and over in his direction. My eyes follow and spot a thin smeared red tarnish on the tip of the tapping toe. It glistens, fresh and probably still warm, as it moves up and down. Options pass through my thought delivery system. The mental image of a vacant, bloodied chest cavity reappears.

All the stale man needs to do is to shut up. To not ask any more questions.

'Which zone are you with?' he asks.

We wait to see who will answer. Grace steps in.

'Zone 1. First division special ops.'

'Oh, special ops? You guys must have different uniforms then, I guess. I haven't seen that combination of boot and body suit before. Unusual.'

My visor flashes and a beep sounds in my ear.

'It's a trial,' says Grace. 'Testing out new gear. I can't say any more than that, I'm afraid. Highest level priority clearance only.'

'Oh. Of course,' he says. 'I suppose that makes sense.'

The lift stops and emits a tonal series of three beeps.

'Sixth floor,' he says.

'Yes, thank you,' replies Grace.

Our bodies exit the lift, and my head turns to see the stale man stare as the sliding doors close.

All he had to do was not say anything.

'Shit,' says Grace. 'We may have a problem. Keep moving. It's not far now.'

91|

Consider using mindfulness training technique…

The voices, the display, the boots, the suit. It feels as though these things are disconnected.

'Come on, keep up.' Hushed urgency enters my ears. 'One more right turn and then we are at the entrance to the room.'

The tiny rectangle in the corner of the visor display acts like a rear-view mirror and shows the world as it moves behind me. There is something that draws my eyes towards it. They flick down the menu pattern and the image enlarges. There, further down the corridor, walking in the same direction as us is the stale man. He cannot be missed even though he looks as though he is trying to be.

'Grace, the man from the lift is following us,' my voice bewares.

'I know. I can see him too. Don't panic. Don't do anything stupid, you hear me? We are almost there. Okay. Turn right now.'

The turning arrives and leaves and another corridor begins to pass under our feet. The stale man is no longer represented in my field of vision. A woman peers up from a file and her eyes bore into me.

'Fifteen feet.'

He now reappears behind us, looking down as he taps something into an interzoner. There is a bead of sweat on his forehead.

'Ten feet.'

Heavy breathing.

'Five feet.'

Flashing red. *Consider using mindfulness training technique…*

228

'Two feet.

'Meloy, move to the back. We are here.'

A black door. A panel with buttons and a scanner juts out from the wall beside it.

'Take off your helmet,' she says to me. 'Scan your eye.'

'What?'

'Take off your helmet. Scan your eye. Do it now.'

'Why?'

'Just do it. Come on.'

'But it won't work. You said you had something for the entrance into the room.'

'Yes, we do. It's in your eyes. The implants. Your eye has been con-figured. I'll tell you more later. Come on, get on with it.'

The stale man has stopped about fifteen feet behind us and is now talking to the woman with the boring eyes.

'But if I take off my helmet then they'll see my face…'

'We'll sort it, okay? Now isn't the time for this. Christ, you need to do it. Now!'

My hands raise to lift the helmet from my head. The visor deac-tivates and the world reappears in its unfiltered form. It is nauseating and vulgar. It feeds the ache. My feet steady themselves. Grace nudges me on the arm.

The scanner sends its blue line of light across my eye up and down, then side to side. A red light turns green and the door opens.

There is a one man security chamber on the other side. Grace pushes me through. The entrance door closes again and the chamber seals around my body. A whirring sound begins and is followed by a series of different pitched tones. There is a moment when everything is black and silent and all I can feel are aching bones. Then a door on the other side of the chamber opens and my feet step through.

92|

It is dark. This appears to be some kind of entrance corridor. There is a door a few feet away at the other end. Dim orange lights line the floor leading the way. Another scanner and communications panel adorns the wall to my left. No air is entering my lungs. Everything is on high alert. My ears strain but in this space, there is literally nothing to be heard. It must be sound proofed. Or the world has disappeared.

In the rush to return it to my head, my hands drop the helmet on the floor and it makes a metallic clang. The sound dies in the air the moment it appears. As if it never existed at all. Fumbling on the ground, the fallen headwear is retrieved and restored.

'Grace? Grace? Meloy? Can you hear me? Where are you?'

Nothing.

The comms light is flashing as normal.

They can hear me.

'What is going on? Grace?'

A silent pause.

'You are on your own now.'

'Grace?'

The voice is cold and unemotional.

'The implants have been designed to record what you see. Ensure that you get a good look at everything you can. Your comms won't work once you are through the inside door. The video will get uploaded automatically once you are out of the building.'

'Why aren't you coming in? Where are you?'

'We are returning to the slider.'

'What about Sasha?'

'We won't be able to get her out.'

'What do you mean?'

'Did you honestly think that three of us could break into the FPD jails and set a prisoner free?'

Is it even possible to think honestly?

'You can try to save her if you want, if you get out of that room alive. We need someone to get into that room, James, even if it's only a one-way ticket. That was the aim of this whole mission. That's why we brought you back. That's why we fixed your eyes. We need this moment to be a real *story*, to capture the hearts of everyone, not just Thaw. If our intel is right, footage of this room is more important than you or Sasha, or any of us. We knew the risks and that's why we all came with you – to make sure you got in. Rest assured, your legend has been solidified here today. And so has her's.'

'What?'

'You will be a genuine martyr. A real hero this time.'

'What?'

'It is far more than you deserve, after what you did.'

The comm shuts off.

What did she say?

The dark corridor closes in and engulfs everything. My body hits the floor soundlessly.

93|

The things that this life does to us.

What happens in the spaces between my particles when they become clogged up with emotions? How am I supposed to feel them? How am I supposed to express them? With everything so bunged up and stuck together, how am I supposed to cry?

Since my brother died, being alone and always waiting has meant that my body barely sleeps. Bodies aren't meant to exist in such ways. It falters and it stutters. It decomposes and decays. And it dreams. It dreams dreams that occur in the gap between consciousness and unconsciousness. The space that touches reality, but tampers with it. This is a painful, torturous configuration. There is some control in this space, which makes it feel more real. Each night it feels as if it is all really happening. If only I could leave the dreams behind.

When my mind shifts to the conscious realm, I used to think of this as waking up. But now I'm not so sure. Now it seems to be the opposite of reality. The underside of reality. The world flipped back on itself and inverted. The waking world is where all of the uncertainty happens. Everything seems somewhere *between* now. I'm lost somewhere between in the twilight.

94|

Lens flares of orange lights on my retina. The warmth of the suit. The edges of the metal floor on my temple. How long was I out? It can't have been long because there is still no one else here. My brain decides it needs to keep the rest of me moving.

A scanner reads the implant again and a door at the far end of the corridor opens.

The room on the other side is the size of a small hall. Lighting is mid-level and my high-definition eyes hunt quickly for any humans. There appears to be none. On the left-hand side of the room there is a set of display screens and wall mounted panels. Eight in total. Large, dull, black reflective rectangles sunken into the wall like voids. A row of shiny metal tables runs along beneath them. On each of these is a set of interzoners, perhaps twenty or thirty, all docked and on sleep mode. The quiet whirring hum of their chargers is the only detectable sound to hear. Further along this side of the room is a large collection of pulse rifles racked in rows. They are hung neatly in specified places and each one is clearly marked with a numbered code.

As my eyes reach the far end they see doors with signs for toilets, showers and changing rooms. Another sign has a knife and fork on it. In the far-right corner is a door with a picture of a bunk bed. All of the doors have keypads where the handles should be and are flush to the wall itself. The right-hand side of the room is lined with some FPD suits on hooks. There is something odd about them; they are different. Different colours. Less armoured. More lightweight. They too are marked with the same numbered codes on their helmets and shoulder pads. Folded metal chairs are stacked up in the corner nearest to my gaze. The tiled floor zig zags its way around the room without any interruptions. Everything is spotlessly clean and organised. There are air vents in the ceiling and no windows. My feet take a step towards the suits and stop dead. The click and hiss of a door opening sounds behind me.

'Freeze! Right now! Get down on the ground!'

What did she mean, after what I did?

95|

Hands are locked behind my back. Forefingers and thumbs tensing against each other. Legs bruising from the baton strikes. Feet aching from all the walking. Shoulders hold themselves high and tight. Ears hear the footsteps of the boots on both sides of me. Eyes remain immaculate but foreign. Heart is pounding a staccato beat. Brain descending into the darkness. The ache is there keeping everything held together. Sometimes I wonder whether all these parts would disassemble if the ache weren't there. Break off and float away into nothingness leaving an empty container behind. It is my glue. My invisible chains.

The centripetal force within me pressures and pushes everything to its outer limits and yet they are held there somehow by the ache.

There are four FPD troopers with pulse rifles surrounding this insurgent. They are bringing destiny in a highly efficient, organised manner. They are not in the standard street uniforms and their heads are clear but for smart glasses and earpieces. They look like regular human beings. People who have children, mortgages, arguments, shits, tears and fits of laughter. Cars, takeaways, night lights and bean to cup coffee makers. Friends and girlfriends and hugs and fights. They probably have brothers and sisters. Ones that aren't dead.

The red and white capsules have all but worn off. Along with the ache, the edges are returning. Nearly everything seems to have edges now. It takes all of my concentration to avoid them.

Eyes in offices follow the atoms that identify me through the corridors. There is some curiosity in their stares, but more satisfied vengeance. They don't know who I am, or why I am here, but I must have done something wrong to be in this position and they are happy about that. They are enjoying it.

'This way. Keep moving,' says the trooper in front. He is square shouldered and precisely gym built. His hair is slick and trim. His walk deliberate and methodical. He is afraid of death. That level of controlled, polished and defined self-construction is driven by a fear of the unknown. My fear manifests itself differently, but at least mine is authentic. Acknowledged. It is only possible to defeat death by confronting it and addressing it. The face of death is human and weak like the rest of us.

There is a prod in my back from the trooper behind and my legs respond instinctively.

After another corridor that looks the same as the others, we reach a door and the lead trooper punches in a code and retinal scans.

'In,' he says.

We walk into a small room and standing inside is a man with sharp edges in a matt blue suit.

'Take a seat,' he says. 'It's great to have you back. We must get started. I have many questions.'

96|

'You can leave,' he says to the trooper. 'He's not going to hurt me.'

The troopers nod and then exit out the same door.

'You're not here to hurt me, are you James?'

'What?'

'We are friends after all, are we not?'

My mind tries to place the face in front of me. There is something there, but it is as if it has been etched out or scrubbed away. Parts feel familiar but the whole seems alien.

'You do remember me, don't you?'

He tips his head to the left and peers at me. There is a smug look on his face. He slides hands forward on the table. His eyebrows raise.

'My goodness, you don't, do you? Well I knew you had problems, but I didn't realise you were quite this messed up. We've kept an eye on you for a while, James, waiting to see if you would give us another lead. But all we got was your sad, depressing little lifestyle. Week after week of watching you gradually wasting away in that sewer of a house. Drowning in a pool of your own self-pity and regret. I almost felt sorry for you at one point, seeing you rot and wither away into this tiny little man I see before me. I thought you would probably end up solving the problem of what to do with you by yourself.

'But then I get news that you moved. Re-joined the *cause*. Ran away with the lovely Sasha Shiverstone. Such a beauty. I wonder: what must she have made of you when she saw this animated corpse in front of her? Poor you, you had such feelings for her. Enough to betray your own brother as I remember. Yes, I remember it very well.'

He pauses. 'But you don't, do you?'

Everything is scraping and clawing and scribbling black. He needs to stop, but he won't.

'Allow me to fill you in – this will be fun. Another tragic tale of a broken heart. You couldn't stand it when she fell in love with Jake, could you? Such a troublesome thing having a brother who looks just like you. I always wonder how lovers of identical twins could choose one over another. Surely if they are attracted to one of them, they must be attracted to the other too? How could you not be? So how does one decide? It must come down to personality and strength of character, I suppose. Integrity perhaps. Loyalty, maybe.'

He leans in until his angular face is right in front of mine.

'You lack those, don't you James? It seems to me that you must do. To sell out your own brother to the FPD just to get a girl back. Not only that, but to give up the whole trip and everyone on it too. I mean, that's cold. What *were* you thinking? Even I wouldn't do that. And I've got real problems. Still, it worked out well for you, didn't it?! Look where you are now!'

He tilts his head back and laughs brashly.

'I still remember my colleague bringing you in. What a scared little ball of anger you were – a few threats and empty promises was all it took. I suppose I have to allow you some credit. Coming back here must have taken some guts. It was brave, I'll give you that. Stupid, but brave. How the hell you got in here I have no idea. And what exactly were you hoping to achieve? To find your precious Sasha and break out of a maximum security FPD headquarters? Run off into the sunset and move in together and make lots of little Jameses and Sashas? A very well thought through plan. Excellent idea! And as for Grace, your imperious leader. Well, she sold you down the river, didn't she? You're

238

in here and she's gone. Where? I'm hoping you'll tell me, but we'll get to that.'

He shifts back in towards me and exhales slowly. There is a moment as he looks down at the table before raising his eyes.

'You need to listen to me, James. Grace doesn't give a shit about you. Sasha hates you. She knows what you did and despises you for it. There is no future for you two; you destroyed any chance of that a long time ago. Your little rebellion is nothing more than a bunch of crackpot kids who are soon to be removed. There is nothing for you out there, James. You are not wanted by Thaw, Grace left you here to die. You have no friends, no family. Nothing, you hear me?'

He slides back in his chair and his hands move together, slowly interlinking their fingers.

'To put it bluntly: you're screwed. But, I can offer you a new life. We can set you up somewhere outside the city. Away from all this. A new place, a fresh start. A way to begin again. This is a genuine offer this time. Forget about all this. Put the past behind you, move on. Build a new origin story. Be reborn. I just need a couple of things from you.'

He looks straight into my high-definition eyes.

'You are going to tell me how the hell Grace got in and out of this building and why she did it. And, most importantly, where Thaw's little setup is and how to get in. Give me that information, James, and you can get out of this mess.'

He stands up from his chair and arches his back.

'I'm going to get something to drink. Take a minute. Have a think. I'll be back.'

The door closes. A white light flashes and the room is as bright as lightning.

97|

The metal of the floor is cool against my cheek. There is a tiny circle of condensation appearing and disappearing each time I breathe. Waves upon waves of feelings and sickness. The whole of reality feels wrong. What was he saying to me? How did he know all those things? Could they really all be true? The surface layer of my memories has been struck with a blunt instrument and now I'm left with the raw, unprotected depths underneath.

My body pulls itself and the chair from the ground and sits back down. Fingers rub the back of my head in an attempt to self-sooth.

Some small set of rodent teeth is gnawing at me, tugging and pulling at the scant flesh on the carcass of my conscious recollections. There is doubt and doubt spreads like a disease. He has placed one rotting apple in the basket. If I don't get rid of it the whole bushel will go and I'll be left with nothing but a putrid mess.

He can't be right. The FPD killed my brother, not me. We were on a trip and they killed him along with a bunch of other people. They are the evil ones here. They are the ones who deserve to be punished. The ones who ruined my life. This is all their fault.

The door reopens and my fists clench in their cuffs.

'Well, James. How are we doing? Have you had a chance to think about my offer?'

'Stop talking.'

'James, I'm trying to…'

'You're trying to get into my head. To screw me up so that you can get me to hand over the location of Thaw. It's not going to happen.'

'Why would I do that, James? Think about what you're saying. Come on,' he smiles, 'you sound like a crazy person. Hell, maybe you are a crazy person given your reaction. The crazy ones never know they're crazy, right? I know your brother had some issues, maybe it runs in the family after all? Somewhere in there,' he leans forward and taps me on the temple, 'are the memories of all this. It's not my fault if you're so messed up you can't find them.' He sits back down nonchalantly. 'You've got real problems here James, and not simply psychological ones either. I have you and Sasha in custody. Why would I need to concoct a story in order to get you to cooperate? You have no power here.'

My jaw clenches and the confusion balls up into anger.

'Yes, I do. I'm the only one here who knows how we got into this dump and how to get to Thaw's base. I have all the power. You can do what you want to me, shithead; I don't care anymore. I gave up on all this a long time ago. I'm dead already.'

'Well, that is a novel way of describing this bag of bones in front of me. Not too far from the truth, I'd say. Unfortunately, you may think that you are already dead, but Sasha Shiverstone is very much alive.'

He holds up and taps the screen on his interzoner. A stream of Sasha in a cell begins to play. A uniform walks in and brandishes a sting stick.

'Do it,' says the sharp suit in front of me.

'No, no, please,' she screams, 'not again.'

The sting stick strikes her on the arm and she falls to the floor, convulsing. Her body wretches and wretches but almost nothing comes out. A small puddle of yellow coloured bile emerges. Sasha's face slowly turns to reveal tears running down her cheeks. He touches the side of the interzoner and returns it to the table.

'So, you see,' he says, 'she does not share your nihilistic tendencies, James. You can bullshit me all you like, but there will be direct consequences and, seeing as you have made it very clear that they will make no difference if acted out on you, they will be necessarily conducted on Sasha. Which all points to the fact that, really, I have all the power.'

'You're an arsehole.'

'Well, that is a matter of perspective. I know a lot of people who would say the same about you. Regardless, all your *I don't care* crap won't wash with me. I know what you care about and she is under my control.'

He stands and grasps the back of the chair in his hands. His eyes look up to the left.

'Seeing as you don't believe me about your brother, James, I think you should go and pay Sasha a little visit. You've got a long time here with us if you don't cooperate, so I think it's time that you made your reacquaintances.'

He taps on the door and a guard walks in.

'Take him to see Miss Shiverstone.'

'Yes sir.'

My arms are lifted and my whole body rises from the chair.

'Maybe seeing her will jog your memory,' says the man with the sharp edges. 'Ask the delightful Sasha what you did. Ask her about James. See if she still loves you so.'

98|

The cell is dark. There is only one dim light bulb lit in the corner and no window. The air smells of stale body odour and sick. Metal bars hum and then clink. A grating sound as the door slides open automatically. Curled up in a corner is a person. Her body is hunched over itself in a primal protective pose.

'I don't have any answers to your questions,' she says without looking up. 'I've told you what I know. Please let me be.'

The door closes again behind me.

'Sasha, it's me.'

Her neck twists and her eyes turn to mine. There is fire and water in her stare.

'What the fuck are you doing here?'

'They...'

She coils from her position and lunges at me. My body falls against the back wall of the cell. Her scream splits me in two.

'Why did you run off? You just left me on that street to die, you fucking coward! Do you have any idea what I've been through in here? All because you ran away.' Her fists are flailing and she is yelling. 'I'm going to die in this cell because of you! I should have known I couldn't trust you. God, I hate you! I hate you!'

Her punches slow down to lumbering pushes against my chest, each one thudding hard.

'You've ruined my life,' she says through slow and painful sobs.

Tears force their way through my immaculate eyes. Two broken humans crying for the things that they have lost.

'I'm sorry,' I say. 'I never wanted any of this. You must know that? I tried to help you…I have always…I haven't stopped loving you, Sasha.'

'You love me? You love me? Like you loved your brother? You don't even know what that word means. How can you love someone and do what you did to him? To all of us? You're a fucking psychopath.'

'But I don't know what I did to you, Sasha. If you mean on the street, I didn't just leave you behind; I had been spotted, I was trying to draw them away from you. I didn't think they had seen you. I was trying to do the right thing.'

'The right thing? Well you fucked that up, didn't you? Just like you fuck up everything else. How did you even get in here?'

Her energy exhausted, she flops to the floor in tears. Her hands barely holding her bodyweight.

'We broke in to try and get you out. At least, that's what I thought we were doing.'

'We? Who's we?'

'Me, Grace, Edmundsen, Meloy and Maddox.'

'Oh, so you managed to make it to Thaw's base okay then? How nice for you. I'm sure you had a lovely time there whilst I was stuck in here being sting sticked every day.'

'Not really. They fixed my eyes, which was kind of good. But I don't like the way reality looks perfect now…I keep fainting. I don't understand what's happening. I'm a mess.'

Her breathing is heavy and laboured and wheezy. There is no physical fight left in her. She stares at the tiles on the floor.

'I'm sorry. For everything. Whatever I've done to hurt you; I'm sorry,' I say.

The apology hangs in the air awaiting its fate.

'I don't care,' she replies. 'Sorry doesn't fix any of this, does it? It's easy to say sorry. You were always fine with words. But your words don't mean anything. Guards! Please get him out of here. I don't want him in here with me.'

'Wait, I've got questions. I need answers, Sasha.'

'Fuck you. Guards! Guards! Please, someone! Can you please get rid of him?'

A guard approaches the door and it slides open again.

'Time for you to come with us. Boss says if she wants you out, you're out.'

'Wait, wait. Just wait. I just need a few more minutes.'

My arms are pulled out of the cell and my body follows.

'I will fix this, Sasha,' I shout. 'I promise. I will.'

She doesn't acknowledge me as the guard pulls me out of the cell and down the corridor.

'Wait! What happened with Jake, Sasha? Just tell me. Please. I need to know.'

99|

I can't tell how long I have been inside this cell. The lighting is always the same. Nothing ever seems to change. It's like the whole room is frozen and I'm tripping through it. They have given me three meals so far. Three bowls of synthetic sludge. Does that mean I've been here one day? Or three? Or more?

All that happens is the same thought loop on repeat. The same search for a coherent story to make sense of what happened with Jake. My mind replays the events as if it is watching a videotape that deteriorates a little more with each viewing. The problem is I don't know if this video that I'm watching is veridical. How was it created?

I can see myself on the trip. Jake is there. So is Sasha. And four others from the group. Two of them were men, but their names escape me. We had just come through the slipway and were running through the frozen street. Everything was silent and deserted as we had expected. We were headed towards one of the federal buildings. I had my spray paints and they were carrying the flags. We were going to set up a message on the front of the building. But as we turned the corner towards the main entrance, the FPD troops appeared. On the video it is as if they appear out of nowhere, but they can't have done. But it really feels as if they entirely weren't there one second and then completely were the next. Instantly we are surrounded. Their guns pointing at us. Who started shooting first isn't on the tape. My mind rewinds and rewinds but it isn't there.

The next scene involves our group running for cover and a shootout taking place. I can see Sasha handing me a gun and screaming at me to shoot. Pulse rifles are destroying the scenery around me. Someone shouts *grenade!* but there isn't enough time and the fragments of the wall in front of me shatter into my eyes. Bodies are falling everywhere and there is nothing to this part of the tape except a feeling of immediate and consuming panic. The next thing is my brother tapping me on the head and signalling to an alleyway behind us. Sasha, my brother and I make a run for it. As we pass through the alleyway, there is a fraction of an instant between rounding a bend and reaching the slipway. That fraction was all it took. In this instant the sound and images in my loop heighten and grow. The crack of a pulse rifle. My brother falls; his insides all over the road. It is as if it happened in slow motion. He looks up at me with a terrified expression, spluttering his line that everything is everything and there is nothing more, and then taking his last breath. Sasha is pulling my hand and yelling at me to run. Then we are in the slipway and out of the frozen zone. We jump into the waiting escape vehicle and the tape cuts off. There is no more reel for the projector. The next scene sees me waking up at my flat with eyes that can't see properly.

There is nothing more.

100|

A voice sounds out in the twilight.

'Are you ready to work with us now, James?'

'Who is that?'

'I want you to come with me, I have something that I think may interest you.'

Bright lights render me sightless until muscles relax. The world is moving past me. Another room. This one has a table and a chair and a man with sharp edges again.

'How are you, James?'

This seems an odd question.

'Never mind, don't answer that. I'll be honest with you, I don't really care. But I'm sure that's not a surprise to you. However, the fact that no one else seems to care about you might. I heard about your conversation with Sasha. Tut tut, leaving her alone like that. She really wants nothing to do with you, does she? But that's not why I brought you in here.'

He flicks on his interzoner and points at it. 'Watch this,' he says.

It shows a video. In the centre of the tiny screen is an image of a tiny man. He looks like Edmundsen. He is being transported by four FPD agents. He is in handcuffs.

'Oh, we soon figured out who you came in with, James. He was arrested in his car the very next day. That wasn't too difficult. But wait, here's the interesting part.'

Three people burst out from behind a building and start firing. There is a blaze of gunfire and two FPD troopers disintegrate. The two remaining troopers raise their arms, and the three figures cease fire before rushing to surround Edmundsen. They gesture for the troopers to lower their weapons, which they do, and then the figures grab Edmundsen and begin to run. The camera follows them for a few seconds before the whole screen flashes white. Briefly, there is nothing to see. It is as if a drift of snow has fallen over everything. However, patches of the world slowly return to existence, and when the smoke clears there are some small remains of four bodies scattered on the sidewalk.

'Do you see that, James? Edmundsen is dead. Nothing more than he deserves, the traitor. But that is not why I wanted to show you this. Did you see what your fellow members of Thaw did? They tried to *rescue him*. Now why would they try to do that? Let's have a think about that for a moment.'

He clicks his fingers sardonically. 'Oh yes, because he is important to them. Because they care about him. Because they *need* him.'

There is a pause and inhaling through nostrils.

'Do you know how many people have tried to rescue you, James, since you have been in here?'

His head is lowered to my level. He looks into my eyes.

'Would you like to take a guess? You can have as many goes as you like. It really isn't that difficult…No? Well, okay then, you caught me in a generous mood; I'll tell you. None. No one. Nobody at all. Nobody. Do you understand what I'm saying to you?'

My eyes look away.

'They don't care about you, James. You mean nothing to them.'

He lifts my chin with his hand, forcing my gaze back on his. He smells of something strange.

'You will die in here. In here, you will see nothing but pain. You will rot. And they will do nothing about it.'

He pushes my head away.

'Guards, put him back in his cell. This piece of shit deserves nothing else.'

101|

The time is passing slowly. Moment by moment twilight sits upon more twilight. Nothing moves anywhere in here. It all heaps on top of what is already there and makes the space unbearably thickset and heavy. Everything is glued together. My mind can't wade its way through. Especially not without my tablets. The perfect cylinders of white and red.

It is hard to tell whether I am awake or asleep. Sometimes I try to kick the wall to see if I am still awake. Only, whatever happens would be the same if I were dreaming or not, so it is no use. The indistinguishability terrifies me at times. But it comforts me at others.

Sasha loved me once. I know she did. But was it so long ago? It doesn't feel long ago. It is the only thing that seems immediate when I think of it. The feelings and perceptions are so clear. So vivid. They have to have been real. Otherwise there is no hope for me at all.

Could I live in my memories? If I were always asleep, I might be able to. Maybe this is where I need to be. The other reality only brings me confusion and rejection.

I deserve nothing else.

102|

'Okay, James. We've waited long enough now. I've asked an elegant sufficiency of times. Always polite, that I am. But every man has his limits and I have reached mine. Time's up.'

I think I am awake.

'You need to come with me and make a decision. I have a special job for you. You are just going to love it. Oh, and there's more good news. Sasha will be coming too. How wonderful! The two lovebirds back together again. A reunion tour! I am sure it will be just like the old days. Come on, get up. No time to waste.'

'I am unsure if my legs will stand.'

'Oh, I'm sure they will if you try hard.'

'Did I just say that out loud?'

'Oh, you really are in the shit, aren't you?! For God's sake, stop rolling around and just stand up.'

My body tries for the third time and manages to stand.

'There's a good boy,' he says before handing me a tube of filler. 'Now come along now. We've got work to do.'

103|

Sasha is slumped in a chair. When she sees me enter the room she looks away.

'What is he doing here?' she asks.

'Aren't you glad to see him, Sasha?'

'No.'

'Oh, that is a shame. He loves you, you know? Deeply and desperately. It's quite tragic, really. You could be at least a little bit pleased to see him. You'll break his poor little heart!'

He laughs like he owns the world.

'Well, let's get right down to it, shall we? No point wasting any more of your time. I have an opportunity for you. One in which, I think you'll find, everyone can come out happy.'

'That sounds unlikely,' mutters Sasha.

'Oh ye of little faith, Miss Shiverstone! You haven't even heard my offer! Shame on you!'

'Well get on with it then,' she spits. 'And then I can say no, and you can put me back in that hole.'

'Oh, it's not going to be as simple as that,' he ushers in lowered tones. 'Your time in that cell is over.'

He turns to look at me.

'You are going to take us to Thaw's headquarters and find Grace for us. Once you have done this, we will let you and Sasha, out of the kindness of our hearts, go and live in one of the outer territories. There isn't much there, but I'm sure you'll be able to survive if you can find some of the locals to help you.'

'The locals outside the EPRL?' Sasha shouts. 'They'll kill us before they help us.'

'Oh, well, maybe. Who knows! You can be very persuasive, Miss Shiverstone. I'm sure a beautiful woman like you will find some way to work something out.'

'Screw you, I'm not doing it,' she asserts.

'No, me neither,' I say.

'Well, that is disappointing. But, you see, not entirely unpredictable. Believe it or not, I did think that this scenario might eventuate. So, I have a counteroffer. If you don't do it, we will kill Sasha.' He leans forward onto his elbows. 'In the spirit of clarification, I should relay to you the full offer in relation to other potential outcomes. If you go and try to run away, we will kill Sasha. If you lead us to the wrong location, we will kill Sasha. If you try to be a hero and attack one of us, we will kill Sasha. Do you get the picture?'

'You can't do that.'

'You see, that is where you are wrong I'm afraid. I very much can do it. In my line of work, when there is a terrorist threat upon us, I can do anything that is deemed necessary. New anti-terrorism laws. You really should look them up sometime.'

He signals to one of the troopers and they smash a baton down onto Sasha's back. She screams.

'You are my responsibility. I can do with you as I please. So, what'll it be, loverboy?'

There is a pause. He indicates to the trooper and Sasha is struck again. Her cry makes me wince.

'Fine. Just stop. I'll do it.'

'No you won't!' she yells.

'Oh, but it sounds like he will, so that's lovely. Splendid, in fact.'

The sharp suit straightens out his tie and collar. 'Sasha will be going with you on the trip, just to give you a reminder of why you need to stick to the script. You'll have my other two troopers with you as well. It'll be a nice little party!'

'I won't go, I won't do it,' says Sasha from the floor. 'You can't make me.'

'He'll show us where the headquarters is with or without you, Miss Shiverstone. But I do think you'll serve me better on the trip than elsewhere. I'm sure my friends will find a way to get you along. They can be very persuasive, just like you. Only their skillset is rather different. Right, let's get everyone ready to go.' He tucks his chair under the table. 'How exciting!'

104|

Wheels from the FPD squad van create a dull grinding noise. Inside the windowless back of our vehicle, it is twilight. Sasha still won't look at me. She has spent the whole journey staring at the floor. There is anger and sadness in the shape of her body. She hates me.

The anxiety in the air keeps my body pressed against the seat.

I hate myself.

I know what they will do to Thaw when they get into their compound. I know what is going to happen. But I can't let her die. I've put her through too much already. But this act feels like the end of our relationship. There is no coming back from this. She can't even look at me now, let alone after what is going to happen next.

The high-pitched dog whistle whine of the electric engine lowers and our van slows down. A hatch from the front compartment of the transport slides open. A bolt of light blasts in. Sharp lines twist and turn to face me.

'This is as close as we can get to the location you gave us. From here you walk. Someone will come to collect you in a minute.'

The hatch slides shut. It then opens again quickly.

'I will be monitoring the situation from here via the troopers' bodycams. Remember this: if you try to screw us, Sasha is right here, and she will be the recipient of my temper.' He takes a deep, slow breath. 'I have a short temper; it is one of my unfortunate weaknesses, but I am trying to work on it. Strive towards my self-actualisation, perfect my chi and all that. Realign my chakras, build up some positive karma.

It's not easy but I'm trying. I am. My point is, if you mess with me and make me lose my shit then I'm going to be really pissed. Okay?'

My head nods.

'Marvellous!'

The hatch slams shut and it is twilight once more.

'Sasha,' whispers my voice. 'I'll figure something out. I will.'

She doesn't even look at me.

The door slides open and a superhero shape appears.

'Time to go, Mr. figure-it-out,' says the guard inside the van.

A thick, muscular arm reaches in and grabs my shirt.

'If you survive this,' says the painful voice from the twilight, 'I don't want to ever see you again.'

105|

A quietish shuffle. Too deliberate. Conspicuous. Being the centre of attention and walking with the knowledge that FPD troops follow near behind tracking every move is not usual. For me, it is avoidance. Abstention. Seclusion.

Not this.

The planet rotates under my feet. Turning and turning. Circumvolving towards the point of no return.

Got to figure something out.

This morning is clean and crisp. The sun warming my cheeks in the brittle cold of a biting breeze. Clear blue hangs blithely above the buildings. To my left, a bird flaps its wings in a dead tree before flying off into the unending colour that surrounds it. My eyes watch it slowly disappear. People walk past. One replacing the other who in turn replaces the other. Each one a life with a private theatre of performance in their minds. Billions of secret worlds, all different to the last.

The flapping wings of the bird are gone now and sounds of people are all that remain. A throbbing skitter and scatter of voices and bodies and heels and clothing. Buttons and ties and trousers and zips. They are crawling and writhing all over the pavement and brushing their ignorance on my shoulders. Oblivious to the end point that will soon occur.

Got to figure something out.

My feet stop.

Everything washes past me, and I stand as a statue in a stream. My head looks up to the blue and feels it pulling me toward it. Disintegrating and dismembering my parts, the bonds between them tumbling away, the blue becomes me. Everything passing into it until there is nothing left but shapeless colour and I am a pure perception ready to become a part of someone else's experience.

'Hey, James!' the voice crackles in my ear. 'What are you doing? We don't have time for stoppages here.'

There is nothing for me to say.

I've got to figure something out.

'Do you need a friendly reminder of your motivation? I've got a sting stick here somewhere. Hang on, just let me find it…'

'No, no. I'm going.'

'Then go. There's a good boy. And hurry up.'

Picking themselves off the pavement, my legs start moving and become part of the stream once more. Not far now. Only two more turns and I'll be at the street. I could run but they have Sasha. I could fight, but they have Sasha. I could hide, but…There's nothing else to do.

The first turn happens onto a smaller side street and my head glances behind me to see the troopers following round the bend. I have to do this. The busy world moves further away from me as the final turning approaches. My footsteps slow and my eyes look. A moment of quiet.

This is the end.

Crack! A whistling scream slices through the air and thuds into a superhero shape ten paces behind. His body crumples to the floor in a heap.

'Snipers!' yells a voice in my ear. 'Get down! Get down!'

106|

The air is ablaze with splintering cracks and blinding flashes. Bodies are dropping on the ground behind my curled-up cowering mass. It seems that even a dead man is frightened of gun fire.

'Get out of here! Get out! Pick up the target and return to the vehicles. Abort! Abort!'

Tentatively lifting my hands from over my eyes, amidst all the chaos it appears that no one is aiming at me. They aren't trying to kill me. Are they trying to save me? Inch by inch, I raise my body up from the ground and turn to look around. There are at least five or six shooters firing pulse rifles from the rooftops. They seem to be well-protected because the FPD troopers are not managing to hit any of them. There are shouts and clatters and cries but in all this madness there is a quiet around me. My eyes catch a wisp of smoke rising off a rooftop in the distance. It disappears into the sky that surrounds it and my lungs take a deep intake of breath. Lifting my arms into the air I turn slowly. This must be what it feels like. This must be the moment.

'Come on, someone! Do it! They're using me to get to you! Just end this now!'

My eyes close and wait, arms aloft. The silence feels empty and I realise that in the middle of all these weapons and people I am entirely alone.

'Do it!' I yell, my face contorting.

'Stop this, James!' says the sharp voice in my earpiece. 'You get down, now! If you die, she dies! You're killing her if you do this! And not in a way that you want, believe me.'

Suddenly she is there, and I am no longer alone. I die, she dies. Maybe this is inevitable, maybe it has to happen. Maybe it is for the best. We could die together and I would never have to face a world without her in it. But then there is a picture of her face in my visor. She is crying and I realise that I can't do it to her. I'm not strong enough. My arms start waving.

'Stop! Stop!' I shout. 'They've still got Sasha. They'll kill her if you do this!'

A trooper appears out of nowhere and piledrives me to the ground.

'I have the target,' he says. 'Extracting now. Let's go! Move, move!'

He yanks me up and lugs me away back down the direction from which we came.

Sweat is beading its way down my forehead.

'If you screwed us, James, you cannot fathom how much misfortune you have just brought upon yourself.' The voice in my ear is followed by a painful scream. 'You better hope this wasn't your doing, James. My temper has been lost.'

107|

There is blood trickling slowly across my cheek. When it reaches the corner of my mouth it mixes with the saliva resting upon my split lips. It tastes sweetly metallic and feels loose and sticky. I can't stop tonguing the cut. My jaw slowly moves from side to side, clicking as it does so.

I spit the bloody mix onto the floor. Each breath scrapes its way in past my bruised ribs. The ache is now not only in my bones but throughout my muscles and flesh. There are no pills to numb it anymore; the effects of them are completely gone. This is what the real world feels like.

In the real world, the floor is solid, cold cement underneath my naked body. Every potential place a bug or tracking device could have been hidden on my body has been examined and then re-examined again. Every time that they found nothing, they hit some more and then looked again. A line of blood moves from under me and rolls in the direction of the drain. Sharp suit says that I set them up, but he can't work out how so he's going to punish the both of us until I tell him. My mind knows that the only way that they will find out means losing my sight. And I need it to get Sasha out of this mess, so I can't tell him about my high-definition eyes and the fact that once I'm out the firewall of this building, they show Thaw everything I do.

I've got to figure something out.

How can I get them there without seeing where I am going? There must be another way.

Everything feels swampy, sodden and impure. Tears start to fall down my face as the familiar feeling of meaninglessness mauls me from the dark. My head rests in bruised hands and battered eyelids close as my chest and shoulders shake in sobs. Is this everything that I will ever become? There must be a way that this can mean more than nothing.

My mind remembers the first time that I cried for the death of my own dreams. At that moment, late at night, I told Sasha that I was afraid that I wasn't going to be magnificent. She replied by laughing and asking me who the hell was? I said that I didn't know, but that I always thought that I might be. As if I had a chance at least. She looked at me as if I were a child and then held me in her arms as I cried. What an idiot.

My nose is running down my face and all I want is a tissue to wipe it clean.

I've got to sort myself out. In that moment, amidst the gunfire, I still couldn't do it. I still wasn't strong enough. Her name brought me back to life. That must mean something. I've got to be honest. Right now it's different. I'm not ready to die.

No more tablets. No more twilight. No more messing around. I need to be present for long enough to get Sasha out of here. That means I have to do what I haven't been able to. I've got to beat it. I need to own the ache. Make it *mine* so that I can turn it into something purposeful and use it. I owe her that.

I drag myself off the floor and sit on the stool.

PART 3:
NEXT

108|

Time passes and I realise that I have to pick at the open wound in my memory. To tease out some of the truths that I must have buried in the twilight. I cast my mind back to the last time that Sasha and I were alone together. The last moment before everything went wrong.

'I'm sorry. I can be a better person. I can change,' I said.

'But you will still be you, won't you? I'm sorry. It's over. I'm trying to let you down gently here, but you have to accept that I don't love you anymore.'

'But I can work on that. I'll improve. You'll see. You loved me once. You can love me again. It's not like you're in love with him, is it?'

She paused and rubbed the back of her neck.

'You're not, are you?'

Her fingers smoothed across her forehead and her breathing was slow and deliberate. My heart started to beat double time.

'When did…? You've only been together a month.'

Looking at the floor, she mumbled. 'Love is complicated. We didn't mean it to happen.'

'That's exactly what he said. What does that even mean? Does anyone ever mean anything to happen? Are we simply doing things all the time without any sense of ownership?'

'No.'

'Then, in what way did you not *mean* it to happen? Own your actions. You're lying to me. I hate liars.'

'I know you do. I said I was sorry.'

'Oh, well, I don't suppose you meant that to happen either?'

'Yes, actually, I did. And, you know what? It's more than you deserve. I haven't been happy for ages. I was going to end it with you anyway. This happened first, that's all.'

'Well, lucky you. Dating identical twins at the same time! You are such a sophisticated woman. So refined. Did you get off on it? When were you going to ask to have us both at once?'

'Fuck you.'

She started walking away and I reached out to grab her.

'I'm sorry, I'm sorry. I'm angry, I didn't mean it.'

She stopped sharply and spun around. Her face was a frightening force of emotion. My body started to shake.

'You hold onto anger. That's your fucking problem. You never just let it go, and it means you reek of it after an argument. I can't take you being like this. We aren't the problem here. You are. You understand that? There's something wrong with you. It's this constant negativity and toxicity that's slowly killing me. You used to be…I don't know. Fun. You used to be fun. You have no joy anymore; it's always safety and escape with you and it's boring.'

'What – because I don't believe in the cause? Because I'm fed up with this fake bullshit fight? Because I don't want to go to jail?'

'No. Yes…I don't know. I don't know what happened to you, but I know that I don't want to be around you anymore. You make me a worse person.'

'Well when you look at him, you'll think of me!' I shouted after her as she walked away.

The door slammed shut and I started to cry.

I banged my head against the doorframe. Everything felt sunken and empty. There was nothing left to love anymore. And that place felt dead.

I'm going to get her back, I thought.

In the cold black of the prison cell this thought seems utterly absurd. I can't get her back. But I have to try to get her out.

109|

An electronic lock clicks and a rectangle of light appears with a human shadow.

'Get up.'

'Please no more,' I beg. 'I don't have an answer to your questions. I'm telling the truth.'

'Not that. Get up. You're coming with me.'

The shadow moves forward and picks me off the ground. A bucket of water tips itself over me and my whole body shudders before the soft feeling of a towel envelopes everything. He pushes me out of the doorway and into the light.

We walk through a series of corridors and arrive into one of the many interrogation rooms. It is warm inside and, wrapped in the towel, I can feel my body wanting to fall asleep.

I arch my back over the chair and feel the individual vertebrae click into place. A low buzzer sounds and a door at the far side of the room opens. The sharp suit walks through and sits down opposite me.

'So, how are we?'

I don't know how to reply.

'Never mind. It was just a pleasantry. Would you like to ask me how I am?...No? Well, perhaps I'll tell you anyway. It does seem to be up to me to keep this conversation going, after all. I am feeling frustrated, James. You keep confounding us. Did you know that? There really does appear to be nothing on your person. Which begs the question, how did those rebels know that you were coming? We've trawled that entire area and can't see any evidence of any lookout points. Did they just get lucky? It's a possibility but, well, it is rather unlikely. Have you heard of Ockham's Razor, James? I must admit, I am rather a fan. When presented with a problem, the simplest solution is usually the best. The option with less explanatory baggage, if you will, becomes the best option until further evidence presents itself. Now, seeing as no further evidence has presented itself, no matter how hard we tried, I am confronted with an interesting quandary. Should I overlook the simplest explanation and start looking elsewhere? I am not ashamed to tell you that this problem has kept me up a few nights recently. Up late, I have been. A bit like you, eh?'

He reaches forwards and pats me heavily on the arm.

'But, last night a clear realisation came over me. And I had such a good sleep, you wouldn't believe. The best I've had in, well, a very long time. Only now, it's like my body has realised what it's been missing so I'm even more tired than before. Most frustrating. Anyway, excuse me, I digress. Do you know what it was that I realised? Hmm?'

'No.'

'I realised that it doesn't matter in the slightest. It doesn't matter how they knew, because you still know where it is, and we still have Sasha. Which means you will do whatever we say. And if we are going to avoid a very public firefight, we are going to have to do this differently. And they can't interfere if they are frozen. So there's nothing for it but to trip there and revisit the place in freeze state.'

'It's ages until the next rotation in Zone 1.'

'Oh yes, that's true and now that they know we are onto them, the longer we wait, the more time they have for preparation. Or worse,' he leans in, 'to move their base entirely. Wouldn't that be absolutely terrible for all of us? Really very discouraging. But luckily we don't need to worry about that. We are going right now. We don't normally do this, you must understand, but exceptional times call for exceptional measures. And this needs to be done now. Guards, take him to the preparation chamber.'

'What? Why don't we need to wait? What do you mean?'

'Oh you'll see, you'll see. You've been there once before actually. Not that you knew it then. If you had, we could have all been in a real pickle, so thank you for your ignorance.'

The guard picks me up and pulls me towards the door.

'This will be quite the surprise for you,' says the suit. 'Won't you just kick yourself when you find out.'

110|

I walk down the identikit corridors for the second time. This time, I am surrounded by troopers and every pair of eyes in each tiny uniform cubicle window tracks my movements with fascination. The dressing gown hangs around my knees and does little to alter the surreal nature of the experience. I keep tonguing the cut on my lip and it brings with it the kind of exquisite pain that makes me do it more.

Up in the lift and onto the same floor again. I wonder what Grace and Meloy are doing right now. I wonder whether or not they are moving away from their previous headquarters. Our footsteps approach the end of the corridor. There was a voice in my ear before, but I don't need it to know the directions now. I know exactly where we are going. Quite why it is called the preparation chamber, I am yet to work out. There is one possible reason. But that can't be right.

We arrive and the sharp suit scans his green eye against the panel on the wall. The door hisses open and we all walk back into the dark airlock.

'Remember this?' he asks. 'You'll love what we can do once we get inside. Everyone always does.'

The second door opens and I am ushered through to the same space as before.

'Welcome to the preparation chamber, or as we like to call it: Zone 5.'

111|

'You do realise that I am only telling you this because you'll never be a free man again?'

I can vaguely hear him, but his words aren't registering.

'Yes?'

I nod my head.

'Good. I wanted to get that off my chest and clear the air before we went any further. It's nothing personal, you understand? Simply humans doing what humans do. We are interesting creatures, aren't we? So highly evolved and yet so…primitive.' He puts his hands firmly on each of my shoulders before continuing. 'You are now one of the minute number of people on this whole planet who know about Zone 5. Such a revelation, I'm sure. I'm also sure you have lots of questions, but given that you will only be in possession of this newfound knowledge for a very brief period of time, now is not the moment to sit down for a parlay about the whole thing. Suffice it to say that those crackpots at Thaw got a few things right and a few more things wrong. All you need to know is that from here we can freeze all of the other zones as and when we choose. Right now, once we are geared up and ready to go, we will temporarily freeze all other zones and then enter into Zone 1 so that you can safely lead us into Thaw's headquarters and we can finally clear up this whole unfortunate mess.'

His head turns back towards the airlock entrance. 'Ah, good. Miss Shiverstone is here. Excuse me, I really must be the one to tell her about this place. The look on her face is going to be absolutely price-less!'

He walks past me and over to Sasha as she stumbles through the door. In the harsh lighting her face is gaunt and drawn tight over cheekbones. Dark purple moons stain the space under her eyes and her hair is bedraggled and matted with grease. She looks frail and thin. Sharp suit stands in front of her, speaking his sharp words and shining his sharp smile. As he gestures around him with a flourish, she collapses onto the floor. Her hands cover her face and her body shakes with loud sobs. She throws her arms down to her sides and screams. It is a scream that scrapes the hope out from my heart and leaves it with nothing but emptiness. Sitting back on her heels, she begins to shake her head and repeat the same words over and over.

'I knew it,' she says. 'I knew it. I knew it.'

112|

Sasha lost her mum when she was almost a teenager. The police said that her mother had simply left. Left for another zone or gone outside the walls. People do it all the time, they said. Mothers get bored, don't feel loved, meet someone new. It's a tale as old as time. There's no body or evidence of a struggle, they said. Her possessions weren't all there; a few random items seemingly packed and disappeared with her. Sasha said that anyone could have done that. That her mum's favourite things were the ones left behind. She wouldn't up and leave like that, she said. It wasn't her nature. The detectives tilted their heads sideways and softly relayed the fact that people can be surprising. Sometimes you think you know a person, but really you don't. After all, she was a person of interest in an ongoing investigation, so she had every reason to leave, they said.

Her dad never knew what to think. An absence of resolution didn't sit well with him, but he got tired of being angry and, over time, managed to accept that he would never see his wife again. Sasha, on the other hand, never reached acceptance. That lack of a settlement gave her this dark, deeply ingrained suspicion and mistrust for others. I always thought that this was why she believed in the cause; why she was so insistent on the government having something to hide. I supported her for as long as I could because I thought that she simply needed something to believe in. I thought that she might get over it at some point and move on. That she might heal from her trauma.

But she always said she knew something wasn't right. The murmurs and distant tales of others going missing in freeze state didn't help either. So and so said that they knew someone who knew somebody who had also heard about someone being snatched when frozen. These accounts became fables, myths and cautionary bedtime stories for children who had been misbehaving. Stories shared amongst trippers when they were trying to impress each other. Anecdotes that bound together the first founders of Thaw.

Of course, there was never any proof.

113|

A nudge in the back.

'Right, let's go. We need to get you in some gear. You can't go out there in the nude, you'll get arrested.'

Grating, gruff laughter from the grunts that surround me. One of them reaches over to the suits that are hanging on the racks and picks one off.

'Here, try this on, he says. And be quick. Boss wants us to get moving fast on this one.'

He pulls down my dressing gown and hands me the suit. It is lightweight and the spotless fabric has a smooth, engineered texture. I've never seen any FPD troopers wearing it before. This must be a special Zone 5 uniform. A uniform for silent assassins and government kidnappers. Was I wrong about everything?

It is painful to bend down and put on the trousers, but I try to hurry so that I can cover up my naked body. I feel ashamed of this ugly flesh that has become me.

I glance over to see Sasha being forced into a suit of her own. She is silent now and staring at a fixed place on the wall. Her body is manipulated into the sleek grey suit and her limbs seem to have given up. I am glad that she can't see me looking.

The grunt gives my sleeves a tug before handing me some gloves. 'We need to keep this clean,' he says. 'No trace.' He clicks something on the shaft of his pulse gun with his palm and coughs. 'This never happened,' he adds, smiling. 'Keeps idiots like you guessing in the dark.'

'Fuck off.'

'What did you say?' He leans into me so close that I can smell his foul breath.

I push him hard in the chest and he stumbles backwards. Regaining his balance, he pivots back towards me and shouts, 'Who the hell do you think you are?'

'Now, now, play nicely please.' Sharp suit is back. 'Can everyone gather on the chairs now. I have a few words to say before we begin.'

The grunt elbows me out of the way as he heads to a seat. Somebody has set up a number of folding chairs in the middle of the room. They are positioned in front of one of the screens that are attached to the wall. One of the grunts pushes me to the front row and points at the seat next to Sasha. I begin the process of sitting down but there is too much pain to do so, my body naturally righting itself. I try to bend over again but everything cries out and I fail once more. The grunt pushes me over and I collapse into a heap bent over on the chair. It takes me a minute before I can pull my torso up from a hunched position. Sasha's body flinches fractionally as my shoulder brushes hers but other than that she offers no reaction. She is so close to me and neither of us has the energy to fight it.

'I'll get us out of this,' I say. 'I'll think of something.'

There is no recognition of my words. Did I definitely say them? I feel more sure of the answers to these types of questions since the pills wore off, but I could be wrong.

'I said I'll figure something out,' I repeat, speaking loudly so that I can be sure to register the sound of my own voice. That definitely sounded real.

Her eyes look over. They are shot through with something awful. So much so that her glare is incredible and I have to turn away.

'I can't hear a single word you say,' she says. 'You are nothing to me. You don't exist.'

Then she fixes her stare back onto the place on the wall. I bite the cut in my lip until it splits and I can taste blood.

114|

'Right then, let's go over the basics. You've already been briefed on the specifics, but as mentioned this is a simple locate and remove operation. You've all done these before. The only significant difference this time is that there are potentially a large number of targets to be removed. We are not sure of the exact number, but it could be anywhere between one and two hundred people.'

There are some whistles from the grunts in the crowd before sharp suit continues. 'We are taking three cargo trucks with us, which should give us the space to fit in as many as we need in order to…'

The airlock door opens and a young man with a slight frame, brown blazer and thin spectacles walks through. He seems aware that he is late and flustered because of it.

'Ah, Dr Hillier. Welcome, please take a seat.'

The slight man quickly slides over to the chair next to mine and sits down silently.

'Dr Hillier is one of the scientists at base,' continues the suit. 'He will be joining us on the mission for research purposes. We have never removed this many frozen bodies at once before so he will be along to monitor our progress and any potentially unusual effects of the transition. Isn't that right, doctor?'

'Yes, yes, absolutely,' he says in a half-mumble.

'It is his first mission into freeze space, so ensure that you look after him carefully. He is also here to document and capture any technology or evidence of note that we find in the rebel's headquarters. Please be extra vigilant and careful when moving around the area. Do not touch anything unless specified. Is that clear?'

'Yes sir,' they all grunt together.

'Do you have anything else to add, doctor?'

'No, no. Nothing else at this point, thank you.' He shifts to the side as he speaks.

'Well, okay then. Be advised that the two captives attending the mission have been to the rebel headquarters before and will need to be monitored at all times. They are both experienced trippers, as they self-identify, and are familiar with the process of moving around in frozen state. They are very important to this mission and are not to be left alone at any moment; I hope that I make myself very clear in this regard.'

He looks down to check an interactive display strapped to his wrist.

'With a four-zone shut down today the current temporal delay will be approximately eleven percent below normal. Remember to keep this in mind when considering reaction times. We have a couple of hours to get the job done, so we need to remain focused throughout. Stay alert and good luck out there. Okay then, let's go!'

I turn to the scientist beside me. 'What's a temporal delay? What does he mean eleven percent below normal?'

He picks up a small backpack that lies at his feet. 'I'm not allowed to talk to you,' he says as he stands and moves towards the far side of the room.

The grunt whom I shoved appears in front of me and motions with his gun towards the end of the room.

'Come on, hero. Let's see if you really know where this hideout is. You had better, otherwise you are going to be in so much shit you won't believe.' He looks down to check his pulse rifle before continuing. 'I almost want you to fail just because I'm curious to see how many ways they are going to mess you up.'

115|

Everyone is standing by the door marked exit. The slight scientist has joined us too, now resplendent in a grey suit like everybody else. He is chatting with one of the troopers next to him. My ears catch the end of their conversation.

'It is exciting to finally wear one of these suits,' says the scientist stretching out his arms and admiring the fabric that covers them. He pauses before continuing. 'They were so long in development that I wasn't sure if they would ever make it out of the laboratory. Getting the correct materials and permeability of the membrane was incredibly difficult. Too thin and the wearer would simply slow down excessively as with the rest of their surroundings. Too thick and they would not be able to achieve basic functionality. Most ordinary fibres couldn't cope with the sub-atomic anomalies and were about as good as wearing nothing!' he snorts. 'It was a fine balancing act and took many months to perfect. Without wishing to sound arrogant, I am rather proud of these. How do you find the suits? Any comments on their functionality or composition?'

He looks over expectantly at the man to his left towering above him.

'Fine,' says the trooper, lifting his arms up and down and twisting from side to side. 'Does the job, sir.'

'Good, good.' The doctor looks down at his feet. 'Good,' he says again.

'Get yourselves into squad order!' barks a voice from the front. 'Begin boarding of cargo trucks! Squad A into cargo truck one, squad B into two and C into three. Let's move!'

All the humans move through the exit door two by two. The other side opens up into a partially lit concrete cavern with three large, all-terrain rugged green trucks lined up next to each other. The nearest grunt pushes me in the direction of the second truck and I use all my effort to climb into the back without screaming. Everything hurts. My arms. My stomach. My legs. My head.

But what hurts the most is my heart.

116|

We are sitting on benches that span the inside of the truck. In the uncomfortably close quarters, everyone has found a neutral space to stare at and is ignoring each other. Besides myself, there are five troopers in this van as well as the scientist. We are waiting for something but I do not know what.

I think about the end and how long I have been waiting for it. For over a year, I would have embraced it. Only now that it's here, I need more time. I would laugh at the irony if it weren't so frustrating. I suppose that this could be the end. Why shouldn't it be? Everything ends and humans have no special right to a meaningful ending. Millions of living organisms die every day; people are no exception.

In the back of the truck, it strikes me that owning the end might be one of the greatest things that a human can achieve. Authenticity in life; dignity in death. Some people must achieve it. But this is another thing that appears out of my grasp. There is no sense of ownership here.

How much ownership do I need to take of the situation that I am in right now? If I hadn't disappeared when my brother died, would I be here now? If I hadn't sunk down into the depths and folded in Zone 4, would I be here now? And if I hadn't agreed to help Sasha? At what point do I become responsible? Maybe Sasha was right; things just happen and we move along with them. Life simply occurs and no distinctions are to be made. I am the steam from the steam train. I am the flame from the fire. I am the fly on the horse's back that believes he is pulling the carriage.

But I am still the steam, the flame, the fly. I need to bellow and burn and buzz. And, regardless of my causes, I know what I need to effect. There is something I must do.

A recollection seizes me. There is a way.

I have figured it out. Provided the memory is real, the flame will burn.

An electronic signal sounds and a large sliding shutter begins to raise with a skitter and a clatter. The trucks pull out into a motionless world.

117|

There is a certain glueyness to everything. Every movement feels partially stuck to the last. As if a very strong wind is blowing against my body at all times. It's all marginally slower. I try to shake my head clear of it, but the decision to do so is too slow itself to have any real effect. The bubbles of my ideas float a little longer before they pop.

Staring at my hand, I watch as the slight delay between my thoughts and my movements acts itself out. It is an unnerving sensation. A frame is missing in between the thought and the movement. Scrabbling around for ideas, there is a sense of frustration that itself takes too long to arrive.

As the truck moves on to its destination, reality is one page behind in its own flicker book. I have always had the sense that time can subjectively move more slowly in certain situations, but now it's definitively moving at a different pace.

'What's happening?' I ask one of the troopers opposite me with some effort. 'Why is everything shuffled backwards?'

There is a slight pause. 'It's the temporal delay,' he says.

'What's that?'

'When they freeze this much space it affects the things moving through it. Eleven percent, the governor said. You'll get used to it. Now stop talking.'

My decision to move my head happens before my head turns, but once the action arrives, out of the front window there is a recognisable sight. The street where we were attacked by the snipers before. There is no gun fire today. My mind imagines men and women up there on top of the roof completely unaware that they are frozen. Unable to know until it is too late, and they become aware again of the passage of hidden time that sentences them. I try to think of something else and the image slowly moves out of focus until it is gone.

I mentally track back through the layout inside Thaw. So much of it is black and white, frayed around the edges. It's an addled mess of operations and speeches and blackouts and red and white pills. There is a main entrance court which is clear and the route into Grace's office feels present enough. The layout of her room is especially clear, as are the objects. These memories are pertinent and have to be correct. The objects must still be where they were for the plan to work. If not, then there will be no ownership over the end at all.

The truck slows a little slower than usual to a stop. The driver in the cabin turns around and shouts in our direction.

'Time to disembark! Take the prisoner and allow him to direct towards the entrance. I will await your signal when you have arrived.'

'Yes sir,' the men all shout in unison.

The scientist is waving his arms around in front of him with a look of wonder over his face. 'This is truly remarkable,' he comments to himself. 'Better than I could have ever hoped. Such remarkable things of which a human is capable.'

Such things.

287

118|

We are walking down a passive side street. Each step wades its way closer to the destination. There are troopers behind me, tracking my movements as before. The difference is that this time every step hurts. My left leg is limping and although every muscle around my waist is tense, I feel strangely calm. Can something ever be inevitable? Life is so unpredictable it seems hard to feel certain of anything, but right now I feel content with the events that are about to unfold. If my memory holds up, then this will work. I reach the corner and turn towards the hidden console in the wall.

Groping for the right place, I begin pushing different bricks in front of me. My wrist is still sore from the ties, and it is too easy to fumble because of the slight delay between my choice to press and the action of pressing. The group of troopers look on as I flounder.

'It is here somewhere,' I say. 'It'll only take a moment.'

It takes a heightened, lengthy minute, but eventually the correct brick is found and it indents into the wall creating a recess which spurs the smooth, artisan, dead stone façade to move as it did before, but eleven percent slower.

My hand wipes away the sweat from my forehead.

'It's open,' I say.

The troopers push past me one by one and Sasha is brought to my side. She spits at me in semi slow motion. It lands on my cheek and all the stuck together thoughts can't decide whether or not to wipe it away.

'Why did you do it?' she seethes. 'They could have just killed us and that would have been the end of it. Now you've potentially ruined the whole rebellion. I don't understand you. You've been told the truth and you know it's them behind the whole thing, but you are still letting them in. It's like you *want* to help them.'

'I do want someone to help *me*,' I reply quietly. 'When the time is right.'

'What are you talking about?' she hisses.

'You'll see when we get there,' I whisper. 'Keep an eye on me, please. I've got a plan. I'm trying to get the end right, Sasha. I owe you that.'

'Enough talking you two,' barks a grunt moments after we have already finished talking. 'Keep moving, prisoner. Now that we are inside, you need to show us around.'

'There is another door to go through yet,' I remember out loud.

'Well hurry up and open it then,' the grunt replies.

'This one is a retinal scan; I don't think that I will be able to open it.'

'Let's hope for your sake that you can.'

He pushes my body up to the panel and both legs give way, dropping me to the floor. I use the wall to help myself up and he grabs a handful of my hair. Holding my head firmly, he presents my eyes to the scanner. Nothing.

'Blink!' he shouts. There is nothing wrong with my eyes, I want to tell him. They are the only part of me that is perfect. I blink anyway and stare again. Still nothing. 'Blink again!' He forces my head into the scanner, and I can feel its polished plastic pressed against my cheek. It hurts.

'Let go of him, for God's sake!' The grunt lets go of my hair immediately and I see out of the corner of my eye Dr Hillier appear next to him. His wiry straight arms are crossed. 'We are in a frozen state,' he continues, 'the scanner is suspended in time just as everything else is, you fool. Physical manipulation is required to make change in a temporal suspension, have you not been told that as part of your training? The button worked because he pressed it; the scanner is still frozen, it will not operate. You need to find another way to open the door.'

The doctor looks at me with something that I can only describe as close to sympathy, before melting into the background again.

'Alright, you heard the doctor. Let's set up another method of opening this door.' The grunt puts his finger to his ear and I remember that they are all connected. Sharp suit is probably on the other end of it all. They need his permission. After a delay the grunt slowly pulls his finger back to his side and shouts, 'demolition force approved! Prepare the area!'

119|

The grunts scurry about and fuss over a collection of explosives. There is a sense of grave seriousness around them as they work. I think they prefer munitions to people. As a human, I understand them on this. Destruction is so easy that it seems purposeful. Why would it come so naturally if it weren't natural? Humans aren't built to create alone, annihilation is part of us too.

Sometimes all I want is to ruin things. Anything, everything. I have spent a year feeling like this. Although I think it started before. It doesn't matter the cost. In fact, the greater the cost the greater the desire to sabotage. Why is it that we have to discount the urge to disfigure? If I am the flame then I should burn; I don't choose the fuel.

I watch the grunts work and remember that I am ready to destroy something too. I think about what I used to be. I think about the future I thought that I would have. When everything seemed open and nothing was finite. When I had aspirations that were unburdened and achievable. A pathway that wasn't fixed. That is when I am ready to dismantle, gut and consume. When I want to ravage and shatter and wreck. To ruin myself and anything that I care about. It is as present as a desire to eat and sleep. Why should I deny myself this?

The grunts move away from the wall and create an invisible cordon to demarcate the blast zone. One of them holds the remote and then begins the brief countdown. When he hits the button, the explosion lights up orange and yellow and red and green and blue. I enjoy the moment as it lasts eleven percent longer than any other that I will ever experience. A flash of magnificence that burns and breaks and then it is gone.

A pile of smoking rubble lies in front of us, and the grunts all grunt their approval before sharing a quiet moment of reverence. Silent, agreed mutual perception. I am in it with them and it is a clean experience that should not be rationalised or second guessed. I'm tired of trying to explain everything. Some things just feel the way they feel. Even though the potential consequences of this act of destruction are horrendous, the act itself is inert. It is amoral and awesome and frightening and wonderful.

120|

The smoke disappears and the dust begins to settle.

'Right, let's move. You first, hero. Take us to where we can find Grace. Everyone else, get started on clearing any frozens you find in the compound. Do not kill any of them; they will all be needed for interrogation during the debrief.'

The other side is packed with people. Motionless, passive, temporally dysfunctional people. As we walk through the communal area, we pass bodies that are in mid flight. No person is standing still. Some are hovering in mid air as their stride takes them from one location to the next. Others have arms outstretched in different positions, trying to gather or arrange or beckon. Humans assembled over bags and sacks of shared possessions or food.

They were trying to leave.

A dog is mid-bound. His tongue half out of his mouth and every muscle and sinew seem to be stretched.

'Leave the animals,' a voice asserts. 'Right, where will we find Grace, hot shot?'

'It's this way,' I say, pointing towards the shiny door that reflected the torch light the last time I was here.

We walk towards the stainless-steel door and stop in front of it. I push the button on the wall and we walk through. I have to be ready. It needs to be the same.

At this point, our group has diminished to myself and two guards. This needs to change. I need Sasha and I need Dr Hillier. My brain functions in a below average way and creates an idea which eventually impregnates my consciousness.

'This is as far as I have been before, I say. You need Sasha to direct us from here.'

'No, you take us,' says the trooper on my left.

'I don't know the way. They told me that they set up traps for any kind of frozen entry. We need Sasha to direct us, there is no other way to be safe.'

I look over to the two troopers that stand before me. They ask permission and then touch their earpieces and wait for what seems like an unnecessary amount of time. One of them finally nods to the voice in his ear and turns to the other.

'Go and collect Miss Shiverstone,' he orders. 'You wait here,' he says to me.

The other trooper disappears in a hurry and reappears moments later. Sasha is being dragged along behind him. She looks at me and can barely maintain eye contact. In my expression, I try to say that she needs to follow my lead without saying anything. Her eyebrows crease and she stares into the shadows that surround me. It takes a glutinous second, but I begin to wonder if she doesn't understand after all.

I remember the time that we didn't need to say anything to each other and there was a complete understanding. Love as life without limits; it felt as if it was a truly original experience. I think that something of that remains, however small, and that we are ready to keep moving.

'Sasha, is it this way?' I point and gesticulate and hope.

She averts her gaze and shifts her weight. 'Yes,' she replies. 'It is that way.'

Something pure enters my heart and fills a tiny part of the empty oblivion.

121|

'Leave the war with me,' I said.

She was still half asleep and facing the closet. I had woken up early and had an unusual feeling of optimism. I pictured a future that involved a small community outside the city walls. Where we built our own house and there was a village green, and we grew our own vegetables. Where we could build a playground and families and a sense of shared ownership. A shared interest amid a sparse landscape. Where people knew each others' needs and tried to help them fulfil them.

Sasha rolled over and stretched her body out. 'What did you say?' she asked.

'Let's leave. Today. Why not? We could just go; we know where there's a hole in the wall. I talked to that guy about Cornwall again. We could start a new life together. A life without all...this. I know I could do with a change. We could have kids there and bring them up without all the baggage from the freeze. None of the zone shit to deal with. A simpler life, don't you think? What do you say?'

She didn't respond.

'I love you, Sasha. We could do this. We could make this work.'

She pulled the duvet over her head. 'It's too early for this,' she grumbled.

'No it's not,' I replied. 'It's the perfect time. Come on. Let's do it.'

'Are you being serious?'

'Yes, why not?'

She turned in bed to face me. 'I thought we already went over this? Anyway, it's not the right time,' she said. 'There's too much happening, and we barely have any money.'

'That doesn't matter, we can figure something out.' I grasped her hand. 'Don't you want to escape with me?'

Her hand went to her forehead and then rubbed her eyes. 'What about the rebellion?' she asked, propping herself up. 'The movement? Don't you think that is a consideration? It is really beginning to take off now. We have a big trip planned for next month; your brother's going. You should be in on it, it's going to be great.'

'I don't know if I want to be part of that anymore. I've had enough. I want to get out. We can't save the world, Sasha. I would love to, but it's too complicated.'

She moved away from me and turned back towards the closet. 'If nobody tries to save the world then it definitely will not get saved,' she asserted. 'A collection of drops makes an ocean, you must not forget that.'

'I know, I know. But haven't we given our drop? Haven't we done our part?'

'No. No we haven't. Not yet.'

'How much more will it take?'

'I don't know, but we obviously aren't there yet. Has the world changed? Are there still four zones? Is there still mass inequality? Are people's lives still being ruined?'

'You know the answer to those questions.'

'Then we haven't given our drop.' She looked at me with gravity that sank my optimism. 'We can't leave. It's not time. There is too much to do. I can't leave the war with you, because who will be left to fight?'

She kissed me on the cheek in the way a victor might a challenger who had been vanquished.

That was the last time we spoke about leaving.

122|

Myself, Sasha and two troopers walk towards Grace's office. Sasha is next to me and the other two are behind. Two frozens stand part way through the door gesticulating to each other. I can see Grace inside the room. She is bent over her desk and bathed in the warm orange glow from the lightshade. One hand is putting papers into a cardboard box whilst the other has something small and black in it. I recognise it right away. The shelves are still there as they were before. I stop in front of her desk and turn to face the troopers.

'You're going to need to call the scientist,' I say. 'Grace has got something here which he will need to take a look at.'

'What is it?' peers one of them.

'It's a subatomic slider.'

'A what?'

'Exactly. Go get the scientist; we aren't supposed to touch anything of note, remember?'

'Yes, alright, alright. I'm the one giving the orders around here.' He turns to the other one. 'Go grab Dr Hillier quickly. He's in the main square, I think.'

The trooper turns to walk away with a finger to his ear. 'Coming to collect Dr Hillier,' he announces.

We all watch as he exits the room and I quickly whisper to Sasha. She looks at me strangely but does as I ask.

'Hey, trooper,' she says, 'there's something else over here you should see.' She leads him to the corner of the room where there is a pile of books and folders. She begins to carefully pick through them.

'What is it?' he asks.

'It's in here somewhere,' she replies.

Softly stepping towards the shelves, I pick up the antique sword and unsheathe it silently.

'Have you found it yet?'

'Nearly there,' she replies.

I walk as quietly as I can until I am standing right behind him. The pain in my arm is gone as adrenaline courses through it. This is the moment. I pull back my shoulders and then lunge forwards with as much force and anger as I can muster. The bitterness and frustration boils inside me as, eleven percent more slowly than normal, the blade plunges through the finely balanced mixed fibres of the trooper's suit and then the flesh and muscle and tissue and sinew that lies within. It continues its way all the way through until it comes out the other side. Sasha reels backwards and gasps with her hands to her mouth. The trooper collapses to his knees and just as he is about to say something I pull the sword out and swing it across his face. It carves through his cheek and instantly creates a bloody mess. As his body drops to the floor, there is a raging destructive glee everywhere inside me. I stand over his body with my knuckles white and my heart pounding and an antique samurai sword dripping with blood in my hands.

Sasha looks up at me and I can see that she is afraid.

'Come on,' I say, reaching out towards her. 'I told you I would figure it out, didn't I? Let's get out of here.'

123|

Sasha is frozen on the floor. There is a bright crimson pool of blood slowly edging its way towards her.

'Come on!' I shout. 'We don't have much time until the trooper comes back and we need to be ready when he does.'

I run as fast as the temporal glue will allow over towards the shelves and grab the shotgun. Opening the barrel, I can see that there is a round in the chamber. One shot, that's all that we have. I hurry back to Sasha and hand the firearm to her. She looks up at me and frowns.

'This isn't going to work,' she says. 'We're really screwed now.'

'We were screwed already. We were screwed the minute we set foot into Zone 5. Look, we only have one chance to get this right. Any minute now that trooper will be back with Dr Hillier. We need to kill the other trooper, grab Hillier and use him as a hostage in order to get out of this dump. Okay?'

'Is that your plan? Is this you *figuring it out*?'

'Yes, come on. Let's go.'

My body is hurting again now that the adrenaline is wearing off. I need more.

'And where do we go after that?' Picking herself up, some of the old fire is coming back.

'I don't know. Anywhere. The whole city is frozen. We'll figure something out.'

'I thought you already had figured it out?' She snatches the gun from me and cocks the hammer. 'We are never going to make it out of here alive, you know that don't you?' Her head turns towards Grace. 'And we can't just leave her here.'

I can hear footsteps approaching down the corridor.

'Quick, Sasha! Hide the gun! Move over to Grace where they can see you. Go!'

She drops the gun behind the desk and I slide along the wall and wait behind the door gripping the sword tightly.

'Okay, we're back. So where is this tech stuff you need to show the scientist?'

Dr Hillier sidles round the grunt and looks past Sasha at Grace.

'It's over here...' gestures Sasha, pointing to the desk, but he is already leaning in to grab the slider.

'How on earth did you get your hands on one of...?'

It's too late. The trooper tilts his head to the side and catches a glimpse of the body lying on the floor. As he reaches for his gun, I leap and a flash of metal glints in the orange light. The blade sinks into his shoulder and the force of it pivots his body sideways knocking the gun from his hand. He staggers away from me and drops to his knees desperately scrabbling for the weapon on the floor. I grab the sword and tug it from his body before roaring and sending it back in again. This time the blade goes all the way through and stops him dead. He collapses on the floor and falls silent. I pull the sword from him and feed it, still dripping, back into its sheath. Panic removes the pain once more.

I did it.

When I turn, I see that the scientist is hiding in the foetal position by the desk in the corner.

'Don't worry, I'm not going to kill you, Doctor. We need you.'

My entire body begins to shake and the sword slips out of my fingers. It tumbles frame by stilted frame to the ground.

124|

'Are you ready? We need to go.'

The question asks as I reach down to pick up Dr Hillier. He tries to push me away and drops the slider.

'What is that thing?' asks Sasha, bending down to collect it.

'Careful with that!' bleats the scientist. 'Do not press any of the buttons!' He reaches for it but she moves her hand out of the way in time.

'It's a subatomic slider,' I say.

The scientist abruptly turns to me. 'How do you know that?' he asks, shaking slightly. 'This is top secret, prototype technology. Only a handful of people on the planet know that these even exist.'

'We used one to break into the FPD headquarters.'

'Wait. What? You've used one?'

'Well, it was used on me.'

'You were deconstructed?'

'Yes.'

'Incredible!' He seems to have momentarily forgotten about the two dead troopers and gets lost in his curiosity. 'What was it like? You must tell me. I co-designed this but have never seen it used on people.'

'Strange. Look, we have to go. It didn't work very well anyway. One of the guys didn't reconstruct properly. He was a bloody heap.'

'One of them? How many did you use it on?'

'Four.'

'Four! No wonder it didn't work properly. It was never designed for more than one person, two at the absolute most.'

'Hold on, this box can deconstruct people and then put them back together again?' interjects Sasha.

'Yes, I'll tell you about it later. Enough about this, we have to get going before someone else arrives.'

Sasha holds up the little black box in front of her. 'But we could use this to escape,' she says.

My mind is too stuttery to keep up. I catch sight of the dead bodies in front of me. I just want to leave this room, and forget this ever happened, but Sasha looks like she has an idea.

'What? How?' I ask.

'You put me, the shotgun and the scientist in the box. You tell the next guard who comes that I killed the two troopers and escaped with Dr Hillier. They'll put you in one of the trucks with some of the frozen rebels and then you can reconstruct us at some point once it starts moving.' She slings the shotgun over her back. 'I'll use the gun to take over the truck and we can drive it away and escape. There are only three trucks that are out here; all the other FPD troopers and gear are frozen like everything else. We have a chance at escaping for long enough. How long 'til this freeze ends, doctor?'

'I don't want to say.'

I lean down to retrieve the samurai sword. 'Are you sure?' I ask with no need to fake authority anymore. It flows unnervingly through me.

'Okay, okay...The longest they can stably freeze everything at once is about two hours. If they don't unfreeze things after that time, then the temporal delay gets steadily bigger and bigger until you end up frozen too.'

303

'So if we can stay escaped for long enough, they'll have to unfreeze everything. Hopefully at that point Grace will have some idea on where we can go next. It'll give us a shot at least.'

She is still her brilliant self, so much more than everyone else.

'Right, okay...this could work. But what if they think that I killed the troopers? If they kill me then you'll be stuck inside the slider.' A slow thought bursts open. 'You need to cut me with the sword. It's going to have to be bad. I'll say you attacked me too and left me for dead. They know how much you hate me. They'll go for it.'

She looks at the ceiling and touches her forehead. 'There has to be another way,' she says.

'There isn't. You know there isn't. And we don't have time for any discussion. We just need to do it. Doctor – what do I do to get you both out of the slider?'

Sasha passes it to him, he presses the button on the top and the mechanism within the box begins to whir quietly. 'I want to make it very clear that I do not want to be a part of this plan,' he asserts. 'But seeing as I clearly have no choice...'

His words fade out as he fiddles with the tiny touch screen on the top of the box. His fingers move slowly and this clearly frustrates him. 'Nearly there,' he says half to himself.

Sasha looks at me and her eyes meet mine. I emphatically feel like I exist once more.

'Okay, it's ready. I've calibrated it so that you simply need to press the button on the top to deconstruct myself and Miss Shiverstone. The same button will reconstruct us when you decide that the time is right. There is a failsafe reconstruction point which occurs thirty minutes after entering the device in order to ensure that no one re-mains stuck as subatomic matter for all eternity.'

He reaches over to me and hands me the slider.

'Please,' he says. 'Please be careful with this. It is still only a proto-type and isn't yet completely stable.' He pauses, before continuing quietly, 'I don't want to die.'

'I will be, don't worry. Sasha, this is your last chance. Are you sure you want to do this?'

'It's our only chance,' she says.

I hand her the sword. What's left of my upper body muscles tense together. 'Right, do it now.'

The sound of footsteps filters into the room. 'It's now or never. Do it. Come on. I deserve it anyway.'

She raises the blade above her shoulder. 'You do deserve it,' she says. 'But that doesn't make it right.'

'Quickly, come on!'

There is a moment of time when all our eyes are fixed on the length of perfectly crafted, slender curved steel poised in the air beside Sasha's head, before it swings down and cuts a gash across my chest. It sears with pain and jolts everything into stimulated alarm. I fall over, drop-ping the matt black box momentarily. Lying on the floor, my hands begin to feel around desperately. The shock feels as though it makes up for the missing eleven percent and my fingers manage to find the box and its button. Just as I point it at them and push it down, I think she says, 'I'm sorry, James.'

And then she is gone.

125|

I feel around inside my suit for a pocket and the slider stows itself safely inside. Gingerly, my fingers touch the cut. It is bleeding extensively, but it isn't too deep. Sasha has hurt me well.

The footsteps are almost in the room. My feet shuffle the rest of me along the floor until I lie right next to one of the troopers. He has a nothing expression on his face, as if he isn't real anymore. I can feel his warm blood soaking into the back of my suit.

'What the hell happened here? Unit three to control! Unit three to control! We have two troopers down. I repeat two troopers down. Looks like Unit 12. Checking the scene. Be advised, only one of the prisoners remains. Shiverstone is not here.'

The second trooper kneels down in front of me and checks the pulses of the two dead bodies. Dead bodies don't have pulses. When he realises this, he grabs my suit by the scruff and pulls me up towards him.

'What did you do?' he shouts in my face. Some spit lands on my cheeks and it feels foreign and infectious.

The voice of the other man continues. 'Both troopers from Unit 12 are deceased. Looks like some kind of blade has been used. One prisoner remains. He is injured but alive. Awaiting instructions.'

'What happened?' grunts the man in front of me. 'You'd better start talking.'

'It was Sasha. There was some kind of sword on the shelf over there. She led us in here and seemed to know exactly where it was. As soon as we got in here she grabbed it and just went crazy. I've never seen anything like it. She was trying to kill me, but the troopers tried to stop her and she turned on them before coming back for me. After she hit me, I just lay here as still as I could. She thinks I'm dead. She's completely lost it, I'm telling you.'

'Where is she now?'

'She struck us all down and just ran. She took the scientist guy with her. She's taken him hostage. She left out of that door. I don't know where she's gone.'

'Yes sir…Okay…Right away sir…Yes, Grace is still here too…Yes…Thank you, sir.' The other man is getting his considered, intelligent orders. 'Right, we have to take this idiot and Grace out of the compound and lock them securely in one of the full trucks. This guy'll give us the full story when we get back, but for now we need to get on with the evacuation operation.'

'Okay. You're coming with me.' The trooper has kept hold of my suit this whole time in a tightly clenched fist and now pulls me up off the floor. He takes a big swing with the other arm and strikes me across the face with all his might. 'You're going to pay for this,' he snarls.

'Leave him. He's dead once we get back, just like the rest of them. Let's just get him out of here.'

'I hope they kill him slow.'

I've been slowly dying for over a year now, but being this close to death is the most alive I've felt in a very long time.

126|

The courtyard is bustling with activity. I have never seen this many people moving around in a frozen zone before. Troopers are running back and forth carrying objects and weapons and boxes of documents. Mostly, though, they are carrying people. Frozen people unaware of their movements, their bodies in a diverse range of freakish, fixed positions. Some are hunched over picking something up, others seated with knees bent. Some are on tiptoes reaching for an object overhead, others curled up asleep. One mother and child go past, entwined as one. A silent mortuary of mannequins all on their way to the end.

The trooper hurries me through the organised mayhem as best as he can. I can't walk all that well so this is taking longer than he would like. Also, everything feels as though it is slowing down a little more than eleven percent. Experience is beginning to glitch a little, as if reality is taking longer to render or load. It is becoming harder to think about anything clearly, but it certainly feels as if this is the case.

We finally make it through all the congestion, past the rubble and outside the main gate. I notice two troopers standing guard and another one by each truck throwing in the lifeless bodies as they are handed them. The trooper who wants me to die slowly lifts my collar up into the back of a waiting truck and lets go, pushing the rest of me in. On my knees, I raise my eyes to see rows of frozen people lined up one by one. There must be about thirty people in this truck, packed in like cattle. All unmoving. All perfectly still.

The other trooper hurls Grace in next to me and slams the door.

Everything goes very quiet. I kneel for a minute without moving. There doesn't seem to be anyone else coming in. Carefully, I check for the box in my pocket and gently tease it out. It looks like it did before I was thrown into the truck. Plain and black. There is no visible damage.

Crawling down the central aisle, in between the deformed bodies, I can hear my heart pounding in my head. A slow, heavy drum beat with which to march. The cabin is only a few more paces away. There is a wire mesh covering most of the area at head height that separates the front seats from the cargo behind. There is a small rectangle of meshless space through which items are designed to pass. It looks about big enough for the slider to slip through. I use the knee of a frozen rebel to prop myself up in order to reach the gap. His face looks at me through one continuous stare. There are theories that, akin to being in a coma, the subconscious mind somehow remembers what happens in freeze state. As he looks at me, paralyzed and impotent, I really hope they are wrong.

Turning away, I begin to stretch up towards the gap in the mesh. As I do this, the cabin in front of me opens and in climbs a trooper. Slamming the door behind him, he reaches forward towards the wheel and touches his key. The engine starts up, the truck rumbles with a slow, low groan and begins to pull away.

The driver turns back onto the road and it knocks me off balance. He hears the thump and looks behind him whilst driving.

'Hey, get away from the grill! Get to the back where I put you!'

Sliding in the slippery surface of my own sanguine soaked suit, I pull myself up once more and hold on tight to the knee of the listless man next to me.

'I said get to the back!'

She has to be able to manage it.

I stretch with everything I have left and inch the slider towards the gap. It sneaks through and I press the button in the last moment before I let it go and collapse back onto the floor of the truck.

There is a thunderous clangour.

'What the hell?' shouts the trooper.

The vehicle swerves over a bump and moves around violently from side to side. I slide again and am now lying on my back on the truck floor. The world is slowing and fading and dimming but there is a palpable sense of panic in the air. A scream and a shout and a flurry of frantic movement. Mad voices bark and squeal in desperation.

'Get off me! What the hell is this?'

'She kidnapped me. Please help me! God, I can't move anything.'

'Aargh! Move you idiot!'

'Why doesn't anything work? I can't feel my legs!'

Fists and arms and elbows and knees are forcing themselves into others.

'Get your hands off me, you pig!'

Desperate deep breaths punctuate the struggle.

'Aargh! Come on, come on, come on!'

'This isn't happening. This isn't happening. I'm not here, I'm not here…'

'Shut the hell up! Hold her legs down!'

'I can't! I can't!'

'No! No! No!'

Another thump and a big shift in something.

'Screw you!' she shouts.

'Wait…Please, no…'

There is a tiny click that leads to an almighty bang and a shatter of glass and the lights dim some more until the truck disappears.

127|

My interzoner is next to my ear and I can hear a man talking. His voice makes me feel sick. Something is very wrong.

'So what time are you aiming to arrive?'

'What? Sorry?'

'At the federal building, James. What time are you due to arrive?'

'Oh, right. About two o'clock, I think. It'll be just like I told you before.'

'Yes. About that, can you come in again to go over some of the finer details?'

'No! Do you know the risk I took going in last time? Putting that suit on to get into your office was humiliating. You've got more than enough info anyway. Remember, you are just going to scare them, right? Only arrest a few to make it seem real.'

'Yes, absolutely. And we will be sure to arrest Jake.'

'Yes, but only *arrest* him. That's what you agreed when we made this deal. I'm giving you the details of one the rebels' trips and you are getting to arrest him and some of the organisation's big guns. But once this is over, he gets to go free somewhere outside the city, okay? That was the deal.'

'Right, of course.'

'Okay then…And no pulse guns, right?'

'Our officers will act with caution and restraint as always.'

'Sure, but without guns? Yes?'

'We will see you tomorrow. Thank you for the tip off. Your safety will be guaranteed, James.'

'What do you mean *my* safety? Hey? Hello…?'

The conversation has ended. The sick feeling is in my stomach and a burning feeling stretches across my chest. My breathing is heavy and slow. Consciousness is raw and indiscreet. Something is moving around me and as my head turns there is no interzoner in my hand.

Everything is dark and I feel afraid. I can't be here anymore. I need something to help me escape to that perfect spot. The spot that's not quite real, but not quite fake either. A spot that feels like genuine, designed human experience. Like God intended it to be. The precise exposition of everything that sets a human apart from its lesser cousins. The phenomenal point that is sad and hopeful and desperate and complete. It's warm and it's cold and it's vibrant and it's alive. And it's beautiful. I can't describe it any better than that. Especially not now with my mind swimming in glue. The pills used to give me parts of that perfect experience, but it was never complete. Drinking gave me glimpses of it too, but it never lasted. Music used to take me there, lift me into that perfect place, but even that doesn't do it anymore. The problem is that nothing in life provides it anymore. Maybe it's perfect on the other side?

I can hear what sounds like Sasha's voice, but there's a madness to it that I can't understand. Unless you're going to give me something, Sasha, I need that spot now. I can't cope without it anymore. Real life doesn't compare. Whatever real life is.

How damaged am I that I need something additional to unlock the very part of me that differentiates me as a human? Don't answer that. I just want something. Anything. I'm trying, Sasha. I really am. I know you hate me, but I'm still here, and I still have to face that every passing minute. Along with what I did.

Help me, please.

128|

'WAKE UP! WAKE THE HELL UP! JAMES! COME ON!'

The absurd voice is screaming again out of the dark. I don't want to wake up. The dark is thick and warm and beginning to set around me. It feels like I need to stay here and allow the deep pressure to finally settle and solidify. It wants me to. It's taking too long for the tiny light to register anyway, it may as well not be there.

'COME ON! JESUS, JAMES! I NEED YOU!'

This time I recognise the voice and hearing those words drags my mind through the layers of viscous fluid one by one, slowly emerging out of the depths and ever closer to the cold. All I want is for her to need me; she is going to be with me after all. The nearer to the surface I get, the brighter the light becomes.

'WAKE UP! PLEASE!'

The world of perception reappears, and I remember where I am.

'JAMES!'

'I'm here.' Cough. 'I'm here.'

'Oh thank God! You have to help get this crazy doctor off me! Stop it! Get off!'

I take a deep breath and it takes a huge effort to heave myself up onto my knees. In the cabin, I can see the scientist leaning over from the passenger seat and wrestling Sasha for the wheel. The truck is moving but only slowly because it keeps veering violently from side to side. The window to Sasha's left is shattered and spattered with blood.

He won't stop.

Their struggle appears to be of equal strength and there is a look of concentrated determination on the slight scientist's face.

'Look, James, you need to listen,' she says in between strained breaths. 'I've unlocked the back door and I'm going to pull over. You have to get out and climb in the front to keep this idiot under control.'

The effort of moving all the way there feels terrifying.

'Can't you kick him out?'

'Stop it...! No, we need him. He's our proof and answers to all this crazy shit. We have to keep him. But we also really have to get the hell out of here. Let go of me!'

'Okay.'

'Right, I'm pulling over. Hurry! You've got to be quick. They must know that we've gone by now.'

The truck slows down and I begin the crawl back towards the rear doors. It is slow and tiring, but I get there and lean my whole weight against the door handle to get it open. It unclicks with a creak before swinging wildly on its hinges, my body falling through onto the pavement as it does so. Head hits the concrete in slow motion and the impact shakes my insides, winding me. Lying there, coughing and gasping for air, my eyes spot the shape of an FPD truck in the distance. It is glitching its way in this direction, one extended second at a time.

I force myself off the floor and use the side of the truck to support my weight in order to stumble to the cabin. Yanking the door open, I can see Sasha holding on to the scientist as he wriggles and squirms in an attempt to escape. In the only way I can, I throw myself in on top of the scientist and he lets out a loud yelp. The door closes in on itself behind me.

There is an oddly low-pitched screeching of tyres and the truck peels away down the road as fast as a temporally delayed world allows.

129|

Sasha keeps eying the rear-view mirror. My tongue is back to pushing at the cut in my lip. We are still driving and now I am sitting in between her and the scientist. He seems to have given up trying to escape. His eyes are fixed on the frozen world outside as it passes. There is something in his expression that reminds me of the first time I went tripping.

The grand stone buildings that are flying by suddenly open out and I recognise where we are. Trafalgar Square with Nelson's Column and the Lions that sit beside it. In the middle of the square is the famous memorial to those fallen from the invisible enemy: it stands equal in height to the Column so that its gravity is not mistaken. It looks even bigger in real life. The nameless old couple that perch atop exist as a stand-in stone for the millions of bodies that had to be buried in mass graves. Like it made any difference. They use it in all their propaganda; that's the whole point of it as far as I can tell. Once someone is dead, it's too late to do anything for them. Your actions for others only count whilst they are alive.

'They are still behind us, but they don't seem to be gaining any ground,' she says as she grips the steering wheel. Everything feels more and more heavy and slow. 'They have to end the freeze soon, don't they?'

'I don't know. I hope so,' I reply.

I am too preoccupied with finding the right words to say. If I don't get them out now, I don't know if I'll ever be able to.

'I'm sorry, Sasha,' I say. 'I remember now.'

'Remember what?'

'Why it was that my brother ended up being killed. Who I really am. Or was.'

'What are you talking about?'

'I'd forgotten what happened to Jake. Or at least, I'd done something with the memory; put it away somewhere, hidden. Locked it up somewhere deep in the dark. Maybe I never really forgot, I haven't figured that out yet, but I'm trying to face up to what I did and I don't think that I have done that before. Everything has been so hard for so long. I thought that it had to end. And now that it is going to, I don't want it to.'

'It's not going to end, James. We will get out of this frozen hell and Grace will take us somewhere we can be safe and fix you up. The world's not done with you yet.'

'I never meant for them to kill him.'

There is a delayed pause and a sigh. 'I know,' she says.

My eyes are starting to close. The lull is starting to pull me back below the layers.

'Hey! Eyes open! Hey! You've got to stay awake. You've got a job to do.' She elbows me in the ribs, and it jolts me back to the surface. 'It's about time you started talking, doctor. You have to keep him awake. If he dies, I'm going to hold you responsible.' She swerves around a bend before straightening up again. 'Talk to him; don't let him fall asleep.'

'What do you want me to talk about? I have nothing to say to you people.'

'Nothing to say! Ha! That's pretty rich coming from Mr. Secret Laboratory. How about starting with how the hell it is you can freeze time, doctor? Try starting with that!'

His eyes are transfixed on the world outside the window, and he begins to talk without glancing in.

'I don't know if you'll understand, but I'll try and simplify it for you.' He inhales deeply through his nose before continuing. 'It turns out that time has a certain mass to it. Like light previously, which we discovered could be identified as either a wave or a particle, time was finally isolated in the same way. Time is its own entity; it persists in the universe as a framework…a kind of container in which everything else exists. Think of it this way: when you make an appointment you necessarily must include not only the physical location, but the location in time. Otherwise your point of reference makes no sense.'

He pauses and Sasha implores him to keep going.

'About twenty years ago, scientists developed the ability to demonstrate that time exists in its own right and were able to finally isolate those subatomic particles that were connected with it. The revelatory breakthrough was the realisation that it is linked in with dark matter.'

He is gesticulating now, and he turns in to face me, immersed in his own explanation.

'For decades dark matter was a source of great mystery for us scientists. It took a paradigm shift in the way that we try to understand it in order for us to able to gauge what it consisted of. The early results were very exciting and what soon began to emerge was the fact that dark matter, when manipulated, affected the way that time passed in its vicinity. It was a remarkable discovery and the next logical step was to try to figure out how we could harness dark matter intentionally.'

'Was it just an experiment then?'

'In the beginning, yes. It started with freezing the entire city, barring what we now identify as Zone 5. With the city walls keeping everyone else out, it was easy to do for short periods without anyone knowing. We did that thirty or forty times – which, of course, no one knew about – in order to test the effectiveness and impact of the time manipulation. There were varying degrees of success at the beginning; it was very much trial and error. But eventually we began to settle on a stable formula which seemed to be working consistently. We couldn't identify any long-term side effects and managed to get the procedure to come in and out as smoothly as possible.'

'Stay with us, James. Come on!' shouts Sasha.

'I'm here, I'm here.'

'That was when the orders came to divide the land mass into different zones. They wanted to see if we could isolate different areas and then freeze them at will. We learnt that dividing the space up into four zones was optimal: there was no slowdown in the other areas, and almost none for those who entered the zone when it was frozen. This meant that the newly created FPD forces had access to whatever they wanted in the frozen area without any hindrance.'

'You mean kidnap and kill people?' snapped Sasha.

'Until today, I had no idea what they were doing in freeze state. I was just like you. I had my suspicions, but never knew what was involved. I don't have all the answers. I simply turn up to work in a lab and perform my experiments and try to invent new technology.'

'Bullshit! You knew, you knew. You knew that there was a secret fifth zone, and you hid it from everyone,' spits Sasha. 'So you weren't just like us, you're one of them! You obviously need to hear this and I'm glad that I'm the one to tell you: the blood is on your hands too, doctor. You're just as bad as they are.'

There was such venom in Sasha's words that the doctor was stunned into silence. She glanced into the rear-view mirror again and frowned.

'They've stopped,' she says. 'It looks like they're turning around. We're getting away,' she smiles. 'We are actually getting away!'

This cannot be right. I look at the doctor. 'Why are they doing that?' I ask.

'I couldn't say definitively. My best guess is to get out of the frozen zone before they unfreeze it.'

'Why? I've been around when a zone has unfrozen before and it's been fine,' Sasha asserts.

'In one zone, maybe. But when they unfreeze an area of this magnitude and you're in it, it can be very harmful. The longer a freeze occurs on this scale, the greater the chance that the sudden temporal jolt back poses a risk of causing cardiac arrest, amongst other things.'

Sasha bangs the wheel, and she twists and turns her head frantically back and forth trying to spot any recognisable landmarks. 'By the looks of it, they are probably a little over five minutes or so from the headquarters. We're going to be stuck out here. What can we do? Is there anything we can do to minimise the risk?'

'What do you mean stuck out here? We have to go back to Zone 5 now! Were you not listening to what I just said? With this amount of change, we'll likely die out here.'

'You don't get to tell me what to do, doctor.' As she says this she slams on the brakes and the truck comes to a stop. 'Okay, I'll make you a deal. I'll turn this truck around, back to Zone 5, if you tell me the real reason for the freeze.'

He is rubbing his thumb against the bridge of his knuckles. 'I already told you how the freeze works.'

Sasha has twisted in her seat to face him. 'No, I don't want to know *how* it works. I want to know *why*. Why are they doing it? What is all this *for*?'

'I don't kn-'

'Don't bullshit me!' She slaps him on the cheek. 'Don't bullshit me! I know you know more than you're letting on. Tell me, or we stay out here.'

'You're going to kill us all,' he says.

'I don't care,' she replies. 'I have to know.'

He looks like he is about to cry. In a strange way, I feel sorry for him right now. But Sasha's wave of righteous indignation is too powerful for anyone and he's getting pulled into the riptide along with the rest of us. The look on his face reflects his acknowledgement of this.

'I don't know everything,' he says quietly. 'But I do know that the vaccines don't work anymore. They haven't done for a couple of years. The virus mutates quicker than we can develop a solution. All the vaccines we give out now are old – they won't work against any of the latest strands. The government knew this was going to happen twenty years ago, all the models predicted it. So, with the new advances in nano-technology, they asked us to try and find a new way to fight the virus. To find a way to freeze it, isolate it in a host and stop it from growing. That's when we started looking into dark matter and time manipulation. That's why. But we couldn't do it, we had the breakthrough but could only freeze large, generalised areas, not specific people or atoms.

'Why use it at all then? Why did they ask you to carry on with the experiment?' she asks.

'They knew sustaining a city this size with no viable vaccines wasn't possible,' he continues. 'And this is the same everywhere – trade with other countries is gradually dying out as everyone tries to protect what they have left and not spread this virus any further. Think of how much this technology would be worth if they could find a way of making it useful. They asked us to develop it so that we could save the city: divide it up so that they could tackle the virus in isolated pockets, slow the spread, track and limit movement wherever possible, remove those infected in freeze state and give more *time* to deal with outbreaks. It wasn't as good as isolating the virus in individuals, but it was better than nothing.

320

'Without the means of mass vaccination, and with dwindling resources, it was a simple utilitarian calculation: to save the lives of some, others had to be relinquished. We can't sustain all zones, it's not possible. Zone 1 was to be protected at all costs, and then the order of importance dropped through the zones. The city needs to shrink to survive, it's that simple. And this technology, through a kind of happy accident, has allowed us to do that longer than anyone thought possible. As a scientist, I did what had to be done to save lives and I don't regret it. We are still working on freeze technology, trying to develop it to isolate individuals, but we aren't there yet. That will be the real game-changer.'

He stops for breath. Sasha is staring at her lap.

'Okay, I've told you what I know,' he continues. 'Now turn around and head back. We're running out of time!'

Sasha looks at the steering wheel. 'We're not going back,' she says, coolly.

'What?!' he shouts. 'I gave you your answers, now turn us around and head back! We'll die out here!'

'I told you we're not going back.'

'We made a deal!'

'Well, I lied – how does that make you feel? Huh?' She reaches over me and pushes his face against the windowpane. 'Huh? Being lied to? How does that make you feel?' She pushes him in the face again harder as she says this. 'How do you feel being taken advantage of for someone else's benefit? Just some fucking pawn in someone else's plan, huh?' She points to the back of the truck. 'Did you really think I was going to take these people back to die? No, we are staying out here and you'd better start coming to terms with that. So if you want to survive, you need to tell us quick if there is anything we can do to get through this.'

'God damn you. You're going to get us killed.'

321

'Just tell us what we can do!' she shouts.

'There isn't much you *can* do! Our only option is to be as still and calm as possible...And during the transition you have to get your heart rate down so that when the time delay disappears, you have the best chance of it not overloading your system.'

'Okay,' she starts up the engine again and pulls away. 'We need to get off this road and find a quiet side street. And I've got to stop driving this bloody truck because my heart already feels like it's going to explode.'

130|

On a tiny, unremarkable street that most people don't even know exists, a truck sits stationary with only just enough room either side to accommodate it. Across the front seats, three bodies sit silently in a line with their eyes closed. Their heads are bowed as if they are in prayer. Their breathing is measured and slow and rhythmic. Each second that passes drags on for how long, I don't know. It begins to feel as though we will never leave this place. Tears start to push their way out from behind my eyes and brim over onto my lashes.

'It might be over soon,' I say.

'Yes, I'm waiting. When are they going to switch the damn thing off?' she asks.

'No. I mean, it might be over soon.'

'Oh, I see.'

'I'm sorry,' I say. I have to say it. 'I did it. You're right to hate me. I met with the FPD and set up that trip knowing we would get caught. I was so...hurt and angry, I wasn't thinking straight. They agreed not to hurt anyone, they were just supposed to arrest people, but they screwed me. I'm so sorry. I wish it could have been different.'

'Sorrys are for nothing now. If we get out of this, then we can talk about it.'

She opens her eyes and breaks the seance. 'I know you didn't mean for him to die...' Her voice cracks. 'But I loved him. And you stole that from me. That is a future that I'll never get back.' She tries to breathe but it waivers and she whimpers instead. Fingers run through her hair. 'But we just let you rot in that house for over a year knowing that you were eating yourself from the inside out. That wasn't right. And I have something I need to confess too; I was only sent to you so that we could use you on that mission. Grace knew I was the only one who could convince you to come back. And I knew if I did it, you would get caught. That was always the plan. We knew we were going to move our base outside the city. We thought it was worth the risk to get the intel and leave you there with everything that they do to people like us…' She looks down at her hands. 'So, really, I'm as bad as you, James. You don't owe me an apology; we've both done terrible things. God, I can feel my heart rate going again.'

She takes my hand and grasps it tightly. 'If we get out of this, we can start again, okay?' Saying this, she returns my hand and runs hers over the back of her neck. 'But for now, we need to stay alive and keep breathing.'

'There's one more thing I have to know,' I ask as my heartbeat starts to change. 'Did you recruit me?'

'Huh?' she half-replies, eyes closed.

'That day when you invited me to the party…Was I just a mark? Another body for the rebellion? I need to know: was any of it real between us…?'

'I don't want to die,' interrupts Dr Hillier so quietly as to be almost inaudible. 'So please, stop talking and shut up.'

131|

The first thing that comes back is pain. An immediate detonation of pain that sends courses of agony rippling through my body with such ferocity that I almost lose consciousness. After the initial wave it dulls a little, and then my heart begins to feel as if it is racing so fast it will burst. Everything seems to become immediately louder and faster and so much more precise all at once. I can't catch my breath and my body doubles over as the muscles in my stomach and chest convulse. Sasha is shaking violently beside me and clutching at the steering wheel. The scientist scrabbles at the dashboard, shouting and coughing before suddenly going silent. His body sags and slumps limply onto my shoulder.

Then I begin to hear the noises from behind me. Terrified screams and piercing cries that bounce around inside the metal container within which they are trapped. Panic ensues as nobody knows where they are nor why they are there. Fists pound and scrape against the metal grill and the thumps of shoulders charging into the back door wobble the truck.

'What is going on? Let us out!'

'I can't breathe!'

'Somebody help us!'

I manage to gain some control over my over-agitated body and turn my head. It happens too fast and I bash my nose on the cage. The frenetic energy of everyone inside the truck spikes the air around me and I can't seem to say anything.

Then I hear the radio. The screen on the dashboard lights up and there is the unmistakable voice of a sharp suit.

'Well now, James. You are proving to be quite the surprise, aren't you? My perfectly designed plan has been ruined because of you. In fact, you really are starting to piss me off. I just wanted to let you know that your little escape party will be over soon, and that I am going to personally see to it that you can never cause another inconvenience of this kind again. I will be sure to kill Sasha first, of course. And make you watch as I kill every other single person on that truck in front of you. This was a completely futile endeavour and you will pay for the lives of those two soldiers. I'll be seeing you…'

I lunge for the old trooper's pop gun that lies on the floor by Sasha's feet and fire at the radio. It crackles and snarls and glares brightly as it is briefly set ablaze. A trail of smoke rises up to the ceiling and my shoulders start to sink. Once the glare dies down, I realise that everything has gone quiet.

'Sasha, you're alive! Wait…is that really you, James?'

Turning with more control now, I can see Grace's face pressed up against the grill. About twenty five other huddled faces are staring at mine too.

'Yes.'

'Then, how on earth…? Please tell me what the hell is happening!'

'There's no time. The FPD are coming for us. We have to get out of this truck and try to escape from here on foot.'

'Why? What is going on?'

'There is no time! Please, just move to the back of the truck so we can get out of here.'

'Okay, okay. Come round and let us out.'

'Wait!' Sasha is rotating her palms on her chest as she speaks. 'Where can we go? Grace, the backup location: Is it ready? Please say it is…'

'It's as good as we are going to get it. After your last visit,' she says looking at me, 'which was sooner than we were expecting, we were all getting ready to head over there when…I don't know what just happened.'

'How much farther is it? I've been trying to get us closer, but I can't remember the exact entry point.'

Grace tried to peer out of the front window. 'Where are we now?'

'Just off the corner of Maple and Treeacre.'

'Oh, well done, Sasha. It's about five minutes on foot from here.'

'Then we have to hurry,' I say. 'They're coming for us and they want us all dead.'

'I thought you were dead,' says Grace, turning towards the back door.

So did I.

132|

Grace takes charge and begins to lead the way now that everyone is out of the truck. I count thirty-six of us in total. The doctor wouldn't wake up, so we had to leave him there. His thin face was drawn out and his eyes still wide open in a childlike stare of disbelief. He didn't deserve to die.

As we reach the end of the tiny side street, Sasha, breaking briefly from her animated conversation with Grace, gets one of the others to give me their long coat to cover up the wound. They force it on me because I can't manoeuvre my arms into the right positions. As they do so, their garbled words of thanks pour out of them. It's too much. Why are they thanking me? Grace props me up with her shoulder and we start to walk. Not so slow as to be unhurried, but not too fast that it will draw any more unwanted attention to ourselves.

'Where are we going?' I ask. My chest feels as if it is burning.

'We have a tunnel. We've been using machinery to dig it out for over six months now. We've been planning to leave for a while, and of course everything sped up after your capture. We didn't know if you would bring them to The Mews, or whether they could use Sasha to get to you, but we had hoped to be out by the time it happened. The tunnel leads all the way to outside the city. The entrance to it is secreted behind one of our nanogates. It has an automated transport vehicle inside that will drive us all out and away from here.'

'But won't they just come after us?'

'If they find the gate, then we will employ the failsafe button. The tunnel was designed so that it could only be used once. It will collapse in on itself and the earth will rearrange around it once we activate the nano-technology. They will never know that it was there. Six months of work from teams around the clock, gone just like that. But it's the only way to ensure a clean getaway. It will work, as long as they don't get to us until we are all through the entrance way and safely down onto the transport.'

We round another corner and some strange looks befall our caravan of deplorables. In Zone 1, there is something not quite right about the way we look. Too conspicuous. We have to hope that no one reports this unusual behaviour *for their own safety*. Not yet.

'We are nearly there,' says Grace. 'Hold on for a bit longer and then you can tell me more of the details about the last few days. Just one more turning and we'll be on the road. I want you to know: I don't blame you for bringing them to The Mews. We kind of expected it to happen – Sasha is worth a lot to us all, and if they kept you alive we knew they'd get to you somehow – we just thought we would be gone by the time it did. She told me all about today, about what you did. You helped get us out and that's the main thing right now. We're square, okay? I told you they were up to something, didn't I? I hope that you believe in us now, because we've…'

Sasha comes running up next to us. 'They're here! They're here!' she screams and the sirens of not-too-distant FPD vans faintly sound the impending onslaught.

'RUN!' Grace yells. 'EVERYBODY RUN!'

133|

The deliberate walk disbands and the question of drawing attention to ourselves is no longer of any concern. We make it round the next bend and Grace darts away from me, feeling her way along a seemingly empty stretch of wall. She moves quickly and methodically and, pawing at the surface, soon finds something. She puts her hand flat against an individual brick and it shifts to the side and a green light emits, scanning Grace's ordinary eyeball. It only takes a second, but time is going too fast now; I wish that we could have back some of the eleven percent. A section of the wall becomes a door and Grace pushes it open.

'QUICK!' she shouts. 'Everybody IN!'

She stands by the door ushering in the first people with her arms before moving over towards Sasha and myself. The sirens are much louder now. They are nearly on top of us.

'We're not going to get everyone through before the FPD get here,' she says. 'Sasha, give me the pop gun. I'll hold them off until everyone's in. They cannot be allowed to see the gateway.'

'But what about you?'

'I'll be fine. I'll keep them away until everyone's got through. Quick, give me the gun. There's no time to hesitate,' she says. 'We need to act now.'

Sasha relinquishes the firearm and puts her hand to her forehead. 'What are you going to do?' she repeats in a voice of panic.

'Once everyone is in, wait ten seconds. If I'm not in by then, close the gate, get going and begin the collapse of the tunnel.'

'No…'

'Promise me! You must. Everyone's lives depend on it. I'll find another way out. Promise me, Sasha! And you, James. You owe us the right thing. You owe us. Ten seconds, that's all. Okay?'

There is a shared look between us and we all know that there is no other way out. Sasha reaches in and hugs Grace tightly.

'Now go!'

Grace pushes her off and runs towards the street corner. She takes up a position behind a perfectly polished racing red sports car and the tiny gun begins to expend itself repeatedly. I can hear a screeching of brakes and then the deep clack and bang of return fire.

'Let's go!' shouts Sasha, pulling me in towards the door. She pushes it open and we tumble through, plummeting our way down a short flight of stairs. My body finally at rest, I lean up on my elbows and see two more rebels dash in from the light.

'Is that it?' asks Sasha as they reach us.

'Nearly,' they shout before a young man bundles through followed by another.

'Is there anyone else still up there?'

'I don't think so, we're the last ones through, says the second young man. Apart from Grace. She's still there.'

The sounds of the firefight echo down the tunnel. The crash of pulse rifles reconfiguring matter. The tinkle of glass on concrete. The thunk of twisted metal and rubbled concrete.

'Come on, come on,' mutters Sasha.

I count slowly in my head. Numbers moving through the passage of time.

'Come on!' she shouts.

Ten is an arbitrary choice. It's really no different to nine or eleven. I guess she had to pick something. I reach up to put my hand on Sasha's shoulder. I have to do the right thing.

'It's time,' I say. 'We have to go.'

'No, just a moment longer. She's going to make it!'

Anxious faces look at me from all directions. They already know what Sasha is refusing to accept.

'It's time, Sasha. We've got to go.'

She lets out an almighty yell before reaching over and slamming her fist down onto the button that closes the gate. The tiny shard of light that connected us to the world outside disappears.

'Get in the transport, quick, sir. We need to move so that we can begin collapsing the tunnel straight away.'

Everything has stopped working. 'I can't...'

Somebody picks me up and I feel my legs being dragged along rocky ground until they hit something metallic and smooth. There is the sound of an electronic engine start-up and a series of small spotlights appear. Cool air begins to move past me and my back is gently laid down next to a collection of people's feet. No one is saying anything. The only sound that rises above the whir of the electricity is that of Sasha's sobs.

'We can't just leave her there. We have to go back. We can't just leave her there,' she repeats.

My eyelids, so heavy for so long, find that the dark weighs on them too much to stay open any longer.

It's time to go.

I can hear my mother's voice. She is talking to me as she strokes my hair. Jake twists sideways and his warm body squeezes in next to mine.

He smells of bath water and shampoo. Our foreheads touch as a blanket goes over us. There is a kiss on my hand before it is laid to rest on his shoulder.

134|

My eyes blink and I awake. I am in a room filled with glowing warmth. A cool breeze is gently blowing through some hanging blinds, making shadow patterns that stretch across the space towards me. Sitting up, the covers slide off and I reach under the pillow for my gun, but it isn't there. Where am I?

A strong gust of wind moves the blinds briefly to reveal morning sunshine that beams down onto the bed sheets. Looking around, I can see that the walls and ceiling are all white and there are several old paintings hanging on pieces of frayed rope at irregular intervals.

I turn and slide my legs off the side of the bed. Hesitantly, I reach towards my chest. Did it all really happen or was it just one of my dreams? The surgical tape and bandage answer my question. As does the pain when I push myself off the bed; not as bad as before, but enough to cause a sharp intake of breath. The feeling of the wooden floorboards on my feet is new; I curl my toes up and down to get a good sense of their grainy, textured surface.

The painting by the bed is of a stormy seascape; I move in closer to examine its rendering of an old lighthouse casting out over a rocky coastline. On the windowsill, nautical decorations crowd together: a miniature seagull, a wooden beach house, a rusty model boat. I push the blind out of the way to reveal the view. And what a view it is.

I think it is the most beautiful thing I have ever seen.

A small stretch of grass reaches out to a wooden fence and all that lies beyond is the sea. A sea that is as rich and blue as the sky that floats above it. Flashes of sunlight sparkle and dance on the ocean in brilliant patterns. The horizon stretches out in front of me for an almost impossible distance. There is so much space, I can't comprehend it.

'You're awake,' says a voice which makes me jump. I spin around too fast and lose my balance, stumbling back onto the bed. Looking up, I can see Meloy standing in the doorway.

'Hey, take it easy! You've got lots of healing to do before you're fully operational yet,' he says, leaning his elbow against the doorframe.

'You're alive?! I thought you were...' I trail off as the memories come back.

'I was on the truck you rescued. Thanks for that, by the way...' he replies with real sincerity in his voice, which throws me.

'Where are we?' I ask.

'We are on the Isle of Wight.'

'Where?'

'It's an island off the south coast.'

'We are outside the city?' Panic rushes back into my body as if the world were being unfrozen again.

'Yes, yes. But don't worry,' he rests his hand on my shoulder. 'We are safe here. At least, as safe as you can be anywhere right now.'

'How did we get here?'

'You've been out for quite a while – over a day. Once we were out of the tunnel, our friends who were setting this place up met us and drove us to the coast. From there we took a boat to the island. Look, you don't need to worry about the particulars. The main thing is: we are out of the city, and at our new location. Here, put these on,' he throws me a jumper and some sandals, 'grab the walking stick on the back of the door too, let's take a stroll.'

135|

As I walk out the bedroom and through the house to the backdoor, we pass several people. Each time there is a vague recognition of their faces as I flashback to a picture of them in their frozen states. It makes me start to tremble and I hold tightly to the walking stick hoping no one notices. The hairs on my arms raise as if they are trying to trap in some sense of security. Everybody nods or smiles at me as I walk past but I can't respond. I want to feel safe; I need to know more.

'What about the locals out here? Aren't there any Brits around? Shouldn't we be carrying guns?'

Meloy holds open a door for me as we make our slow progress out the house. 'With a huge ageing population before the virus spread,' he replies, 'this island was one of the first places to clear when things got really bad. Once it took hold on the island, it spread like wildfire through the oldies and those able enough fled. Since then, it's been pretty much empty. We haven't visited the whole island yet, but we have only encountered a couple of small subsistence families out here on our travels so far. No one who'll cause us any trouble. Given that and the fact that it's surrounded by water and a good distance from the EPRL, we were able to begin setting something up here with as little risk as possible. We are currently on the southeast side of the island, away from any prying eyes on the mainland. This town used to be called Ventnor, but I think we are going to rename it once we get things up and running properly. This town represents the future. And in case you were wondering…no, it doesn't ever freeze here.'

We are making our way through the kitchen now. Every available work surface is covered in tins of food, packets of filler and long-life cartons. A man I don't recognise is sorting all this and pats me on the back as I pass.

'Good to see you up and about, sir,' he says, smiling a toothy grin.

I smile back unsure of what else to do. Leaning into Meloy with a whisper I ask, 'Do they still not know about everything that...?'

'Never mind that for now,' he interrupts. 'We can deal with that later. The added bonus of living on an island,' he continues, changing the subject and ushering me towards the backdoor, 'is that you get to have a view like this...'

He opens the door and my eyes squint in the sunlight. As they adjust, the sight that greeted me earlier out of the bedroom window is drawn into sharper focus and I can breathe in the air properly for the first time. It feels clean and clear. It's inside me and all around me and makes me feel incredibly alive.

And then, as my eyes scan the garden, I see her. She is sitting on an old wooden bench looking out to sea, the sunshine reflecting off her skin.

Meloy turns to me. 'She's been through hell, James. You both have. She's going to need time, just the same as you. She doesn't want to take it, but you have to convince her she needs to stay here for a while. After what happened to her...I don't even want to think what kind of damage that has done. She needs rest. She needs to heal.'

'Why should I convince her to stay?' I ask, confused. 'We have to get ready to go back, surely? We can't just leave the others behind. The government has taken hostage two truckloads of people. They might even be dead already.'

'Yes, I know. That's over sixty souls,' he replies.

'So we can't just leave them there. And now we know, we *know* everything, so we have to go back and get the truth out there. Sasha must have told you everything the scientist said?'

'Yes.'

'So then you know we can't waste any time. We have to reveal the truth to the city.'

He turns away from me and looks out to sea, shaking his head. 'If only that doctor hadn't died,' he mutters, 'we would have had concrete proof...Still, we're figuring this out, we are going to go back as soon as possible, don't you worry. We've got some great leads we can follow up. We have some footage from your eyes which we should be able to use. Nothing uploaded during the time you were in the frozen zone unfortunately, but we have the time you were in the FPD building. Of course, they'll say it's faked, but it's something at least. And now we know, they're going to be very scared of us.'

'Have you heard from Grace?' I ask, hesitantly.

'Nothing. But there's been no news of her death either. That's one of the reasons we have to go back. If she's still alive, we need her.' He reaches out and turns my face to his. 'Make no mistake: I hear you. This isn't over. We've got unfinished business in the EPRL, and once we set our people free and uncover their lies, then we will need this place up and ready to become a new home. Which is why, for now, the best place for you and Sasha to be is here. You can't go back. Not yet. You realise this, don't you?'

My shoulders start shaking and my heart beats fast. 'But it's my fault those people were captured; I have to help them. If it weren't for me, you might all be out here right now. Even Grace...' A heavy blanket of guilt sinks on top of me.

'Maybe, maybe not. But there's no use in blaming yourself for all this. Ultimately, this is all their doing. The relevant fact here is this: you aren't in any fit state to help us. And now that your face is going to be one of the most recognisable in the entire EPRL wanted list – along with Sasha's – I think waiting here is going to be the place where you can do most good right now. You know this, right?'

I stare at a wisp of white cloud trailing across the perfect blue sky and nod. He's right, but it hurts. 'I know,' I reply, sighing.

'Then help me to convince her,' Meloy says, pointing me in Sasha's direction. 'I'll give you two some time to talk.'

Meloy opens the door and walks inside once more. I gingerly walk over to the bench and stop.

'Hey,' I say.

She turns to look at me with eyes so fragile it feels like they could shatter into a thousand chestnut glass shards. A tear slowly falls down her cheek and it's as if we are meeting again for the first time.

136|

I sit down next to Sasha and we both stare silently out at the ocean. From here, I can see that our house is raised up above the water, built into a hillside overlooking the bay. I have only ever seen beaches on the television, and they always looked different to this. The sand here is less golden, grittier and paler, but infinitely more beautiful. It's *real*. I watch the waves roll into a frothy foam as they crash in the horseshoe basin below and then pull out again. The salty smell in the air is something brand new. There is almost a taste to it.

'There's a plaque on this bench,' says Sasha, her eyes still fixed on the horizon. 'A couple lived in this house for sixty years together, spending every day looking out at this view. Sixty years.'

I look over at the writing inscribed on the bench. *Mabel and George lived and loved at this spot from 1964 until they died in 2025.*

'It's not fair,' she continues.

'I know,' I say. We listen to the gulls as their cries carry over the wind. 'I'm sorry. I'm so sorry...I miss him too.' My breathing is heavy and fast. 'I wish I could take it all back. I wish I could speak to him again, even just once. I wish I could explain...I didn't have a choice. I wish...I just miss my brother.'

'He would have loved it here,' she says, her voice wavering.

'He would have,' I reply, picturing him running down to the beach and diving into the surf before pulling me in and ducking me under.

She sniffs and hunches her shoulders up. 'Well, we can't change it now. There's no time to waste thinking about what could have been anyway,' she sighs.

'We've got some time,' I say, with Meloy's words echoing in my ears. 'If we stay here, away from everything, we have a chance to survive and get through this.'

She looks back at me, frowning. 'How can we stay here? After everything that happened...How can we abandon everyone else?'

'We don't have to abandon everyone,' I reply. 'We can take care of them out here. We can help set up a new place for everyone, here on the island. That's not abandoning people, that's *helping* people. Helping to build a new life.'

She sighs and looks back out to sea. 'I see Meloy has got to you too.'

She always sees right through me; I don't think that will ever change.

'You know he's right,' I say. 'I hate it too, but this isn't only about us.'

I tentatively reach out for her hand, not knowing how she'll react. I can't carry this grief on my own anymore. I need to share it with her; our loss is our bond and I think she needs this too. It feels as though somehow my brother has brought us together again. We need each other now, for something much more than before, otherwise we might never get out of this. As I gently touch her fingers, she turns sharply to me and stares into my eyes. I can't tell what's going to happen next, everything is confused and different. But then just as sharply as she turned, she buries her head into my shoulder and bursts into tears.

'What are we going to do?' she sobs, her tears soaking into my jumper. 'What are we going to do now?'

'You'll think of something,' I say, resting my hand on her head. 'You always do. You're the strongest person I know, Sasha.'

341

She pulls back and wipes her sleeve across her nose. 'You've got to start taking better care of yourself,' she commands in a stern tone. 'We need you now more than ever. No more random pills. We'll see if we can find the right medication to help you build the bridge back, help you to heal, but we need you to work hard to keep it together, okay? You're the fucking *hero* of this whole thing. You've got to keep it together this time. We'll find a way to work through all this, but you've got to start talking to people about things. No more holding on to everything inside.'

There is a familiar look and I remember how I used to be willing to do anything for her.

'Okay...' I say. 'I'll try.'

She sits upright and wipes the tears from her eyes. 'We'll both get ourselves together, okay? And then we're going to go and fix this mess, understand?'

'Okay...okay. I'll make things right. I want to. One step at a time,' I say.

A gust of wind blows through both of us and she leans into me, putting her arm around my shoulders. As the waves roll in and roll out beneath us, I realise that I'm free from the riptide now. It's not what it was. We can't be what we were. But perhaps we can be something new.

I close my eyes and feel the sun on my face.

It's time to start again.

ACKNOWLEDGEMENTS

First and foremost, my love and thanks go to A, J and M. You have inspired and challenged me, helped me to grow, and taught me how to be a better person. Thanks to my parents and the rest of my family for your support, love and encouragement over the years. Thank you also to the friends, authors and readers who have offered such valuable contributions to this story in its many earlier iterations. Further thanks go to all the brilliant students whom I have had the privilege to work with over the years - our discussions have helped to shape and inform my views on so many different things, and made me a better writer because of it. And finally, special thanks go to Rowan Thomas, my editor at Vulpine Press, for her invaluable insight and input, both of which have brought out the best in this story.

R. D. STEVENS grew up in Kent, England, with an overactive imagination and a love of big questions. After going to university to study Philosophy, he escaped the UK and travelled the world for two years. On his return, he worked in the charity sector, before training as a philosophy teacher and completing his MA. Outside of writing, he currently works at a school in London and loves to read books, play the guitar, and talk about existentialism. His award-winning YA debut *The Journal* was released by Vulpine Press in August 2022, and *The Freeze* is his sophomore novel.

Twitter: @RDStevensauthor
Website: rdstevensauthor.co.uk/

Printed in Great Britain
by Amazon

17284877R00205